Reap the
East Wind

Other books by Glen Cook

Reap the East Wind

The Last Chronicle of the Dread Empire: Vol I

Glen Cook

NIGHT SHADE BOOKS
SAN FRANCISCO

First Edition

Printed in Canada

ISBN: 978-1-59780-318-2

Night Shade Books
Please visit us on the web at
http://www.nightshadebooks.com

I

YEAR 1012 AFTER THE FOUNDING
OF THE EMPIRE OF ILKAZAR

Armies in Shadow, Waiting

THE BEAST HOWLED and hurled itself against the wall of the cell next door. It raged because it could not sate its thirst for Ethrian's blood.

The boy had no idea how long he had been incarcerated. Night and day had no meaning in the dungeons of Ehelebe. The only light he saw was that of the turnkey's lamp when the man brought pumpkin soup or made his infrequent rounds.

Before the dungeon there had been an unremarkable childhood in the slums of Vorgreberg, capital city of a tiny kingdom far to the west. There had been a strange mother with witch blood, and a father stranger still....

Something had happened. He did not understand it. He thought it was because his father had become politically involved. He and his mother had gotten caught in the backlash. Men had come and taken them away. Now he was here, in irons, in darkness, with only the fleas for companions. He did not know where here was, nor what had become of his mother.

1

He prayed for silence.

The damp stone walls never ceased shuddering to the moans and roars of the Hell things chained in neighboring cells. The laboratories of Ehelebe had yielded a hundred strains of monster terrible and strange.

The scratching and roaring ceased. Ethrian stared at the heavy iron door. A light flickered in the passageway beyond. The beasts remained poised in an expectant hush. Slow, shuffling footsteps broke the abnormal stillness.

The door contained one small, barred opening. Ethrian watched it fearfully. His hands shook. Those were not the steps of his keeper.

His captors had raped away everything but fear. Hope was as dead as the darkness in which he lived.

Keys jingled. There was a metallic scratching at his door. The rusty lock squeaked in protest. The door swung slowly inward.

The boy gathered his legs beneath him. He curled into a balled crouch. Even had he been unchained he could not have resisted. He had been inactive too long.

An old, old man entered the cell.

Ethrian tried to shrink away.

And yet... there was something different about this one. He lacked that air of indifferent cruelty possessed by everyone else the boy had encountered here.

The old man moved as if in a dream. Or as if he were badly retarded.

Slowly, clumsily, the ancient tried his keys on Ethrian's fetters. At first the boy cowered. Then, moved by cunning, he waited for the last lock to fall away.

The old man seemed to forget what he was doing. He considered the keys with a bewildered expression, surveyed his surroundings. He made a circuit of the dark-walled cell.

Ethrian watched warily.

He tried to stand.

The old man turned. His forehead creased in concentration. His face came alive. He moved closer, fumbled with the last lock. It fell away.

"Ca-ca-come," he said. His voice was a crackling whisper. It was hard to follow even in the unnatural stillness haunting the dungeon.

"Where?" Ethrian whispered too, afraid he would rouse the beasts.

"Ah-ah-away. Th-they sent me to ka-ka… to ga-give you to the *savan dalage*."

Ethrian cringed away. The turnkey had told him of the *savan dalage*—the worst of Ehelebe's creations.

The old man produced a tiny vial. "Dra-drink this."

Ethrian refused.

The old man seized his wrist, pulled him close, twisted him round, forced his head back and his mouth open. His strength was both startling and irresistible. Something vile flooded the boy's mouth. The old man made him swallow.

Warmth and strength spread through him immediately.

The old man pulled him toward the cell door. His grip was steel. Whimpering, Ethrian tripped along after him.

What was happening? Why were they doing this?

The old man led him toward the stair leading up out of that subterranean realm of horror. The unseen beasts roared and howled. Their tone suggested they felt cheated. Ethrian glimpsed red eyes behind the barred window in the nearest door.

He gave up trying to hang back.

The old man stammered, "Ha-hurry. Th-th-they will ka-kill you."

Ethrian stumbled after him, to the head of the steps, then down a seemingly endless stair outside. There was a salt tang to the hot, still air. He began to sweat. The sunlight threatened to blind his unaccustomed eyes. He tried to question his benefactor, but could make only limited sense of the garbled answers he received.

This was K'Mar Khevi-tan, island headquarters of the worldwide Pracchia conspiracy. He had been held as leverage upon his father. His father had not performed as desired. His usefulness was at an end. He had been ordered destroyed. The old man was defying those orders.

It made no sense to Ethrian.

They descended to a shingly beach. The old man pointed toward a distant shore. It was the color of rust in the foreground, a leaden hue beyond. The strait was narrow, but the boy's vision did not permit him a sound estimate. One mile or two?

"Sa-sa-swim," the old man said. "Sa-safety there. Na-wami."

Ethrian's eyes grew round. "I can't." The thought terrified him. He was an indifferent swimmer at best. He'd never swum in the sea. "I'd never make it."

The old man settled himself cross-legged, lowering himself with exaggerated care. Intense concentration captured his face. He grunted as he strained to bring his slow thoughts into speech. When he did speak, it was with a ponderous precision. "You must. It is your only hope. Here the Director will throw you to the children of Magden Norath. They are your enemies, those who abide here. The sea and Nawami are indifferent. They allow you the chance to live. You must go now. Before He discovers that I have denied His wickedness at last."

Ethrian believed he was hearing the truth. The old-timer was so intense....

He looked at the sea. He was afraid.

The strength of the drug flowed through him. He felt he could run a thousand miles. But swim?

The old man began shaking. Ethrian thought he was dying. But no. It was the strain of making himself understood.

The beasts beneath the island broke into a suddenly redoubled roaring.

"Ga-ga-go!" the old man ordered.

Ethrian took two steps and flung himself into the chilly brine. He got a mouthful immediately. He stood chest deep while he coughed it up.

He had been chained naked. He had been in the sun only a short time now, but already he felt the fire of its kiss. He knew he would burn miserably before he reached the nether shore.

He pushed off, and paced himself.

After what seemed a long, long time he rolled onto his back to feather and rest.

He was scarcely three hundred yards off shore. He watched the old man climb the steps they had descended, take a few and rest, take a few and rest. The island was long and lean and jagged. The fortress was an ugly old thing strung out along its spine like the crumbling bones of an ancient, gigantic dragon. He turned and glared at a barren mainland that looked no nearer.

He knew, then, that he would not make it.

He swam on. Stubbornness was in his blood.

He had learned four names during his sojourn. The Director. The Fadema. Magden Norath. Lord Chin. He knew nothing about the man who owned the first. Norath was a sorcerer of Ehelebe. The Fadema was Queen of Argon and, apparently, bewitched by Lord Chin. He and she had spirited Ethrian to the island. Lord Chin was one of the high Tervola, or sorcerer-nobles, of the Dread Empire, against which Ethrian's father had striven. Chin was dead now, but the empire that had spawned him remained active....

Shinsan, the Dread Empire, surely was behind all this.

If he survived....

It seemed that many, many hours had passed. The sun had, indeed, moved westward, but it was not yet in his eyes. The grey hills had grown only slightly darker.... He was too tired to go on. His stubbornness had burned away.

He was ready to sink into the deep. He was too tired to be afraid.

Something brushed his leg.

He was no longer too tired. He kicked in panic and tried to swim away.

A dorsal fin slid across his field of vision. Another something touched him.

He began to flail and gasp.

One of the sea beasts flung itself into the air. It arced gracefully and plunged into the brine.

Ethrian was not reassured. He was an inland child. He did not know a dolphin from a shark. Of sharks he had heard from his father's friend, Bragi Ragnarson. His godfather had told cruel, grim stories of the great killers ravening amongst the crews of ships wrecked in fell sea-battles.

His struggles earned him nothing but a belly full of salt water.

The dolphins surrounded him. They bore him up and carried him to the desert shore. With his last spark of energy he dragged himself across the rocky beach into the shadow of a cliff. He collapsed, puked seawater till his guts ached, fell asleep.

Something wakened him. The time was deep night. The moon was high and full. He listened. He had thought he heard a voice calling, but now there was nothing.

He looked down at the beach. Something was moving there, making little clacky sounds... He saw them. Crabs. Scores of them. They seemed to be staring at him, waving their claws like soldiers' salutes. One by one, they scuttled closer.

He drew away, frightened. They meant to eat him! He sprang to his feet and stumbled away. The crabs became agitated. They could not keep his pace.

He seated himself a hundred yards away. Stones had torn his feet and barked his shins.

Again, faintly, he thought he heard someone calling. He could distinguish neither direction nor words.

He stumbled a little farther, then collapsed and slept again.

He had strange dreams. A beautiful woman in white came and spoke to him, but he could not understand her, nor did he remember her when he wakened.

Daylight was almost gone. He was hungry and thirsty. His whole body ached. His sunburned skin had blistered. He tried drinking from the sea. His stomach refused the brine. For a time he lay on the sand in an agony of heaving.

He rose and surveyed the land by twilight. It was utterly without life. There were no plants. No cliff swallows wheeled against the gathering darkness. No sundown insects hummed the air. Even the rocks were barren of lichens. The only living things he had seen were the crabs, which had come from the sea.

A touch of cunning came upon him. He settled himself near the water, watching the waves charge toward his toes, peter out, and slide away.

He used a stone to smash several crabs when they came. He ripped out salty flesh and ate till his stomach again rebelled.

He retreated from the water and slept a few hours more.

The moon was up when he wakened. He thought he heard voices. He crawled out to the sand, where he could stand and walk without further injuring his feet. Searching the line of cliffs, he thought, for an instant, that he saw a woman in white staring out to sea, her arms lifted as if in supplication. Her clothing whipped around her, yet the air was completely still.

She disappeared when he moved to a better vantage.

He considered his predicament. He had to get off the beach and find food and water. Especially water. And something useful as clothing, else the sun would cook him alive.

He could see no way up the cliffs.

He started walking along the strand.

Exhaustion overcame him soon after dawn. He crawled into a shadow and slept among jagged rocks. His tongue felt like a ball of wool.

The tide came in. The sea pounded the rocks, thundering, hurling white spray thirty feet into the air. And again Ethrian dreamed.

Again a woman in white came. Again he could understand nothing she said.

And again he wakened after dark, and ambushed crabs, and thought of walking on down the beach in search of a break in the cliffs.

The tide was out, yet seemed to be in. The crash of breakers seemed far, far away. Over them, he heard the faintest creaking, then clanking and shouting. He settled on a boulder, waited to see what was happening.

Suddenly, he saw what looked like a fleet of a thousand ships out on the white-capped sea. Boats plunged through the surf like raging black horses, scraped on sand and shingle, discharged lean, dark-bearded men in alien armor. Shorter, fairer men in armor equally strange met them on the beach. Their swords flashed and sang.

A voice called out above the roar of battle. Ethrian looked up. A woman in white stood upon the clifftop, her arms outstretched. Blue fire crackled among her fingers.

Blue witchfire played over the white-winged vessels upon the sea. Leviathans surfaced and flung themselves at the ships. Sharks and porpoises swam to the woman's song, ignoring one another as they attacked the swarthy invaders.

Then ruby bolts flashed from the ships, pounding the cliffs. Great walls of stone fell on the combatants on the beach....

Winged things arced across the moon, their mouths trailing tongues of fire. Creatures bigger than men rode their scaly backs, vast black cloaks trailing behind them. In their hands they bore spears of light which they hurled at the woman in white.

She spun webs of blue and cast them into the firmament. They fluttered toward the winged lizards like merry moths, wrapped themselves about the dragons, and brought them tumbling to earth.

One thing Ethrian noted through the flash and flame: The land was alive. Riotously alive. It could not be the desert that held him captive on its shore.

The vision began to fade. He looked this way and that, trying to make sense of it. It was gone before he could grasp anything more.

He looked toward where the woman had stood. There was a gap where the red bolts had bayoneted the cliffs. A gap where, earlier, he thought there had been nothing but solid cliffline.

He crept that way, unsure, cautious. The moon was high now. He could see the tumbled stone well.

It was not a fresh fall. Ages had gnawed at the boulders in the slide.

A voice seemed to call from the desert beyond.

He froze.

It was another of the ghost voices. He shrugged. He had no time for mysteries. His great task was to survive. To do that he had to get off this shore.

The climb was an epic of pain. And he found nothing above but moon-silvered desert vistas. More land utterly without life. Yet... yet he heard the voices. Wordless voices. They called.

What was this land? What forgotten spirits haunted its barrens? Gingerly, he limped in the direction whence the voices seemed to come.

His feet were swollen, raw, and festering. His tongue was fat and dry. His sunburn blisters were breaking. He ached in every sinew and joint. A throbbing pain beat from temple to temple.

But he was stubborn. He went on. And, in time, the descending moon outlined something atop the nearest mountain.

The more he studied it, the more it looked like some gargantuan figure carved from the mountain itself. It was a great sphinxlike creature, facing eastward.

Something crackled beneath his foot. He stooped. It was a twig with a few dry leaves attached. It had been tumbled along by the wind. It was acacia, though he did not recognize it, never having seen the tree.

His heart leapt. Where trees grew there must be water. He limped faster, moving like a man dancing on coals.

Dawn came. He was stumbling and falling more than walking. His hands and knees were raw. The great stone beast loomed high ahead, up just a few hundred yards of slope.

It was larger than he had estimated. It reared at least two hundred feet into the air, and stretched back out of sight over the lip of the flat space surrounding it. It was very old and time-worn. The once deeply carven features were all but invisible now.

He paid little heed to the stone figure. His eyes were all for the scraggly trees around the fabulous creature's forepaws.

The sun beat at his naked back, igniting new agonies. Though he fell more and more often, he pressed on. Crawling, he dragged himself onto the flat area.

Water! A shallow pool lay between the monster's feet... He heaved himself upright and tottered forward, fell on his face half in and half out of the moisture in the depression. He gulped the algae-thick, stagnant water till his belly ached.

Only minutes later he heaved it up again.

He waited, and drank more, though sparingly this time. Then he splashed across the pool into a shadow that looked like it would persist all day. He collapsed into a fetal ball and slept.

He dreamed strange and powerful dreams.

The woman in white came. She examined his hurts. Where her fingers touched the pain went away. He looked on himself and found that he had healed. He tried to mask his nakedness with his hands. She smiled gently and went to stand between the monster's paws. She stared at the moon lifting out of the sea, limning the fortress riding the spine of the island off the coast.

Ethrian joined her. He gazed upon the desert, and saw it as it might have been. Lush, rich, peopled by an industrious, pious race.... But there were fires burning on the island. There were ships upon the sea. They were so numerous their sails masked the waves. And there were columns of smoke on the land, and dragons in the sky. Fell wraiths bestrode the thunderous lizards, raining destruction from the firmament. The armies of Nawami fought, were defeated, and fell back to reform their companies. The woman in white summoned dread sorceries with which to lend them aid. Even that was not enough.

Then the stone beast spoke. It opened its mouth and said a Word. The Word called forth thunder and doom. Skull-faced wraiths plummeted from the sky. Dragons screamed and clawed their ears. The invaders fled to their ships.

They did not remain gone. A Power dwelt on the island in the east. Ethrian could feel it, could sense its name. Nahaman the Odite. A woman of great evil and great Power, possessed by hatred, obsessed with a need to destroy Nawami.

Nahaman rallied her armies and struck again. They rolled across the land and descended from the clouds. Neither the witchery of the woman in white nor the Word of the stone beast could shatter the countless waves of them. Each time they came, their attack crested a little nearer the stone beast's mountain.

Ethrian soon realized he was seeing generations of struggle condensed into a night, an age of warfare reduced to its high points.

The hordes of the Odite did come to the mountain. They destroyed everything they could, and silenced the stone beast's mouth.

Nahaman came ashore. With the aid of her skull-faced wraiths she smote the land barren. The woman in white and the monster of stone could do naught but watch. The beast's mouth was his Power and her life. Nawami's sole preservation, in the beast's wan power, lay between those great rock paws.

Nahaman and the survivors of her host withdrew to the island, and thence overseas, and darkened the shores of Nawami no more.

Ethrian was puzzled. All that drama and violence, just to sail away? What was it all about?

The woman in white became older. He felt her despair. Long had she lived. Long had the mouth of the stone beast preserved her youth and beauty. Now she aged. She withered. She became a crone. She begged for death. The beast would not let her die. Her body became old dry sticks. Even that faded away, till she was no more than an aching spirit fluttering the slopes of the beast's mountain.

Ethrian wakened to the light of dawn. He had slept the clock around. He smelled sweet water. He scrambled to the pool.

Not till he had slaked his thirst did he notice that his hands no longer ached. They remained raw, but seemed on their way to a miraculous healing.

He stood and examined himself. His feet, too, were improving rapidly. His knees were better. Even the sting of the sunburn had disappeared.

He whirled around, suddenly frightened.

Near where he had slept lay a pair of sandals, a neatly folded toga, and a leaf on which stood a stack of seedcakes.

Fear and hunger warred within him. Hunger won. He seized the cakes, fled to the pool, alternately ate and drank. When he finished, he clothed himself. Sandals and toga fit perfectly.

He began exploring. Try as he might, he found no evidence of any presence but his own. He stared at the stone beast. Was there a ghost of a smile on those weathered lips?

He climbed the monster and looked round from the peak of its great head.

For as far as he could see this country was lifeless. The flatter land was ochre and rust. The mountains were bare grey stone.

He knew he would never leave. No mere mortal could storm that wasteland and hope to evade the Dark Lady's eternal embrace.

That old man had not done him much of a favor.

He tried calling the woman in white, the stone beast, even Nahaman the Odite. His shouts did nothing but stir muted echoes.

Some seemed echoes of timeless mirth.

He returned to his place by the pool.

"Deliverer."

The voice came to him out of dream. The woman was beside him, but the word had not come from her. It had whispered down from above.

"What?"

"Deliverer. The one foretold. The one whose coming I prophesied in the hour of our despair. He who shall deliver us from the curse of Nahaman and restore to us the days of glory."

Ethrian was thoroughly baffled.

"Long have we awaited your coming, our powers dwindling to a ghost of what once was. Free us of our shackles and we will grant your every whim. Unchain us and we will make of you a Lord of the earth, as were our servants of old, before Nahaman rebelled and flung her dark horde against us."

Ethrian did not feel like anyone's savior. He felt like what he was, a confused, frightened boy. He had stumbled onto something bigger than he, something beyond comprehension.

He was interested in surviving, finding his way home, and getting back at his enemies. In that order.

"You have fears and hatreds within you, Deliverer. We see them. We read them as a scribe reads the leaves of a book. We say, free us. Together shall we trample your enemies into the dust. Indite. Reveal unto the Deliverer the chained might of Nawami, that shall be his to wield as a spear of revenge."

The woman in white walked into the darkness between the beast's paws.

Ethrian envisioned those who had imprisoned him, those who had carried off his mother and made insupportable demands upon his father. Only Lord Chin had perished. His henchmen remained alive.

Shinsan, the Dread Empire, was their spawning ground. He would destroy Shinsan if the power came to his hand.

"That power is yours now, Deliverer. You need but accept it. Follow Sahmanan. Let her become your first minister in the restoration of Nawami."

The woman in white beckoned from the shadows. Ethrian walked toward her. She preceded him into darkness.

That darkness grew more intense, more tangible with every step. He extended a hand, expecting to encounter the stone between the beast's huge forelegs.

He walked many times that distance. He encountered no barrier. The woman vanished. He kept touch only by pursuing a sort of wordless whisper she trailed behind. He could not take her hand. Unlike the stone beast, she had no substance.

Suddenly, he stepped into light.

He gaped. And a tale came back, told him by his father's erstwhile friend, Bragi Ragnarson, the godfather who might have conspired in the destruction of his godson's family.

The Hall of the Mountain King. The Under Mountain, or Thunder Mountain as the Trolledyngjans called it. The caverns where a King of the Dead held sway, and sent damned spirits riding the mountain winds in search of mortal prey....

He stood on a narrow ledge overlooking a cavern so vast its nether bounds could not be discerned. Sahmanan stood beside him. She gestured. So faintly it was almost inaudible, he heard, "All this is yours to command, Deliverer."

They were arrayed in motionless battalions and regiments, in perfectionist rank and file, an army frozen in time. Their number was beyond Ethrian's comprehension. They were both warriors in white and warriors of the breed that had stormed Nawami in the name of Nahaman the Odite. Footmen. Horsemen. Elephanteers. Fell skullfaces still astride their dragon steeds.

They had been captured in a crystalline moment, like insects in amber. They poised motionless beneath a light from nowhere that neither waxed nor waned nor wavered. An air of tension, of impatient waiting, pervaded the cavern.

"They know you, Deliverer. They are eager to find life in your avenging hand."

"What are they?" the boy demanded. "Where did they come from?"

"Long before Nawami fell it was obvious that Nahaman would work her will. We sidestepped her fury by slipping out the door of time. We allowed her her victory. We devoted our Power to preparations for the day a Deliverer would release us from the bonds she would impose. We did not expect you to be so long coming, nor did we foresee her so weakening us that a sending of dolphins would almost be beyond us."

Ethrian's basic questions remained unanswered. He suspected he would not find the important answers till too late. "Who are these people?"

"Some of the fallen of the Nawami Crusades. They were reanimated, motivated, and preserved by our art," said the voice of the stone beast. "They, too, await their Deliverer." Dead men? Ethrian thought. He was supposed to perform some foul necromancy that would recall the dead?

Revulsion hit him. The dead were much feared in his age.

The woman in white faced him. A smile toyed with her mouth. She began to talk. Her words did not synchronize with the movement of her lips.

"You have your enemies, do you not?" Her speech seemed to come from afar, like a whispering breeze through pines. "Here lies the power to lay them low, Deliverer."

Ethrian was young, confused, frightened, and dreaming, but he was not stupid. He knew there would be a price.

What was it?

"Free us," the woman insisted. "Deliver us. That's all we ask."

Ethrian gazed upon the armies in waiting, the armies of the dead, and reflected on the fall of Nawami. Should such fury be released again? Could it be controlled? Was revenge so important?

What other force could face the might of the Dread Empire? Only these elder sorceries could withstand those boiling in Shinsan today.

And he had himself to consider. If he refused them, would Sahmanan and the beast help him survive? Why should they bother?

He would become one more bone monument to the deadliness of this land.

He walked away from the woman, back whence he had come, till again he could see the silvered scape of the barrens. There were lights on the island in the east. He glared at them, hating the people who had lighted them.

He was nothing in this world. He was as powerless as a worm. How else could he punish their crimes?

Sahmanan had followed him from the darkness. "How do I release you?" he asked.

She tried to explain.

"When next we meet," he said, cutting her short. "I'll give you my answer then. I have to think first." He went to his sleeping place, curled into a fetal ball. He was learning a whole new breed of fear.

Dreams came. They never stopped. And this time he did not waken for a long time. He lay in that one place for what seemed an age, unmoving, while the stone beast used the last of its power to show him the world, to proselytize him, to teach him what was needed of Nawami's Deliverer.

Seldom were Ethrian's dreams diverting.

2

YEAR 1016 AFE

A TIME OF CHANGES

"HE'S COMING! He's at the Gate of Pearl!" Chu enthused.

Ssu-ma Shih-ka'i looked up from the morning reports. He was a stocky, muscular man with a bull neck. He possessed a porcine air. He looked more like a wrestler than the Tervola-commandant of a legion of the Middle Army. "K'wang-yin, comport yourself as befits an Aspirant."

Chu snapped to attention. "I'm sorry, Lord Ssu-ma."

Shih-ka'i stepped from behind his desk. "You're always sorry, K'wang-yin. I find your endless apologies offensive."

The youth stared over his commander's shoulder. "I'm sorry, Lord."

Shih-ka'i ground his teeth. This one was hopeless. Tervola-spawned or not, this one would not have been elected in the old days. War losses should not justify lowered qualifying levels.

Shih-ka'i remembered the old standards with an almost reverent pride.

Ssu-ma Shih-ka'i came of peasant stock. His brethren among the Tervola never forgot that his father had been a swineherd. He did not let them forget that he had come through his Candidacy in the days of the Princes Thaumaturge, when only the best of the best had scaled the slippery ladder leading to membership in Shinsan's elite.

Jokes about his paternity still haunted Tervola gatherings. They no longer mocked him to his face, but his successes had not changed their secret prejudices.

He had learned much during his Candidacy. He had developed a thick hide and a perseverance which had carried him far beyond the heights his electors had expected him to attain. He was a stubborn, determined man.

The Tervola made great show of keeping their ranks open to every child of talent, discipline, and determination. The show was mostly illusion. Ssu-ma would remain an outsider to the old-line aristocracy. He would sire no sons on their daughters. His daughters, if ever he fathered any, would not be mated by lean, pale sons of the Power such as this scatterbrained chela of his.

K'wang-yin apologized again, killing the silence born of Ssu-ma's moment of introspection. His commander fought the gratification such obsequiousness caused. He had them in his power for a time. He made or broke them. That was sufficient. Only the strong survived. He growled, "K'wang-yin, if I hear one more apology, you'll do a month of primary training."

Chu began shaking.

Shih-ka'i looked at pale, twitching cheeks and knew this one would never be accredited Select. Not while Lord Ssu-ma cast the deciding vote. He was too damned timid. "Make a proper report, K'wang-yin."

"Sir!" Chu spat. "Lord Kuo Wen-chin has approached the Gate of Pearl. He requests audience with your Lordship. Commander of the Guard's respects, sir."

"Better. Much better. You're on the right trail. Step outside. Wait two minutes. Compose yourself. Do it again. Knock before you enter."

Chu's cheek twitched. "As you will, Lord."

Shih-ka'i seated himself behind his desk. His gaze returned to the morning reports.

He did not see them. Lord Kuo! Here! He was amazed. What did the man want? Why would he waste time visiting a peasant-born training legion commandant?

Shih-ka'i's legion was the Fourth Demonstration. It accepted a crop of three-year-olds each spring. Over the next eighteen years of their lives it made of them the most dedicated and feared soldiers the world had ever known.

With the exception of a few brief postings, Shih-ka'i had been with the Fourth since childhood, his talent and will driving him upward against the prejudice and inertia of nobly born Tervola. He had been the legion's commander for two decades. He was proud of the soldiers and Selects he produced. They advanced swiftly wherever they were posted. His superiors believed he was the best at what he did. They extended themselves to keep him happy with an assignment usually given Tervola in heavy disfavor. There were no honors to be won commanding a Demonstration legion.

Shih-ka'i had drifted into a professional cul-de-sac. He knew it. Recent changes in the political climate, with younger Tervola ousting Ko Feng's older circle, made his future appear all the more bleak. Though apolitical himself, he was among the oldest and most tradition-bound of the senior Tervola.

Lord Kuo had come. What could he want but to rid himself of another of the old guard? Already Ko Feng's followers had been stripped of their army and corps and Council positions. They had been awarded unimportant postings in the moribund Eastern and Northern Armies. Ko Feng himself had been stripped of his immortality and honors. He had gone into a self-imposed exile rather than endure demotion. Had the purge acquired a life of its own, like a demon carelessly summoned? Had it begun to strike simply on the basis of age?

Shih-ka'i was frightened. And he was angry. He had survived the Princes Thaumaturge, Mist, O Shing, the Pracchia conspiracy, Ko Feng, and had given offense to none. He was a soldier of the empire. They had no right, no grievance. He ignored politics and power struggles.

The door responded to gently tapping knuckles. "Enter."

Chu stepped in and reported. This time he was perfection itself. He had conquered the electric excitement Lord Kuo generated wherever he appeared.

"That's better. Much better. Our first mission is to conquer ourselves, is it not? Lord Kuo, eh? What do you suppose he wants?"

"I don't know, Lord. He didn't say."

"Uhm." Shih-ka'i was not satisfied with the hand now guiding Shinsan's destiny. From afar he perceived Kuo Wen-chin as too idealistic, naive, simplistic, and uninformed. Two years ago he had been a corps commander of Shih-ka'i's own Middle Army. He was too young, too inexperienced. Still, he had momentum. He had charisma. He filled a need for new leadership, new ideals, given birth by the failure in the west. Maybe new perspectives could mend the wounds in the spirit of the legions.

"Shall I greet him, Lord Ssu-ma?" The Aspirant glowed with eagerness.

"Can you comport yourself with restraint and respect?"

"Yes, Lord."

Shih-ka'i was disgusted by the pleading note in the youth's voice. Nevertheless, "Go, then. Bring him directly to me."

"Lord." Chu whirled, and surged toward the door.

"K'wang-yin. If you embarrass me, you'll do a whole year in primary."

Chu froze. When he resumed moving his face was calm and his pace sedate. His frame stood rigidly erect.

Shih-ka'i permitted himself a small smile.

Lord Kuo Wen-chin waved a thin, almost feminine hand as he stepped into Shih-ka'i's office. "Don't rise, Lord Ssu-ma." Kuo doffed his cruel silver-and-jet wolf's mask. Perforce, Shih-ka'i accepted the informality and removed his own facepiece.

This was his favorite jibe at his brethren. It mimicked a boar in a killing rage. One tusk was of quartz, the other of ruby, as if to imply that one tusk had just ripped an enemy. The mask as a whole had a carefully crafted battle-scarred look.

Tervola invested a great deal of thought and Power in their badges of station. It was said that a skilled observer could read a whole soul from a well-made mask.

"You honor us, Lord Kuo."

"Not really. I need you, so I'm here."

"Uhm?" Shih-ka'i considered his visitor. Almost feminine features. Smaller than the run of Tervola from the older lines. Attractive, but in a female sort of way. He reminded Shih-ka'i of the Demon Princess, Mist, whom he had encountered occasionally during her brief reign.

"You know what I represent. Change. New blood. A clean sweep of associations with Ko Feng's ill-starred ventures."

"Don't forget that Lord Feng's group brought us annexations of epic scale."

Kuo waved one of those delicate hands. "Nevertheless... There's Western Army. Twice defeated. Once under the Dragon Prince, again during the Pracchia gambit." In this empire, an empire unaccustomed to defeat, even an appearance of defeat was unpardonable.

"Ko Feng could have won at Palmisano. He withdrew rather than risk losses which might have damaged the stability of the legions. He was a methodical man. He would have anticipated the cost to himself. He withdrew anyway."

Kuo looked irritated. He took a moment to control himself. "We can't, of course, know what would have happened had he chosen to stand. Lord Ssu-ma, I didn't come here to argue. I don't want to exhume our yesterdays."

No, Shih-ka'i thought. You want to bury them deep, and with them everyone who made them. And with them all the good of them, lest someone remember and compare. "Tomorrows. Those interest us all, don't they? Speak to me of tomorrows, Lord Kuo."

Kuo brightened. He smiled an effeminate smile. "You mis-estimate me. I'm not here to dismiss you. I do want to rusticate you, though. To Eastern Army."

Shih-ka'i's stomach dropped a hundred feet. So. The purge *had* burst its political bounds. "I'm not a political creature, Lord. My business is the creation of soldiers. I do that quite well."

"I know. I did my Candidacy with the Fourth Demonstration. I'm sure you don't remember me. You were a brigade leader at the time. But I remembered you. You impressed me."

"Uhm?" Shih-ka'i kept his feelings concealed. He did not remember Candidate Kuo. Was the man about to requite some slight?

"Lord Ssu-ma, I want you to command Eastern Army."

The world fell away again. "Lord! I... I've never held a field command."

"You've directed the Fourth in field exercises. It's been at corps strength because of our replacement demands. I think you can handle it. You're the man I want. You have the stubbornness of Ko Feng without his limitations. You think on your feet. You get jobs done. More, you're an older Tervola. You have no discernible political bias. You'll fit into the gap between myself and the recidivists I rashly banished to what looked like a sessile frontier army."

Kuo's brief rule had bewitched Shinsan with its amazements and marvels and unpredictable decisions. Here was another of the same.

"But my background..."

"Irrelevant. Completely irrelevant. You're Tervola. You're trained to command. If I set you to command, none will deny me. Lord Ssu-ma, will you accept Eastern Army?"

Outwardly, Shih-ka'i remained a man of stone. Within, he flailed about, trying to grasp something, anything, that would give him a grip on a turbulent reality. Command of an army! Even of the diminutive Eastern Army... It was an honor he never had dared hope to attain.

"When?"

"Right away. I need you out there."

"What's happened?"

"No one is quite sure. For lack of anything better to do, they're exploring the desert that stopped their advance. Patrols have vanished. They'll fill you in when you get there. Will you accept the command?"

"Lord... Yes. I will."

"Good." Kuo smiled. "I thought you would." He produced a small scarlet badge that resembled the face of a man with a beak instead of a nose. The badge of an army commander. There were just a handful in existence. It took the convocation of the entire Council of Tervola, with mighty sorceries, to create one. Shih-ka'i accepted it humbly, wondering who had worn it before him. He would have to learn its history and honors.

"You should start east with whatever staff you need as soon as I find someone to replace you here. Your army will consist of the five legions currently posted. I had planned to withdraw two before the disappearances began. Northern Army will be available in reserve, though I'm reducing it to corps strength." Kuo went on to explain that he was stripping all the armies in favor of the southern frontier.

"But... we have twenty-six legions there already."

"The Matayangan situation is worsening. They're trying to lure us into giving provocation for a pre-emptive strike. They want to hit us while the legions are still under strength. We'll give them a surprise if they do."

Shih-ka'i nodded. Shinsan had expanded too fast recently. Civil and foreign wars had drained the legions. The army was strained, trying to hold the present frontiers. Losses denied it manpower usually devoted to assimilation and re-education of conquered peoples. The empire had become a fragile structure. "What about the west?" The Tervola feared the west more than the numerically stronger south.

"I've told Hsung to normalize. To avoid confrontation. To shift his emphasis from the military to the political. They're vulnerable in their disunity. Intrigue should be his weapon of choice. It could be decades before we avenge our dead. We have to digest what we've taken."

Lord Kuo impressed Shih-ka'i now. His inflammatory demagoguery had been, apparently, a device to push Ko Feng aside. Today he was talking a more realistic response to the empire's problems. Maybe he could reverse the trend toward chaos that had set in with the deaths of the Princes Thaumaturge.

Their swift parade of successors had shattered stability by warring among themselves while launching unwise foreign adventures.

"I'll be pleased to command Eastern Army. I'm honored that you think me competent. I'll begin selecting staff today."

A faint irritation flickered across Kuo's face. He was being dismissed—he. Then he smiled. Ssu-ma could not shake old habit. Younger men were trainees... He rose. "I wish you luck, Lord Ssu-ma."

"Thank you." Shih-ka'i wasn't really listening. He was engrossed in his work once more.

He had to hide in the training reports for a while. This stroke of fortune would take some digesting.

Shih-ka'i found that he had to guard thirty-four hundred miles of border with thirty thousand men. The eastern legions were, at least, at strength. None had been involved in the ill-starred western campaign.

He also had to govern and keep the peace in the military frontier zone.

His predecessor had done the obvious and employed local auxiliaries. They weren't much. The peoples of Shih-ka'i's new proconsulate were all savages. Only a few tribes had a Bronze Age level of technology, though storytellers spoke of a past age of greatness. They had revealed a few ruins in support of their claims.

Shih-ka'i followed the lead of his predecessors and made his headquarters with the Seventeenth Legion. The Seventeenth's zone of responsibility faced the questionable desert. The legion had taken all the reported losses.

The Seventeenth had raised a stout new fortress just miles from the edge of the badlands. Shih-ka'i arrived to find the commander engaged in a vigorous program of exploration. One wall of the fortress's main hall had been plastered smooth. Legionnaires were painting in a huge map, bit by bit, as exploratory teams contributed details. Shih-ka'i did not bother visiting his new quarters before going into conference.

He strolled along the one-hundred-fifty-foot length of the wall, studying and memorizing each detail. At one point he asked, "Does it truly begin this suddenly?" He indicated a line near the floor, where green gave way to brown along a well-defined line.

The commander of the Seventeenth, Lun-yu Tasi-feng, replied, "Virtually, Lord Ssu-ma. It fades from forest to grassland to dust and sand within a mile. Were the wind not blowing consistently eastward, the desert would crawl this way like an unstoppable army."

"Rainfall?"

"Considerable, Lord. Both here and there. In the desert you can watch the clouds pile up against these mountains, but nothing grows."

"Uh-hmm." Shih-ka'i studied the sketchy outline of the mountain chain. "Rivers?"

"Several flow out. The only life we've found is a few fish that have swum upstream. They don't travel far. They find nothing to sustain themselves."

Shih-ka'i let his gaze wander. In time, he asked, "Elements of the Seventeenth were involved in the war with Escalon, were they not?"

Tasi-feng replied, "I was there myself, Lord."

"Does this compare to the desolation created there?"

"It's even more thorough, Lord. The thought occurred to me too. I'm operating on the assumption that the land was smitten by the Power, though we've yet to find certain proof."

"Historical research?"

"Nothing on record anywhere, Lord."

"It's very old, then. What about oral traditions among the tribes? I've heard there are ruins in the forests. Have you tried to determine their age?"

"The tribes say there was a war among the gods. The ruins are at least a thousand years old. Probably a lot older. I have my leading necromancer working in the best preserved city. He hasn't been able to determine more."

"Have you consulted Outside?"

"Demons either don't know or won't tell."

"I see. How many men have you lost?"

Shih-ka'i listened to an exact recitation of every detail known about a dozen group disappearances. Tasi-feng indicated their last known positions on the map. Each party had reached the mountains. No other pattern was apparent.

"Have you tried high altitude search?"

"Birds refuse to fly over the desert, Lord. I wanted to send a dragon, but my request was refused. Too many perished in the western campaign, they say. They say they need to breed their numbers up. Personally, I think they're as frightened as the birds."

"Oh? Have they been interrogated? Some would be older than those ruins."

"If they know anything, they're not saying. They're less talkative than the demons."

"Curious. Most curious. Lord Lun-yu, I commend you. You've been thorough."

"There's little else to do out here, Lord. The centurions complain that it's just make-work."

Shih-ka'i smiled behind his mask. "They would. I'm curious. Lord Kuo seemed to think this a critical puzzle. He was quite concerned. Could you guess why?"

"I'm not certain, Lord. Perhaps because there have been flickers of the Power beyond the mountains." He raked a pointer along the top of the wall, over a distance of twenty feet. "They emanated from somewhere here."

Shih-ka'i's gaze bored into the map. In time, he asked, "What's the quality of the water in those rivers? Fit to drink?"

"Heavy with minerals, as you might expect. But potable, Lord." Tasi-feng seemed puzzled by the question.

"So. We begin narrowing the scope, Lord Lun-yu. The lost missions face the area you just indicated. Accept it as a pattern. We'll send expeditions immediately, on parallel tracks. A Tervola will accompany each. At evening camp a transfer portal will be opened." He took the pointer. "When the expeditions reach this line, we'll set up movable transfers. Five centuries will remain battle-ready at all times. They should be prepared to transfer at a moment's notice. Hourly reports will be returned, and news of any anomaly immediately. The parties will travel light. Weapons and equipment only. They'll be supplied through the transfers. They'll continue their advance till we have some answers. We'll keep fresh people out there by rotating through the portals."

"Lord, that ambitious a program will require the support of the entire legion."

"You yourself said there's nothing else to do. And Lord Kuo expressed a more than passing interest in obtaining answers."

"Of course, Lord."

"Is there anything else I should know?"

"No, Lord. That's all... There have been two reports of dragon sightings, Lord. From natives. There was no confirmation. The dragons themselves deny making overflights."

"I see. I commend you again, Lord Lun-yu. You've been as thorough as anyone could ask."

Shih-ka'i retired to his quarters. His batman had everything prepared. He allowed the decurion to remove his mask. "Are you tired, Pan ku?"

"Not if my Lord has a task for me."

"It's nothing immediate. When you have the free time. Mix with the legionnaires. See what they're saying. Find out what they're talking about most."

"As you wish, My Lord."

"I'll rest now." Shih-ka'i stretched himself on his new bed. He did not sleep, though he closed his eyes. He felt a presence in the east. It was something strange. Something alien. It was not tangible, yet it was disquieting. He wondered if Lord Kuo had felt it too.

The exploratory parties had advanced seventy miles into the desert. They were past the last known positions of the lost parties. Of those the only evidence so far found was a single cracked piece of lacquer off the elbow joint of a soldier's armor.

"That's suggestive," Shih-ka'i said. "They wouldn't travel in armor. Too hot out there. Search the area more carefully."

The search turned up nothing. This party had vanished six months ago. Nature had obliterated all trace of their passing.

Two days later one party reported having reached the crest of a mountain. The range dropped away beyond. Shih-ka'i donned his battle gear and transferred there himself.

The slope fell away in a long grey slide. In the distance the grey became rust. For as far as he could see nothing stirred. Nothing lived. The sheer magnitude of the desolation overpowered him.

Another party crested the range a few miles to the south. Its Tervola sent a signal. Shih-ka'i responded. He told the commander of the party he was with, "Remain here. Watch them as they descend." He returned to the legion's headquarters.

The fortress was in turmoil. Tasi-feng explained, "Yang-chu is under attack. He requested reinforcements. I sent him a century."

"Take prisoners. Return them immediately. Bring another century to the ready."

Fifteen minutes later two prisoners came through the transfer portal. They were short men in strange armor. They were dead.

"I want them alive," Shih-ka'i said.

Tasi-feng conferred with the Tervola on the scene. "Lord Ssu-ma, Yang-chu says they were alive when they transferred. They had to be driven into the portal."

"Tell him to send more."

Two more pairs came through. They were as dead as the first. Of the last pair one was a tall, dark man whose armor did not resemble that of the others.

"Have them examined," Shih-ka'i said. He strode back to the map room. Another party had reported itself under attack. He wanted to confirm his memory of their positions. "Uhm," he murmured. "Come, whoever you are. Hit me one more time."

He got his wish within the hour. Two minutes later he had strings attached to the points where each attack was taking place, stretching toward the top of the map. Soldiers were shading areas where the three would cross. The launching of additional attacks allowed Shih-ka'i to begin reducing the size of the shaded area.

"Keep it up," he murmured. "I'll have you pinpointed." He glanced at the log of the times the attacks had been reported. Might the attackers have departed the same point at the same time? Their dispersion and lack of coordination suggested that might be the case. "Lord Lun-yu. Let Yang-chu's position be a point on a circle. Let the other attacked positions be points outside that circle. See if you can describe the circle using the lag in the times of attack."

Lord Lun-yu looked puzzled for a moment, caught on, went to work. He received data from two more assaults. He developed a crude, skewed arc. "It doesn't look right, Lord."

"Guess me a maximum and minimum radius. The terrain they crossed should account for the irregularities." He peered at the map. Neither of his methods was working well. The first, in fact, now looked a little foolish. He had, in effect, collected a lot of lone legs of triangles. He did not know any lengths or angles.

The scope of search did seem to be narrowing.

He accepted a casualty report from a messenger. "Hmm?"

"Lord?" Tasi-feng inquired.

"These people are reasonably good fighters."

Another runner reported that the force attacking Yang-chu had withdrawn. Soon similar reports arrived from the other attacked parties. Shih-ka'i observed, "Their communications are fair."

Tasi-feng asked, "Shall we pursue, Lord?"

Shih-ka'i glanced at the map. "Slowly." He indicated two parties which had not been attacked. "Move these people to pincer the group dropping off here. We'll take more prisoners. Tell Yang-chu to hold his position. I want to see what he's got."

Yang-chu's group had received the most attention. The

slope below his perimeter was littered with bodies. "They took some of their fallen with them," the Tervola told Shih-ka'i. "As many as they could carry."

Shih-ka'i looked across the desert. Among the dust devils he could see a cloud raised by the retreating enemy. "Any wizardry used?"

"Neither by us nor them, Lord."

"Good." He watched the dust. Where could they have come from? How could people exist in this? He glanced at the bodies, quickly averted his gaze. He was not accustomed to seeing the aftermath of battles.

The corpses were of men who had been well-fed, well-clad, and well-armed. "Yang-chu." He indicated the dead. "Collect them. Strip them. Keep each man's things separate. Send the bundles through to the fortress." He summoned his will, looked into a few lifeless faces. They told him very little. All dead men had the same message for the living. It was a message Lord Ssu-ma did not want to hear.

They were a curious breed. Both kinds. Shih-ka'i had never seen their like before. But how were they so different?

He shrugged. The legion's surgeons would dissect them and let him know.

He took a last look at the dust cloud. It was moving straight out the line he had drawn on the map. He returned to the fortress.

Tasi-feng greeted him with, "Lord, Hsu Shen says there were soldiers of the empire in the band that attacked him.

"Ours?"

"They wore our armor. Their badges were of the Seventeenth."

"Your missing men?"

"Perhaps. I told him to keep it quiet till we can explain it."

"Good. Shift those two intercept groups around. Tell them to double-time and get into position to stop that party. Tell Hsu Shen to go after them and resume contact. I'll want a portal open out there when our people are in position. I want to see this myself."

"As you will, Lord."

Shih-ka'i observed while the legion's Candidates went through the clothing and effects recovered from the enemy dead. Each man had borne much of what a soldier could be expected to carry: the tools of his trade and a few personal items that set him off from a thousand more just like him. The things gave no clues. Shih-ka'i examined the lettering on an old coin. He had not seen its like before. "What would you say this head portrays?" he asked one of the Candidates.

"Some sort of fabulous monster, Lord?"

"Perhaps." When he looked directly at it, Shih-ka'i felt an increase in his awareness of the existence of something in the east.

Tasi-feng appeared. "Lord, there seems to have been a continuous, low-grade emanation of the Power since some time before the first attack. The source appears to be near the heart of your circle."

"So." Shih-ka'i reflected momentarily. "Let's take no chances. Establish portals connecting us with the other legions. One cohort each to be ready for immediate transfer here."

"Lord, we're already straining ourselves with the portals we... As you will, Lord."

"Yes. The remainder of each legion is to be placed on first alert. Begin assembling a package that can be sent to Lord Kuo instantly should anything dire happen."

"Lord? You think there's that much danger?"

"No. But I don't believe in leaving anything to chance. Keep the package at a portal. Update it continuously."

"As you will, Lord."

"Also, I want a battery of ballistae readied for long-range work. Let the Candidates handle it. Start now. It'll take them several hours to prepare all the spells."

"Accuracy or destruction, Lord?"

"Destruction."

Shih-ka'i went to the room where the legion's surgeons were at work. One paused to say, "There's something strange here, Lord. We can't be sure, what with the desert heat and so on, but these men look like they've been dead for a long time."

"Oh?"

"Look. Ostensibly, the bodies are less than an hour old. Some of the organs should still show signs of life."

Shih-ka'i looked away from the open cadaver. "I thought you might find something of the sort. Take a good look at the blood."

"Lord?"

"See if the blood is dead or alive. Then make a guess at how long it's been dead." He turned to leave. He had to get out before his gorge rose and betrayed his dignity.

Tasi-feng stood in the doorway. "You've discovered something, Lord?"

"I think they were dead before they attacked. They have the look. It's been a long time since I've seen their like. I imagine it was before you were born. The Demon Prince experimented with reanimated soldiers. He shelved the idea. Control was too cumbersome."

Tasi-feng could not keep his horror hidden behind his mask. He took a moment to control himself. "The new portals are open, Lord Ssu-ma. Our support is standing by. We're still trying to contact Lord Kuo's party. He's reconnoitering the Matayangan border. The parties you sent to establish a blocking position are ahead of the enemy and trying to locate a suitable site."

"Very well. I'm returning to my quarters. Call me when they open their portal."

He had to get away for a few minutes, to conquer the animal in him. He hadn't realized there would be so much difference between the training and battle fields. Once in his quarters he seated himself on a small carpet. He used the basic tool given every child legionnaire. He went through the Soldier's Ritual, the calming mantra-prayers with which soldiers began and ended their days. He regained himself.

Lord Kuo was right, he thought. There is something here. Maybe something bigger than Wen-chin suspected.

Pan ku came in. "Oh. Excuse me, Lord."

"I've just finished, Pan ku. Have you taken the pulse of the legion?"

"They're bored, Lord. They resent being stuck on a dead frontier. Today seems to have perked them up."

"No serious problems?"

"No. This is an old legion. A good one. Well trained and disciplined, with conscientious centurions and decurions. It'll do what you ask of it."

"Good. Good. Thank you, Pan ku."

"Is there anything I can do for you, Lord?"

"Don your battle gear. We're going into the desert."

Shih-ka'i flashed through the portal an hour later. He found that his hunters had chosen a good position in which to wait. After surveying their dispositions, he prepared a number of magicks. "Just in case," he told Pan ku.

The soldier nodded. He was familiar with his master's obsession with being prepared.

Two dust clouds came closer and closer. Hsu Shen was doing a perfect job of pushing without pushing too hard. Shih-ka'i took a look off the back side of the low hill where he waited. Dust clouds were converging on a point several miles eastward. "Setting an ambush of his own," he murmured.

Pan ku came round the hill. "Lord, they just had word from Lord Lun-yu. Two of those bodies jumped up and tried to kill him."

"Uhm? I should have warned him. He's all right?"

"Yes, Lord."

"Good."

Their quarry moved into the pocket. Shih-ka'i counted twenty-five. Someone said, "I thought they were supposed to be carrying their dead?"

Shih-ka'i did not tell the man that the dead were walking again. That none of the attackers had been alive. He gave the signal.

His men revealed themselves. The party below halted. They were badly outnumbered, and Hsu Shen was right behind them.

Shih-ka'i stared. Hsu Shen had been right. Three were legionnaires.

The group formed a turtle, ready to fight. Shih-ka'i's men closed in.

The surrounded men dropped.

Shih-ka'i felt something electric stir the air. "Down!" he bellowed. "Everybody on the ground!" He whipped his mind into his bag of prepared tricks.

What looked like a great black boot sole blotted out the sky. Its heel descended swiftly. For an instant Shih-ka'i pictured himself as a bug about to be crushed.

He loosed a spell.

The air whined with the sound of a thousand giant whetstones scraping steel, then the cracking of a million tiny whips. He looked up. The boot had vanished.

"Get down there and carve those people up before they come alive again!" he thundered.

He did not wait to see if his orders were carried out. He closed his eyes and reentered the realm of spell. He seized one, pictured himself hurling a spear. He painted a big bull's-eye on the map from the fortress wall.

Thunder rolled across the cloudless wasteland. A flash extinguished the sun. Shih-ka'i opened his eyes. A thousand dust devils danced across the barrens like frenzied, drugged dancers, often colliding and collapsing. A few minutes later he heard a remote rumble. He smiled into his mask. "That'll make you keep your head down."

He waited for several minutes, his Tervola-senses extended. Nothing came. His enemy seemed cowed.

For the moment, he thought. Only for the moment.

He joined his men. "We'd do better to burn the bodies," he told Hsu Shen. "But there seems to be a shortage of wood."

The Tervola nodded, untouched by Shih-ka'i's dry humor. He was a man nearly Shih-ka'i's age, one of the old guard banished by Lord Kuo. He too remembered the Demon Prince's experiments. The dead could keep rising and rising, and could recruit their foes to their own cause. They could not be permitted to win battles. They would become stronger with each victory.

"Send those three back to the fortress," Shih-ka'i said, indicating the dead legionnaires. "We'll have that necromancer of Lun-yu's call up their shades."

His neck hairs prickled. He opened up, feeling for some new threat. There was none. He nodded to himself. Something was watching.

He went up the hill and looked to the east. Somewhere out there. In all that nothing. He studied the dust raised by retreating foemen, projecting their lines of march.

There? That heat haze hidden hump on the horizon? He oriented himself by the map. Yes. The hump would be smack in the middle of the suspect area.

"You should have kept your head down, friend," he murmured. "Now we see you. Now we're coming for a closer look."

A wind rose. It was hard and hot and dry. The dust it carried gnawed like sandpaper. Lord Ssu-ma Shih-ka'i ignored it. He stood on that hill like a sturdy little statue, immobile and unmovable. Behind his mask his eyes narrowed thoughtfully.

3

GATHERING OF THE MIGHTY

THE WOMAN FOLLOWED her husband through a corridor in Castle Krief, the Royal Palace in Vorgreberg, the capital of Kavelin, one of the Lesser Kingdoms. Her steps were plodding, rolling. An unkind person would have called her walk a waddle. She was very pregnant. And very distracted. She caught herself falling behind, hurried to catch up. Her husband paused, a slight frown crinkling his brow. "Nepanthe, what's the matter?"

"What? Oh, nothing."

"Nothing? I don't believe it. You've been brooding since we got here. You've been dragging around puckered up like a mouth full of crabapple." He raised her chin, peered into downcast brown eyes. "Come on."

Nepanthe was in her forties. A lot of hard years lay behind her, yet her long raven hair showed only traces of grey. Her figure wasn't the wisp it had been at nineteen, but neither had lumpiness conquered all. Her face did not record all the tragedies that had dogged her life. Only her eyes betrayed the melancholy caged within.

Those eyes were old, sad windows, aged by sorrow and pain the way glass is purpled by the endless assault of the sun. They said they would never sparkle again. They would believe in no good fortune, for luck and happiness were but pitfalls and taunts cast in one's face by a malign fate. She had lost her zest for life. She was marking time, waiting for the big sleep, and knew it would be an age arriving. Her husband, the arch-sorcerer Varthlokkur, had learned to hold Death at bay. He was over four centuries old.

"Come on," he said in his gentle, coaxing voice. "What is it?"

"Varth... I just don't like this place. It brings back so much that I want to forget. I can't help it... Vorgreberg is accursed. Nothing good ever happens here." She met his stare. A shadow of fear brushed her face.

"I won't stay a minute longer than I need to."

"Bragi will keep you..." She ground her teeth on words too harsh for the situation, "Why did you come?" She heard the whine in her voice and was disgusted with herself.

He accepted the question at face value. "I don't know. We'll find out in a few minutes. But Bragi wouldn't have called me if it wasn't important."

That wing of fear stroked her face again. "Important to whom? Varth, don't let him get you involved. He's accursed too." She had begged and begged her first husband, just like this, and he hadn't listened. And so he had died, and left her alone....

Varthlokkur smiled. "I wouldn't call him accursed. Things just happen around him."

"I would. They're bad things. Killing things. Varth... I don't want the baby born here. I lost two brothers, a husband, and my son here. I couldn't stand it if...."

His thin fingers teased through her hair. She stared at the floor. His arms slid around her and he held her a moment.

"There'll be no more of that. No more pain. I promise." And, "We won't stay long. Come on. Buck up. You'll get to see a lot of old friends."

"All right." She tried to smile. It felt like a death grimace tearing at her face. "I'll be brave." I'm good at being brave, she thought. I've spent my whole life bravely bearing up. Then she snorted. I'm also a little long on self-pity.

Varthlokkur drew ahead again. She watched him walk. His tall, lean frame was more rigidly erect than usual. His shoulders did not dip or bob but glided in a constant, unyielding relationship to the floor. He was all tensed up. Something was gnawing him too. King Bragi's summons worried him more than he would admit.

Gods! Don't let this be the start of another of those horrible things that devour everything I love. He's all I have left.

What could it be? Shinsan again? The peace had lasted three years now. The Great Eastern Wars seemed to be over. The Dread Empire appeared to be appeased.

The memories began yammering in the shadowed reaches of her mind, besieging her in earnest. She battled them till tears came. The recollections would not be driven back into their tombs. Too many dear ones had gone into the darkness before her. Too many memorial ghosts haunted her. She had nothing left. Nothing but this man, whom she could not wholly love or trust. This man and the life developing within her.

Her own life she held of little consequence. A wasteland lay behind her. The future looked as barren. She would live for the child, as she had lived for her son before.

Varthlokkur paused a few steps short of a smartly uniformed Palace Guard. Impatience peeped through his customarily neutral expression. He sensed the past rising inside her. He always knew, and always belittled her preoccupation.

She screwed up her courage and asked the question that irritated him most. "Varth, are you sure that Ethrian is gone? Isn't there any chance at all? I just don't feel like he's dead." Someday his answer might satisfy her.

His jaw tightened. He glanced at the Guard, controlled himself. "No, dear, I don't think so. I would've found him by now." He whirled, stamped to the door the Guard protected. The soldier snapped it open, clicked his heels as the wizard passed. He nodded amiably to Nepanthe.

She responded with a distracted nod. Was he someone she should remember? But she had known so many soldiers. How could she recall just one?

And then she was inside, bumping against the faces of her past like a swimmer bumping about in cold water crowded with chunks of ice. She did not know which way to dodge, which memory she most wanted to evade.

Two men in their late twenties were nearest her, their heads together as if their conversation portended conspiracy. Michael Trebilcock and Aral Dantice were their names. Once they had trailed her across half a continent in a noble, vain attempt to free her from the minions of the Dread Empire. Such quixotic youths they had been. "Aral. Michael. How lovely to see you again." The romance had fled the two, she saw. They were starry-eyed boys no longer. They had the hard eyes of men who had seen too much. The war changed us all, Nepanthe thought.

Dantice was short, wide, dark of hair. He looked as though he belonged behind a pitchfork in a stable. He responded with a delighted smile and effusive greeting.

His companion was taller, slimmer, bone-pale, and more reserved. His eyes were cold and remote. Rumor said he had become Kavelin's chief spy. Nepanthe's brother Valther had held that post till his death at the battle of Palmisano. She searched Michael's face.

She saw not one spark of humor there. The man was all

business these days, all self-confidence, competence, and lack of acquaintance with fear. Exactly the kind of man Bragi would choose....

"Darling, you look marvelous!" A woman surrounded her in a swarm of arms. "A little peaked, maybe, but pregnancy becomes you."

Nepanthe returned the hug absently. "You're looking well yourself, Mist." Mist, who had been her brother's wife, a sorceress he had lured forth from the east and converted to the western cause.

"Pooh! I'm an old hag."

Aral Dantice chuckled. "The ladies I know should be so ugly."

And Varthlokkur, with an arm around Trebilcock's shoulder, snorted. "You've added false modesty to your sins, Princess?"

Mist stepped back. "Plain Chatelaine now, I'm afraid. The King sent me to Fortress Maisak. You see what I'm worth when there's no fighting?"

"It is the most important castle in the kingdom."

Nepanthe stared at this woman whom her brother had worshipped, who had borne his children, who had been ruler of the Dread Empire before Valther entered her life. She never seemed quite real. More a fairy tale princess than one of the age's most savage and powerful wielders of magic.

Aral put Nepanthe's thoughts into words by observing, "She hasn't changed a bit. Still the most beautiful and dangerous woman alive."

Mist blushed.

How did she manage that? Nepanthe wondered. Aral had said nothing but the truth. Mist knew that. And she was no simpering little courtesan. She was centuries old, honed sharp and tempered hard by the intrigue and struggle for survival round the pinnacles of Dread Empire power. Her blush had to be contrived.

"How are your children?" Nepanthe asked.

"Growing up too fast. Every time I see them they're two inches taller. I'll tell them you're here. They'll be excited. You were always their favorite."

A gloomy, quiet man chewing the stem of an empty pipe shook Varthlokkur's hand. He greeted Nepanthe with a nod and a mumbled, "Nice to see you again."

"Hello, Cham. Business any better?"

Cham Mundwiller, commercial magnate, was a longtime supporter of the King. "Not really. There's only so much I can do while the Gap is closed." He wandered away, became engrossed in the coats of arms gracing the far wall.

Nepanthe turned to a younger man in military dress. "Gjerdrum. How are you? You look glum."

Aral said, "He's sore as a hornet's sting. His knighthood and appointment as commander of the army have gone to his head."

Sir Gjerdrum scowled. "That's not true. It's just that I've got other things to do. Colonel Abaca or General Liakopulos could have sat in on this for me."

Nepanthe noted the Colonel and General among the two dozen or so people she knew only by sight.

Sir Gjerdrum kissed her hand while clicking his heels. They had developed an innocent flirtation when he was younger and less world-wise. He played their old game half-hearted court with a weak suggestion. "Let me treat you to dinner after the little one comes."

Nepanthe raised an eyebrow. What had become of the indefatigably cheerful Gjerdrum of years gone by? Had he been crushed between the millstones of duty? Or was this just a mood?

She glanced around the room. Her friends had all aged, had all grown tired of their responsibilities. Nothing dulls the enthusiasm like the inability to make visible progress, she thought.

She was not unique, then. The same despair-inducing

nemesis breathed down the necks of all her friends. "Where's the King?" she asked. She and Varthlokkur hadn't seen Bragi yet, though they had reached Vorgreberg the previous afternoon.

"I don't know," Gjerdrum mumbled. "You'd think he'd be on time, wouldn't you? After calling us here... He dragged me in all the way from Karlsbad."

Varthlokkur moved to the room's huge fireplace and stared into the prancing flames. He looked troubled. Nepanthe joined him. She wondered why he was so moody lately.

The gathering fell under a pall. Only Michael and Aral remained immune. They chattered like best friends who hadn't seen one another for years.

Mist took a seat near the head of the huge table which filled half the room. Nepanthe studied her. Exile had made of a once savage conspirator a quiet, gentle woman. A knitting bag lay open before her. A small, two-headed, four-armed demon manipulated her needles at an incredible pace. Its legs dangled off the table's side. Occasionally one head would curse the other for making it drop a stitch. Mist would shush gently.

The door opened. A splendidly attired young officer entered. Nepanthe remembered him as Dahl Haas, the son of a mercenary who had followed King Bragi into Kavelin during the civil war. For an instant she wondered if Dahl had had babies who would follow Bragi in their turn.

"Stand by," Haas said. "He's on his way."

Nepanthe moved nearer the door. The King pushed through. His gaze met hers. He winced slightly, then enfolded her in a gentle, uncertain hug. "How are you?" he asked. And, "I'm sorry I couldn't see you last night. This wart of a kingdom don't give me time to catch my breath. Hello, Varthlokkur."

King Bragi was a tall, powerfully built man. He wore the scars of nearly three decades of soldiering. Nepanthe noted grey in the shag at his temples. Time was gnawing at him too.

He whispered, "I'll try to put on a private supper tonight. You'll want to see Fulk." Fulk was his six-month-old son, whom she had never seen.

"How is Inger?"

He gave her an odd look. Her tone must have betrayed her thoughts. She could not get used to his having remarried. His first wife, Elana, who had died during the war, had been her best friend. "Fine. Full of pepper. And Fulk is just like his mother." He moved away, shaking hands, exchanging greetings. Finally finished, he said, "I hope this thing hasn't gotten anybody fired up... I see it hasn't. Just a roll call, anyway, so to speak. I won't really need you for a few days yet. For now, let me just say that we've had word from Derel."

He explained that his personal secretary, Derel Prataxis, was in Throyes, east of the Mountains of M'Hand, negotiating with Lord Hsung, the commander of Shinsan's army of occupation there. In the three years since the cessation of hostilities not one trade caravan had crossed the mountains. The easterners had kept the one commercially viable pass, the Savernake Gap, locked up tight. Now Prataxis reported a dramatic shift in attitude. He expected the negotiations to be brief and their outcome to be favorable.

The discussion was prosaic and dull, and Nepanthe didn't pay much attention till the King asked Sir Gjerdrum for his guess as to why Shinsan would suddenly alter its policy.

"Hsung over there is a hard-liner," the King said. "He wouldn't do anything that would help Kavelin more than it would his own team."

Gjerdrum flashed his scowl. "Maybe the legions are up to strength again. Maybe they want the pass open so they can run spies through."

"That doesn't make sense," Mist countered. "They have the Power. Anyway, if they did have to have an agent physically present, they'd send him in over the smugglers' trails." Her glance flicked to Aral Dantice. "He'd set up a transfer portal so he could bring in any help he needed."

"All right," Bragi said. "Then you give me a reason that does make sense."

"I can't."

Nepanthe became aware of a subtle tension in the room. There were undercurrents here sensed only by a few.

King Bragi stared into infinity. "Why do I feel like you're not telling me everything? Can't you guess out loud?"

Mist stared at her knitting. The imp's needles became silvery blurs. "I don't feel Lord Ko Feng anymore. There may have been a coup." Cautiously, she admitted, "A few old supporters got in touch last summer. They thought there was something in the wind."

Trebilcock snorted. "Something in the wind? Crap! Ko Feng got his butt thrown out. They stripped his titles, his honors, and his immortality. They as much as accused him of treason because he kept his army intact instead of trying to finish us off at Palmisano. A corps commander named Kuo Wen-chin replaced him. Anybody who had anything to do with the Pracchia got swept out along with Feng. All reassigned to Northern and Eastern Armies. What amounts to internal exile. Ko Feng vanished completely. None of the new bunch were involved in the Great Eastern Wars." Trebilcock's glance flicked from Aral Dantice to Mist, as if daring contradiction.

Michael is a strange one, Nepanthe thought. Dantice and Gjerdrum are his best friends, and *they* say he's weird. Only Varthlokkur seems to understand him.

She wasn't sure what her husband saw in the younger man. She did know he liked Michael, and found him intriguing.

The King asked, "Mist?"

"Michael's connections are better than mine."

Bragi made a slight gesture. Nepanthe caught it. She

watched Michael respond with a tiny shrug. The King said, "Varthlokkur, don't you have anything to contribute?"

"I haven't been watching Shinsan. I've been busy."

Nepanthe stared at the tabletop and blushed. She had mixed feelings about her pregnancy. Excitement and eagerness and way too much worry. She was too old… But she had to try, to replace the son she had lost during the war….

"But…" she started, then shut up. It was entirely her husband's business if he wanted his east-watching kept mum. Still, why should he lie?

Varthlokkur said, "I could send the Unborn, of course."

"No. That would just provoke them." Bragi eyed the group. "My best friends. My advisers and boon companions. Why are you such a moody bunch today? Nobody wants to talk, eh? All right. Be that way. So. That's it. Check your contacts, people. I want to know what's happening over east. Those people won't hurt us again. Not while I have any say."

His tone startled Nepanthe. She took a closer look. Yes. There were tears in his eyes. He had an almost fanatic love for Kavelin.

For a moment she envied him. Would that she had something with as much meaning for her.

The ambitions of eastern princes had cost them both. Him his brother. Several of his children. His first wife, who had been her best friend. His best friend, who had been her first husband, Mocker. And whom he had been compelled to kill himself, because poor tangle-witted Mocker had been convinced he had to make a choice between Bragi and his son…. "Damn!" she spat, and slammed a fist against the tabletop.

Everyone turned. She winced. Softly, she apologized. She didn't explain.

It was not just the past which compelled her now. Something about this nonevent of a meeting argued portent, cried out about bad times coming. The restless armies of the night were stirring. An ill fate was marshalling fresh forces. Dark clouds gnawed the horizon. The air had begun to crackle with foreboding.

King Bragi was crossing a courtyard, headed for the stables, when he spied Varthlokkur pacing the east ramparts. The wizard was engrossed in the distance. The King altered course.

He approached the wizard from behind, settled himself between two merlons. "Care to talk about it?"

Varthlokkur spun. His response so startled the King, he nearly flung himself backward off the wall. Varthlokkur seized one flailing hand. "Don't sneak around like that."

"Like what? Who was sneaking? I walked up and sat down. What the hell is wrong with you?"

The wizard grumbled, "Nothing concrete. Not yet. Something in the east. Without the stink of Shinsan. But I could be wrong."

"Any tie-in with Hsung's change of heart?"

"The world consists of patterns. Mostly, we misread them. In Hsung's case, though, he really wants peace. The question is why."

"You didn't say that before."

"Nepanthe."

"Think I missed something there."

"The years have robbed her of too much. Her brothers. Mocker and Ethrian. Even Elana. I don't want to crucify her on a false hope."

"You're not making a lot of sense."

"It's Ethrian. He might be alive."

"What? Where?" This was staggering news. His godson alive? He owed that boy an incalculable debt.

"Easy," the wizard said. "I don't know anything for sure. It's a touch of a feeling I get lately. Something one hell of a long way off that has his aura. It's like catching one sniff of fresh bread while you're walking down the street, then trying to find the baker. The only resource I haven't tried is the Unborn. I won't unless there's another overpowering excuse to send him that way anyway."

The King sneered his disgust. The thing called the Unborn was a monster which should never have been created. "He's in the east, then."

"If it's him. The far east."

"Prisoner of Shinsan?"

"Lord Chin took him."

"Chin is dead."

"Just thinking out loud. Lord Chin and the Fadema took him. We've assumed they delivered him to the Pracchia, who used him to twist Mocker's arm. But maybe they didn't have him after all."

"They had him. You couldn't bluff Mocker. You ought to know that. They did some fancy convincing to make him attack me."

The wizard peered into the misty east. He did not reply, though he could have admonished the King about romanticizing his one-time friend, or about listening too closely to the guilt he bore.

The King mused, "We never had proof that Ethrian died."

The wizard was proud that he had no scales over his eyes, yet he did have his blind spots. The man Bragi had slain, and whose wife the wizard had later married, had been his son. Sometimes that fact got in the way.

Bragi shifted ground. "Was there anything else?"

"Anything else?"

"Your claim to be preoccupied was unconvincing."

Varthlokkur shifted his attention from the distance to the man. His basilisk eyes crinkled. "You grow bolder with age. I recall a younger Bragi shaking at the mere mention of my name."

"He didn't realize that even the mighty are vulnerable. He hadn't seen the dread ones in their moments of weakness."

Varthlokkur chuckled. "Well said. Don't take the notion too much to heart, though. The Tervola won't give you a decade to find the chinks in their armor."

Bragi stood. "I'll try this conversation when you're feeling more pellucid. Maybe you'll deal some straight answers."

Varthlokkur faced the east. His eyes lost focus. "We will speak later, then," he said.

Bragi frowned, not understanding. The wizard had changed languages. He shrugged, left the man to his mysteries.

The road called Lieneke Lane drew its name from the civil war which brought mercenary captain Bragi Ragnarson into Kavelin. Ragnarson had destroyed then Queen Fiana's enemies. A key victory had occurred near the town of Lieneke.

The road meandered amongst the homes of the wealthy. A lone, rain-soaked rider pursued it westward. A park appeared at his right hand. To his left the homes grew larger and wealthier. He glanced at one. The survivors of the King's family by his first marriage lived there, neither in penury nor in ostentation nor fame. The horseman averted his face. He left the lane just a few houses beyond the King's.

A footman braved the drizzle, took his animal. "The lady just arrived, Mr. Dantice. She said to wait in the library. Bette will be there to serve you."

"Thank you." Aral scampered across the porch. He shed his rain cloak and left it with the doorman. Ambling toward the library, he watched for Mist's children. Usually they were too much in evidence, and too filled with curiosity. He did not see them today, though, and wondered if Mist had moved them elsewhere. Despite the best coaching, little tongues would wag.

"Good morning, sir," the maid said.

"Good morning, Bette. Could you bring me something light? Butter, bread, and preserves, say? I haven't yet eaten."

"The cook has a nice grouse, sir."

"I don't think so. I shouldn't be here long enough."

"Very well, sir. Tea?"

"Anything hot. This rain will give us all the rheumatism."

Dantice prowled nervously after the woman departed. So many books! They represented so much wealth and knowledge they intimidated him. He had no formal education. His limited literacy skills he had garnered from his father, who had troubled to learn only because he was too mean to hire clerks.

Aral was sensitive about his ignorance. His contacts with the court had shown him the value of literacy. His association with Mist had underscored it. She had opened his eyes to uncounted new ideas....

Aral Dantice called himself a realist. He did not believe in the free lunch. His peculiar romanticism lay askew from that of his acquaintances. His relationship with Mist was an alliance of convenience. They were one another's willing tools... so he told himself when he worried.

So why this untamed interest in matters neither commercial nor political? Why did she take time to teach him when the lessons were so elementary they had to be excruciatingly boring? When his long-run value was severely limited and localized? Why did he?... It had come at him from his blind side. It had jumped and mauled him, and had left him with feelings and visions that were new to him. And he was frightened. This was not the right time. And Mist was not the right woman.

She was old. She had been old when his grandfather was a babe. Maybe she had been old when Varthlokkur was a pup, and the wizard had stalked the world for four long centuries. And she was a princess of the Dread Empire. No cosmetic could hide that fact, no term of exile change it. The cruel blood of tyrants coursed her veins. Even now she harkened to its roar.

But she was the most desirable woman alive. When her melting eyes poured fire on a man, he couldn't help but become their slave. Only some gonadless creature out of the same devil's jungle that spawned her could ignore her.

He wondered, perhaps for the hundredth time, just what went on behind her perfect mask of a face. The male thaumaturges of the Dread Empire concealed themselves behind hideous beast dominoes. She hid behind beauty.

He scanned all the titles and finally selected the book he chose each time he came here. Bette brought bread and butter and tea. He sipped and nibbled while studying meticulously prepared, hand-pressed woodcuts of the architectural wonders of the age.

He had seen the real structures during the war. The representations were woefully inadequate. "Damn!" he swore softly. "There's got to be a better way."

Michael claimed there were painters in Hellin Daimiel who could portray people perfectly. Why didn't they try place portraiture?

"Aral?" Her voice was soft. Its edges tinkled like tiny silver bells. Her beauty punished ugliness for existing. He rose, gulped.

"Sit down, Aral." She took a chair beside him. He imagined he felt the heat of her burning across the foot of air separating them. "That book again. Why?"

He swallowed. "The technical challenge. There has to be a better way to illustrate." Did his voice sound like a frog's croak? How could she do this to him? He wasn't a kid anymore.

"Did you talk to Michael?"

"We went riding. He didn't say much. He was even more cryptic than usual. I did get the feeling he was trying to warn me off."

"How so? You think he knows?"

"I couldn't tell. He must suspect something. But he isn't sure. Not yet. He kept changing the subject to landscaping and betting on Captures." He thought, I'm talking too fast, and probably too much.

He knew he wasn't in love. Not really. It was all in the glands. But it was powerful. She destroyed reason by inflaming the urge to mate.

"He knows more than he told the King, Aral. That was obvious. He knew too much about Lord Ko Feng and Lord Kuo not to have known more. He has a good contact east of the mountains. Possibly somebody who's caught wind of us. You'd better have your smuggler friends find out who it is."

"Do we have to do it this way? Mike could help a lot if we let him in."

"He could get us killed, too. I don't trust him, Aral. He's too much his own creature. He doesn't form loyalties, he makes temporary alliances. He's the kind who can change horses without a qualm. I don't think it'll be long before the King is sorry he hasn't kept Michael on a shorter rein."

"Yeah. The riots in Throyes. He admitted he was involved. And he's under orders not to irritate Lord Hsung. The King wants trade reopened bad."

"What about Cham Mundwiller? Is he still sitting the fence? We don't have to have backing from Sedlmayr, but I'd feel better if we did. They could finance another battalion, and that would make my friends a lot more comfortable."

"He's playing it cagey. He wants to be covered both ways. He's got the Michael shakes. He's never gone against the King before."

Mist gnawed a cuticle. "Go on."

"That damned Mike! He's like a ghost anymore. You never know where he is or what he's doing, or even if the guy next to you is maybe working for him. I spend half my time looking over my shoulder. Hell, Mike is just plain bad for business. And now that damned wizard is back, and he and Mike have always been thick. What Mike can't find out for himself Varthlokkur will dig out for him. All he has to do is ask. I don't mind telling you they've got me spooked."

"Has Cham asked for anything?"

"No."

"Don't offer. Let him come around his own way. I don't want to do business with people who have to be bribed. Other people can bribe them too. He'll just have to settle for secure trade."

Dantice nodded. "Far as I'm concerned, trade is the whole point of the exercise." Once a less belligerent, more commercially oriented regime was established in Shinsan, the riches would flow in rivers. All Kavelin could fill dippers in the stream—the way it had been before the Great Eastern Wars.

Aral believed in what he was doing. He was a patriot. His conscience was healthy. He'd had a bad moment when he learned Prataxis was making headway with Lord Hsung, but Mist had calmed him, and had assured him that Hsung was playing diplomatic games, that he had no intention of relaxing his stranglehold on the trade routes.

"What is happening in Shinsan?" he asked. "The wizard had something on his mind."

"I really don't know. They're restructuring army commands and shuffling legions. Lord Kuo's people give the orders. They don't explain. My friends can't tell me much."

"Or won't?"

"I've thought of that, too. There's always a chance they're working the other way, or both ways. I'm considering bypassing them. I have other resources."

Aral shuddered. He had seen some of those resources during the war. She was one of the great wielders of the Power, a fact emotion tended to obscure.

"I'd better get back. When I'm away too long the whole shop goes to pot."

She touched his hand lightly. Her eyes misted. "You're sweet, Aral. You're not quite real. Valther was that way too." She sounded wistful.

If only he were a tad more bold. It had been four years since Palmisano and her husband's death. She should be ready.

Aral took his leave. He tried to distract himself with debate on how to bet the day's Captures matches.

4

A FLASHBACK TO THE WAR

I T WAS ONE of those mornings when spring became an insidious disease spreading disaffection and restlessness. It communicated an undirected desire for action, for movement, for the doing of anything but the task at hand. The dawn breeze off the Kapenrungs had been cool, piney, and invigorating, virile with the seed of unrest. Now the air was still and warm, incubating ill-considered actions.

Nepanthe stood at the window of her second-floor bedroom in her brother's Lieneke Lane home. She stared at the towers of Vorgreberg, visible between the tops of the trees. "I've got to get out of here," she whispered. "I'm going to go crazy if I don't." Her gaze touched the palace. Maybe Bragi could arrange for her to move in there.

Her thoughts turned to her husband, Mocker, who had been gone for a year. An erotic image sprang into her mind. She pushed it away, disgusted with herself. She wasn't that kind of woman. Base physical desire was the mark of a street wench.

She pounded a fist against the windowsill. "I really am going mad," she whispered. And, "Bragi, why couldn't you just leave us alone?" Poor Mocker never did have any sense when it came to Bragi or Haroun. They'd put him up to the stupidest things... This time it had been some kind of spy work for Bragi. And he hadn't come back.

There was no proof that he was dead. Not even a rumor, Bragi claimed. But... if Mocker were alive, he would have come home long ago.

The door to her room creaked open. Her son stood there, looking at her, a confused look on his face. At twelve he already showed a lot of the man that would be.

There was little of his father in him. Mocker was short and fat and brown. Ethrian would stand a hand taller, and would have the broad shoulders and hard muscles of the masculine side of his mother's line.

A rush of sentimentality hit Nepanthe. She wanted to wrap him in her arms, and keep him there forever, safe from the wrath of the world. "Ethrian? What is it?"

In a puzzled tone, the boy said, "There's a man downstairs. He says he has a message from Father."

Something with violent claws grabbed her heart. She babbled questions.

"I don't know, Mother. He just said to tell you Father sent him with a message."

"Where is he?"

"Down on the porch."

"Get him inside. Into the library. Don't let anybody see him." Intuition told her to be circumspect. Mocker wouldn't have sent a messenger had there been no need for caution. "I'll be right down."

She whirled to her dressing table, mind aroil, telling herself to stay calm. She failed utterly to take her own advice.

The messenger was a strange one, a hard, dark, silent man with a big white scar across one cheek. He radiated a chill which made Nepanthe shudder. She ignored the reaction. All Mocker's friends were a little bizarre.

Once the man had identified her to his own satisfaction, he said in difficult Wesson, "I am sent at the command of your husband, Lady, to bring a message important. First, two tokens of faith, that I may be known as friend and not a liar thought. He says you will know the true message they carry." He handed her a ring of plain gold and a small dagger with a tiny silver three-armed swastika inlaid in its hilt.

Nepanthe collapsed into a chair, one item in each hand. Yes. She understood. The messenger had to be genuine. Who but Mocker would know how much these meant? The ring she had given him in token of love soon after their wedding. There was a love charm graven in invisible characters round the inner face of the band. The dagger had been a tenth anniversary gift. It had belonged to her father, and to his father before him, a token of the power of a once mighty family. Someday it would belong to Ethrian. Yes, only Mocker would guarantee a message by sending those. "I accept you as the real thing. Go ahead. What's the message?"

Ethrian demanded, "Where is my father?"

"Be quiet, Ethrian. Go stand outside the door. Warn us if anyone comes." The messenger had chosen the perfect day to appear. Almost everyone was out of the house.

The courier produced a sealed packet. "I am to give you these letters. Read. Then we will talk."

Nepanthe ripped at the packet, fumbling in her eagerness. Finally, she got to the first letter.

It was not written in Mocker's hand. She wasn't surprised. Her husband could write, but unless he worked with uncharacteristic patience his penmanship remained impenetrable even to himself. Anything he wanted understood he would have someone write for him.

The letters were crazy. Bizarre, paranoid, unbelievable. Rambling, tortuous, and only partially coherent.

He flatly accused Bragi and Haroun of plotting against his life. He was in hiding in the middle east, where he had friends. He wanted her to slip away and join him before Bragi took the next logical step and imprisoned her and Ethrian.

It made no sense. He'd never mentioned having friends in the east. And what reason would Bragi or Haroun have for trying to kill him?

The messenger asked, "Have you finished?"

Startled, she looked up at his cold assassin's face. "Yes. What's it all about?"

"Lady, I am sorry. I was not told. I was sent to bring you to him. I have two friends with me. We are to guard you during your journey to Throyes. We are to avoid notice by local authorities. That is all I was told."

"But…"

"I am sorry. Will you come?"

"Yes. Of course." She rose, surprised by the haste with which she had made her decision. It was as crazy as Mocker's letters.

"Pack quickly and lightly. We will travel by horseback, in haste, lest our enemies discover us and give pursuit."

"Yes. Of course." Of course. That was Mocker's way of life. Travel in the shadows, work in the shadows, always moving fast and light. Live and die in the shadows. Don't look back because something might be gaining.

She burst out of the library. "Ethrian, pack some things. We're going to your father. No. Don't ask questions. Just do what you're told. And hurry." She left him looking baffled.

She threw things together with little thought for the journey she faced. Her mind was wholly taken with the puzzle of what was happening.

"Keep up, boy!" Scar snarled. In all the weeks of travel Nepanthe had learned no name for Mocker's messenger. He was in a vicious temper today.

She didn't blame him. His wounds had to be hurting him terribly.

Two days earlier they'd had a brush with bandits, just when Scar was beginning to relax because they were nearing Throyes. His comrades had both been killed.

"It'll only be a little while longer, Ethrian," she promised. "We're almost there." They were among the farms which supported Throyes. A hazy patch of horizon lay ahead. "We should spot the city walls any minute now."

"No walls at Throyes," Scar said. It was one of the few times he'd said anything remotely conversational. "Three hours, we be there."

He was close. Only a few minutes over three hours later they were dismounting before a home as stately as any Nepanthe had known in Lieneke Lane. A grossly fat man met them. He did not seem pleased to see them. He and Scar argued, then Scar terminated the discussion by mounting up and riding away. The fat man fumed and sputtered and threatened his back.

Nepanthe asked, "Can we see him? Is he here?"

The fat man frowned. He thought for a moment. Then, in Wesson worse than Scar's, he said, "Not here. Gone now. On to Argon. You go there too. Yes?"

Nepanthe sagged. "Oh, no. Really? I can't travel another foot."

"You rest. Yes? One, two day maybe. Arrangements to make. Trustful guards." The fat man spat on Scar's backtrail. "Unable to do simple job. Two men lost."

"You're lucky any of us got through. Bandits were after us for days."

The fat man spat again. "Inside. You stay out of sight. Eyes of enemies everywhere these days."

Eager as she was to see Mocker, Nepanthe was disappointed when it took only two days to assemble a new escort.

"My god," Ethrian said. "Mother, it's huge." They were wending their way over pontoon bridges and low delta islands, slowly approaching the city Argon, which stood on an island near the mouth of the River Roë. The high city wall reared in the distance, and just grew more massive as they drew nearer.

Nepanthe came out of her preoccupation with weariness, heat, and humidity long enough to be properly awed. She tried distracting herself by telling Ethrian what she knew about Argon. That didn't help.

The wall was sixty feet high where they crossed a last pontoon and entered a city gate. Ethrian was so bemused he lost all thought of his father. Nepanthe was too miserable to feel more than the smallest flutter of excitement.

Their escort guided them through densely peopled streets to a huge fortress-city within the city. Nepanthe guessed this to be the Fadem, the citadel from which the Queen who called herself Fadema ruled the great city-state. Mocker seemed to have found powerful friends.

They were expected. A platoon in livery met them. The gentleman in command spoke flawless Daimiellian, the *lingua franca* of the western educated classes. "Welcome to Argon and the Fadem. I hope you find our hospitality warmer than that of the road."

"Just point me toward a bath and a bed."

"Can we see my father now?" Ethrian demanded.

The gentleman looked puzzled. "I know only that you're guests of Her Majesty, young sir, nothing of your business here. Someone closer to the throne will deal with that. My Lady? If you'll accompany me? An apartment has been prepared. I've been bid tell you that once you've bathed, eaten, and rested, dressmakers and tailors will be sent to help you form a new wardrobe." They all walked while he talked. Nepanthe soon became lost in the complexities of the fortress.

Ethrian asked another impertinent question. She hissed,

"You behave yourself. Understand? We're guests here, and this isn't the Quarter." The Quarter was the slum where Bragi had found them living before he'd dragooned Mocker into undertaking some harebrained mission.

The apartment was high in a squarish tower. It reminded Nepanthe of her childhood. She'd had her own tower then. This apartment, though, came with a staff of five servants, one of whom was a cook and none of whom spoke any language Nepanthe knew. The gentleman commanding the escort bowed his way out. The servants closed in, using gestures to indicate that a bath was waiting. Nepanthe told Ethrian to go first.

She stood at the one window and stared out over the city's sprawl, now splashed all orange and red and shadow with the light of a setting sun. She was eighty or a hundred feet above street level. In an apartment with its own staff, none of whom spoke a familiar tongue. It was almost as if she were a prisoner.

She slept only a few hours. Awareness of a subtle, unidentifiable wrongness set her to pacing the floor.

Someone tried the door, pushed through. Nepanthe settled onto the edge of her bed. The visitor stepped out of shadow, proved to be a woman.

"Good evening, Madame. I'm sorry you had to wait so long." The woman's Wesson was abominably accented.

Nepanthe rose. The words gushed. "Where is he? When can I see him?"

"Who?"

"My husband."

"I don't understand."

"The men who brought me to Throyes. They said they were taking me to my husband. That he sent for me. They had a letter."

"So that's how they managed it. They lied." The woman

smiled mockingly. "Permit me. I am Fadema, Queen of Argon."

"Why am I here?"

"We had to remove you from Vorgreberg. You might have embarrassed us there."

"Who is us?"

"Madame." Another visitor entered.

"Shinsan!" Nepanthe gasped. She'd seen enough booty after the battle at Baxendala to recognize a Tervola. "Again."

The Tervola bowed. "We come again, Madame."

"Where is my husband?"

"He's well."

"You'd better send me home. You lied to me... I have Varthlokkur's protection, you know."

"Indeed I do. I know exactly what you mean to him. It's the main reason we brought you here."

Nepanthe raised merry hell.

"Madame, I suggest you make the best of your stay. Don't be difficult."

"What's happened to my husband? They told me they were taking me to him."

"I haven't the faintest idea," the Fadema said.

Nepanthe drew a dagger from within her bodice, stabbed at the Tervola. He disarmed her with ease. "Fadema, move the boy elsewhere. To keep her civil. We'll speak to you later, Madame."

Nepanthe shrieked. She kicked. She tried to bite. She tried threats and pleas.

Silent as death, the Tervola held her. The Fadema took Ethrian away. Once the woman was gone, he said, "Your honor and your son are our hostages. Understand?"

She did. All too clearly. "I understand. Varthlokkur and my husband..."

"Will do nothing. That's why you're my captive."

Nepanthe could not stifle a wan smile. He was mistaken. He didn't know the men he wanted to control. Mocker would run amok. Varthlokkur couldn't be blackmailed. He would accept his losses, if need be, and utterly destroy those who had inflicted them.

She was scared. With reason. "I'm *your* captive. Isn't it *her* city?"

"She seems to think so. Amusing, isn't it? One year. Behave and you'll be freed. Otherwise... you know our reputation. Our language has no word for mercy." He turned briskly and marched out.

Nepanthe dropped onto her bed, softly let run the tears she'd held at bay during the interview. "What a fool I've been," she murmured. "I should've known when the letters said Bragi was trying to kill him." Was Mocker dead or alive?

"Ssst!"

The Tervola had said he was well. What did that mean? Nothing, really. They were notorious liars.

"Ssst!"

She tried to recall details of the Tervola's mask. Each mask was unique, they said. The time might come when she would want to identify this one.

"Ssst!"

This time the sound registered. It came from the window. The window? It was eighty feet above nothing. She rose and approached fearfully.

There was a man out there, peering in at her. And he looked familiar. "What? Who are you? I... I know you."

"From Vorgreberg. My name is Michael Trebilcock. My friend and I followed you here."

She was astonished. Followed her here? All the way from Kavelin? "Why?"

"To find out what you were up to. Those men were the same sort who killed the Marshall's wife. And your brother."

My god, she thought. What was the matter with me? He was right. Exactly right. Scar fit the description perfectly. How could she have been so blind? She became extremely angry with herself. All her life she had had this knack for fooling herself.

The man who called himself Michael had a hard time calming her down. Finally, he said, "You're in no real danger while they think they can use you to blackmail the wizard and your husband."

"What are you going to do?"

"I thought about bringing you out the window. But they've got your son. You probably wouldn't go…"

"You're right." The gods themselves wouldn't pry her out of this place while Ethrian was being held here.

"There's nothing I can do for you, then. I can only go home and explain what happened. Maybe the Marshall can do something."

Not likely, she thought. Bragi might try, for friendship's sake, but Kavelin had very little diplomatic clout east of the Mountains of M'Hand. And even less with Shinsan. If he was smart he'd forget her and get on with Kavelin's business.

She leaned out the window. "The rain's stopped. It's getting light."

Trebilcock groaned. "We'll have to spend the day on the ledge out here."

They spoke again before he left. He promised to ride straight through. She gave Michael and his friend a kiss apiece. Poor sad fools. What chance had they? "Good luck."

"We'll be back. That's a promise." There was a playful gleam in Trebilcock's eye.

She couldn't stifle a smile. "You're bold. Remember, I'm a married lady."

Though in her heart she knew nothing would come of it, she could not kill her hope. For months there was a defiant bounce to her step which puzzled and even worried her captors.

She had given up on Michael Trebilcock. Surely he and

his friend had fallen trying to get back to Kavelin. It was a miracle they had made it here. And if they did get home, what could be done? Not a damned thing.

Her nights were long and often sleepless. Insomnia had plagued her most of her life. It was worse now, aggravated by her concern for her son. They let her see him so seldom... He was always healthy when she did see him, if a little frightened and confused by their situation.

She paced, looked out at the night, paced. "You're a damned fool," she told herself for the thousandth time.

Something rattled and clanged outside. She leaned out her window, saw nothing but rain clouds... Wait. That looked like a big fire up on the north end of the island. She ducked back inside, stricken by déjà vu.

Years ago, briefly, her brothers had established her as ruling princess of Iwa Skolovda. There had come a winter night when she had looked out and seen her city burning....

A fat shadow piled through the window. Metal went *shang* as a sword left its scabbard. A man grabbed her.

She panicked, started to scream. A hand covered her mouth.

"Yah! She bit me!"

"Nepanthe! Settle down!"

Several voices talked all at once. "Find a lamp."

"Damn!"

"Marshall, I'm going to clout her."

"Easy, son. Nepanthe, it's me, Bragi. Behave yourself."

She went to the floor with the man holding her, spitting and kicking. Someone struck a light. Someone else seized her hair and yanked her head back. Bragi? Here?

"Can you stay quiet now?"

The panic vanished as fast as it had appeared. She knew she was making no sense, but could not stop babbling.

"Take a minute," Bragi said. "Get yourself together."

She did get hold of herself, and told her story. She was not gentle with herself for her part. "What are you doing here, anyway?"

"I'm here because you are." Just like that. And she had been able to believe he was a threat to her husband.

"But... you're only one man. Three men." She told Michael Trebilcock, "Thank you. And you. Sorry I bit you. I was scared."

Aral Dantice sucked his injured hand. "No matter, ma'am."

Bragi said, "I didn't come alone. That racket out there is Kavelin's army kicking ass."

"Bragi, you're making a mistake. Argon is too much for you." But, oh, did she love him for coming. Just as much as she had hated him for doing things just as crazy for other friends.

Kavelin's Marshall Ragnarson proved her wrong. He hadn't come without sufficient strength. The army of Necremnos, Argon's great rival upriver, was on the attack as well. The Argonese couldn't withstand the twin hammer blows.

She stayed out of the way till she could no longer stand not knowing what was happening. Then she hunted Bragi down. His troops controlled most of the Fadem by then. Only one citadel remained untaken, and he was on the brink of assaulting that. "Have you found out anything?" she asked. "Anything at all?"

"About Ethrian? Some. He's in there." He indicated the target tower. "With the Fadema and the Tervola. We should have him for you in a few hours."

"What if they..." She couldn't say it. Couldn't even think it.

"Why should they hurt him? If there's nothing they can gain?"

She didn't feel reassured. "Spite."

"Hmm. The Fadema might be capable of it. But she isn't in charge. The Tervola has more sense. Why don't you find yourself a place out of the way and wait? We're going in in a few minutes."

The waiting was almost intolerable. The wizard Varthlokkur came and shared it for a while, till he was called into the fighting. His presence was comforting. Though he and she hadn't always gotten along, he had been part of her life since childhood. He represented one of the few stable elements in her life.

The fighting went on for a long time. Far longer than Bragi expected. Despite herself, she nodded off.

Ragged cheering wakened her. She sprang up, rushed to where victorious soldiers were leaving the captured tower. She grabbed at every man she recognized. "Have you seen my son?" Some just looked at her with tired, blank eyes. Others shook their heads and trudged on.

Then Varthlokkur came out, looking more exhausted than any of the men. He was fussing over a man on a stretcher. "Bragi!" Nepanthe gasped. "Varth, what happened? Where's Ethrian?"

In a voice barely above a whisper, without emotion, the wizard replied, "Gone. They escaped at the last second. Through a transfer portal. Just when we thought we had them. They took Ethrian with them."

"But... couldn't you stop them? Why didn't you stop them?" She heard the hysteria creeping into her voice but couldn't quell its growth.

"We did everything we could. Bragi may have lost his sight trying. We failed. That's all there is to it."

The hysteria receded as she looked at Bragi. Lost his sight? Trying to rescue Ethrian? She started crying.

Her world consisted solely of shades of grey. First Mocker had gone, then Ethrian. Her brothers had fallen long before. There was nothing left. No reason to go on. Why even live in a world so cruel?

Varthlokkur was doing his best to soften her despair, and paying gentle court, just as he had done for years. She wasn't ready for that, but hadn't the heart to push him away. And there was comfort in being able to reach out to that one touchstone he represented.

She wasn't alone. Never alone. Varthlokkur wasn't what she wanted, but so long as he lived there would be someone. There was that much security in her world.

Someone knocked. Her security stepped into her room. "We're going to pull out today. Bragi is going to visit the Necremnen King, but that's just smokescreen. We've made a deal with the Argonese." He chuckled.

They were going to leave the Necremnens holding the bag? Good. Recent intelligence indicated that the Necremnens planned to loot Bragi's men as soon as they'd finished their share of Argonese. By seizing the Fadem Bragi's men had managed to appropriate Argon's richest concentrations of wealth.

"How soon?" she asked.

"As soon as you're ready. There's a barge waiting down at the water gate. Do you need any help?"

"Help? With what? I don't have much more than the clothes on my back."

"Well, I'll wait and walk you down. If you don't mind."

She didn't mind. She didn't mind much of anything these days.

The barge was a great fat thing manned by Necremnen rivermen. Michael Trebilcock and Aral Dantice were aboard, along with the majority of the Marshall's henchmen. The two youths spent the morning trying to flirt her into a better mood. By the time the barge tied up near the Necremnen headquarters she was feeling a little gay.

She almost felt a traitor to Ethrian because she was enjoying herself.

She stayed aboard while Bragi and Varthlokkur visited

the Necremnens. Michael and Aral tagged after him, two young men milking their moments near the center of power. Bragi's brother Haaken joined her for a while, trying to express regrets on her behalf, but he wasn't an articulate man. He was a soldier to the bone, a man who had been fighting almost constantly since his fifteenth year. He'd never learned to express his feelings. She touched his hand lightly and thanked him for his concern. She felt a great sorrow for him. He'd had less joy of life than she.

There was a sudden clash of weapons ashore. Men shouted. Haaken bolted toward the action. A fight was something he could handle. Nepanthe followed him.

She came upon the duel and nearly fainted. Michael had gotten into a fight—with her missing husband! "What happened?" she asked Aral.

"He was hiding in the bushes watching us. When we went over to him, he came out fighting."

What was he doing here? Where had he come from? Why hadn't he made his presence known? Surely he had been able to see her at the rail of the barge.

Ragnarson bulled through the onlookers. "Enough! Michael! Back off."

Trebilcock stepped back, dropped his guard. His opponent spun around, face painted with the fear of the hopelessly trapped.

Nepanthe ran into him, closed him in her arms and buried her face in his throat. "Darling. What're you doing? Where have you been?" And so on. She knew she was babbling, that he couldn't answer if he wanted, but she couldn't get her mouth to slow down.

"Back to the barge," Bragi said. "Time to move out. Nepanthe, keep hold of him."

She did. She didn't let go even when it became obvious that her joy in their reunion far exceeded his.

There were long days together on the road home, catching

up, remembering when, sharing chagrin at the way the Tervola called Chin had made fools of them both. Mocker didn't speak much about what had happened to him during their separation. She deduced that it had been grim. He had new scars. And the old wild, unpredictable exuberance had abandoned him. It was impossible to get him to laugh.

For her part, she avoided the subject of Ethrian. He seemed content to ignore the matter.

She thought she was bringing him around, luring the old Mocker out, but then the army paused on the outskirts of Throyes while its quartermasters obtained provisions. Mocker went into town.

Haaken Blackfang brought him back on a stretcher. Haaken wouldn't say much about the circumstances, but Nepanthe soon noticed a cooling toward Mocker by Blackfang, Bragi, and Varthlokkur. When she thought her husband had recovered sufficiently, she started asking questions.

He wouldn't talk about it. She tried everything. He remained as obdurate as a stone. He even lost all interest in sex, a problem she'd never faced no matter how rough times had become.

The army was in the Mountains of M'Hand, traversing the Savernake Gap, nearing Fortress Maisak, Kavelin's easternmost outpost. From its Marshall down to its footsoldiers the army was a-bubble with anticipation. Mocker was the exception. He became more morose with every step taken westward. Then he told her he wanted her to slip away and stay at Maisak.

"Why?" she demanded, almost as suspicious as Bragi and Varthlokkur seemed to be. "Are you going to tell me what's going on?"

"No."

"Then I'm not going."

Anguish distorted his face. He relented a little. "Self, am

in bind. Have decision to make. Job to do, maybe. All would be easier if wife was out of way, safe."

"What kind of decision? Does it have anything to do with what happened in Throyes? Is that why you've been unfit to live with?"

"Since Throyes," he admitted.

"What happened there?"

He tried to share his pain. "Agent of Pracchia contacted self. Said same have Ethrian. Must do something for them, else he dies."

"The Pracchia? What's that?"

"High Nine. Rulers of Hidden Kingdom, secret society trying to take over world. Has members everywhere. Fadema of Argon. Lord Chin of Shinsan. Others of equal power in Mercenaries Guild, in Itaskia, everywhere. Same have no mercy upon such as self." He spoke as a man who had firsthand knowledge.

Fear caressed her. "What do they want you to do?"

He clammed up. He wouldn't say another word no matter what she tried. Her fear grew by the minute. "Defy them," she insisted. "You know they won't go through with their part. Will they? Kidnappers never do."

She might not have existed for all he reacted. His mind was made up. He was betting the long odds, hoping to save their son. She loved him for that.

On that ground alone she allowed him to talk her into staying behind at Maisak. She shut down her fears, tuned out her conscience, and prayed the deed wouldn't be something so heinous the shame would dog them the rest of their days. She sat in the cell-like room the garrison commander had allowed her, numbly awaiting news.

A soldier came one afternoon. A sergeant. He closed and locked the door and went away. Now the room was a genuine cell. He did not tell her why. She knew nothing for days.

No one would speak to her. The men who brought food and removed the honeybuckets looked at her in a way that terrified her. As if they were building her a custom-designed gibbet.

Then Varthlokkur came. His face was long and tired. He released her under Royal parole, and when they were out of the fortress, on the road down to Vorgreberg, he told her.

Mocker had tried to murder Bragi. Had tried and failed. He had died in the attempt.

Her world, briefly reborn, had come to an end.

5

YEARS 1014–1016 AFE

THE GATHERING STORM

E THRIAN SLEPT AND DREAMED. He visited the greatness that had been Nawami before the split with Nahaman. It had been a large and industrious empire, quite unlike any of his own time.

Into his dreams crept whispering voices, arguing.

"It's not worth the risk, Great One."

"He has to be polarized. He has to finish what he started."

"But the Power we'd use… We have so little. If we fail…"

"If we fail, we're lost. And if we don't try, nothing changes. We're as good as lost."

The stone beast and woman in white? Ethrian wondered. Had to be. But how was he tapping their exchange?

He slept, and yet had a feeling of wakefulness, of being outside himself. He could float and gaze down on the curled form of Ethrian, lying there between the stone beast's paws. He could be amazed. That boy had changed. He had grown.

So had the pool. It was bigger, deeper, murkier, and muddier. A few droopy reeds now grew along one side. A frog peeped out from among them. Insects swarmed. A family of dull-colored mudhens patrolled the pond's surface. Swallows had daubed a few mud nests into cracks in one of the stone beast's forelegs. There was a twig nest in the scraggly old acacia that had been there when Ethrian had arrived.

A turtle dragged itself from the pond and paused to take the sun.

"We're growing. He's opened the door…"

"It's a crack too narrow to slide a razor through. All this time. What's been gained? A bigger pond? Ten thousand years of this won't restore Nawami. The door has to open all the way. We need a flood of power. Take him there, Sahmanan. Show him."

"The investment is too big. It would leave us blind. We couldn't see to K'Mar Khevi-tan."

"I know the risks. Nevertheless, you go. The Word has been spoken."

"As you speak, so must it be, Great One." There was more. Ethrian lost the thread. His new awareness slid down a wormhole into yesteryear, into a time when the stone beast was a thing freshly hewn from the heart of a mountain. Artisans clambered over it, polishing away the last marks of hammer and chisel. The thing loomed over the landscape like some timeless guardian, yet at that moment it was just shaped stone.

Nahaman and Sahmanan conducted fell rites between the monster's forelegs. They and a thousand lesser priestesses dragged sacrifices to their altar, tore out hearts, and filled buckets with blood and the air with a stench of burning corpses. They bathed the stone with the blood. Their summons went out.

It was heard, and to them came a hatchling god, a bundle of dark energy so small the women gathered it into a basket. They hauled it up the stone beast's back, and down a stairwell which plunged to the monster's heart. There, with further ceremony, they bound their new national godling, and constrained him to their service.

The god in the stone beast grew. His power waxed. His cunning sharpened. He was subtle. Not till too late did the sisters realize there had been a reversal of the roles of servitor and served.

Sahmanan surrendered to her Great One. Nahaman rebelled and fled. She made herself mistress of another land. She returned with her fleets and dragons and dark dragon riders.

The wars were bitter and pointless. That which had been lost was gone forever. The stone beast was master now. He would not yield.

Who can slay a god?

"Deliverer. Arise."

Groggily, Ethrian abandoned his slumber. Night masked the deserts of Nawami. Tenuous, the woman in white stood over him. Straining, he rose.

Something was wrong. The ground seemed too far away... He had grown. He had to be years older... How could that be? He glanced around. The pool was exactly as he had seen it in his dream.

"Yes. There have been changes. You opened the door a crack before you fled into sleep. You have to open it all the way."

Ethrian did not reply. He reviewed the arguments he had thought out before. He added what he had learned by eavesdropping. And still he could not bring himself to decide. Something down deep told him this was not the time.

"You haven't shown me what to do." How long would they endure his temporizing?

"You know, Deliverer. The Power is in you. Give us Nawami. We'll reward you with your enemies."

My enemies are greater than you know, Ethrian thought. They could not imagine the might of Shinsan. He could not himself, and he had seen it. They believed their Nawami the epitome of imperial achievement.

He suspected the lords of the Dread Empire themselves could not encompass the size and strength of what they had wrought.

"Deliverer!"

He gave her his attention. She was exasperated with him. "Will you liberate us?"

He shrugged.

Angry, the woman faced the darkness between the stone beast's legs. Her stance shrieked *I told you so!*

"Show him, Sahmanan."

"Show me what?"

"Yesterday. A yesterday dear to you," the woman replied. She cast a tremulous glance at the stone beast. "The day your father died."

"Time it well, Sahmanan. Err, and you face my wrath. And my wrath can be eternal."

She told Ethrian, "The Great One wants me to take you back to your father's death, that you might know the revenges at your command."

"I...."

"Close your eyes. Concentrate on staying beside me."

"I'd rather see my mother. Is she alive?"

The woman started singing. Something tugged at the folded-in corners of Ethrian's soul, tenderly pulling him free. He was returning to his out-of-body state. He settled onto his pallet and let go.

But he made Sahmanan work. He had made one decision. No matter what they got, they would work for it. He would hold back. He would make them underestimate him.

He was free. Sahmanan took his hand. They drifted up into an afternoon sky, above the terrible desert. The will and power of the stone beast carried them, higher and higher, farther and farther from the lonely mountain.

A barren Cordillera passed below. The range was but the parched bones of what had been. Not a lichen discolored its shades of grey.

Beyond, fifty, a hundred miles, they reached land where life still flourished. It seemed to leap up and tickle Ethrian's soul with joyful chlorophyl fingers. A surge of happiness swept through him. The desert was not all the world.

Sahmanan murmured, "This, too, was part of Nawami." She sent a vision. For an instant he saw the bustling cities, the endless miles of farms and fields and country carefully tamed. Now wilderness ruled. The descendants of Nawami were savages using stone tools, hunting and eating one another.

Their speed increased. They whipped over a thousand miles of Dread Empire before Ethrian recognized it, and another thousand before he could make Sahmanan understand that this was the land of his enemies.

They passed over another thousand miles, and another, and yet another, before reaching the Pillars of Heaven and Pillars of Ivory, the great twin barrier ranges marking Shinsan's traditional western frontier. "Do you begin to see?" Ethrian called.

The woman's response darkened her face. Nawami could not have matched a tenth of this.

They fluttered across the vastnesses of the Roë Basin, rapidly outpacing the sun. They crossed the mighty Mountains of M'Hand, drifted down on the little green kingdom of Kavelin. Down to its capital, Vorgreberg, which had seemed such a huge city to a younger Ethrian. He observed that it had not changed.

"Be quiet. Don't distract me. I have to reach back and find the right moment." Sahmanan's face became intent.

Down they dropped, gently, till they were among the towers of Castle Krief. Reality began to flicker. Ethrian thought of the quick flashing of distant lightning.

"Now," Sahmanan told him. She squinted with her eyes closed. "Follow me." She drifted toward a wall.

And into that wall and out of sight. "Eh?" Ethrian murmured. Then, "Why not? I don't have a body to stop me." He willed himself to follow.

Two men were fighting on the far side of the wall. One was a big man. The other was short and fat. They tumbled across a bed. The big man was unarmed. The smaller had a knife. The bigger had a wound across his back.

"Father!" Ethrian shrieked at the fat man. And at the big, "Uncle Bragi!"

They did not hear him. Sahmanan reached out, gently drew Ethrian into a corner.

Ragnarson smashed his opponent's knife hand against a bedpost. The blade skittered under a wardrobe.

Mocker, the boy's father, bit and gouged. So did Ragnarson. Ragnarson was doing a lot of yelling, but Ethrian could not hear what he said. The only voice in this dead zone was that of Sahmanan.

Ragnarson seemed to be weakening. His wound was bleeding freely. He stopped blocking the smaller man's blows, tried for an unbreakable hold. He got behind Mocker and slipped an arm around his throat. He forced his hand up behind his own head. He arched his back and pulled.

It was a terrible hold. It could break a man's neck, Ethrian knew. His father had taught it to him when he was five.

Mocker kicked savagely. He wriggled like a snake with a broken back. He slapped and pounded with his free hand, and clawed for the dagger beneath the wardrobe. Bragi held on. Mocker produced another knife, scarred Ragnarson's side repeatedly.

"Why are they doing this?" Ethrian whined. "They've been friends longer than I've been alive."

Sahmanan did not answer. Her lips shaped a weak little smile.

"Father!"

Mocker's struggles were weakening. Ragnarson slowly dragged him to his feet....

The smaller man exploded. He had been faking.

Ethrian foresaw the inevitable. He threw himself forward, shrieking, pounding both men with his fists. He might have been battering ghosts. He felt no impact at all.

Ragnarson leaned forward till Mocker was almost able to throw him. Ethrian begged him to stop. He snapped back with all the strength and leverage he could apply.

"No!" the boy shrieked.

He could almost hear his father's neck breaking.

Sahmanan seized his arm. "Come!"

He fought. "No! I won't! My father...."

Fear filled her eyes. "We have to leave now!" She dragged him into the wall.

The door of the bedchamber burst inward. Bragi's brother Haaken, the wizard Varthlokkur, and several soldiers charged in. Light flooded the bedroom. Ragnarson let his old friend slide to the floor.

Ethrian struggled, but could not break the woman's grip. She tugged him through the wall. He kept pulling back toward that room, but she lifted him into the approaching dawn and carried him back to the east. After a while he stopped fighting.

"Now you have seen your father slain," she said. "You have seen your enemy. Will you deliver us now?"

"Why were they fighting?"

Waves of anger beat at him. "We used the last of our power to show you this. Will you persist in refusing us? Have we destroyed ourselves over you? I warned him...."

Ethrian answered anger with anger. "Enough. I may loosen the ties a little. Let me think."

He had seen his father slain by his best friend, true, but there had been something askew there. The something, perhaps, behind Sahmanan's eagerness to depart before the piece was complete.

He relived that moment of breaking bone... A flash of hatred hit him. It stabbed toward Bragi Ragnarson, then recoiled, twisted, speared toward those who ruled the island in the east. They had choreographed that bitter scene. The old man had hinted at it... Those tools of the Dread Empire....

"All right. I'll free you. A little."

He was sure the woman and stone beast were more than they pretended. They were hiding from him. He was afraid they represented a deadly trap. He had heard all the tales of deals with devils.

The hatred remained with him, twisting his thoughts, telling him to take what they offered. The stone beast had known, and had sent him where the black emotion would be triggered. It had placed its bet well. The hating was too strong to deny.

He would loose them slowly, shaping them to his will. Forcing their cooperation.

Sahmanan brought him through the long eastern day, into the twilight, over the desert, and down to his place between the stone beast's paws. She was now but a ghost of the ghost she had been. The monster's voice was the whisper of a petulant child when it questioned her. It hadn't the strength for anger.

Ethrian decided to release them a little more, for his own sake. He went down inside himself and found the key to it, and tried to replenish them.

The will of the stone beast smashed against him. He staggered, fought back. It had deceived him. It was not as weak as it pretended.

He controlled his panic, used his will. Gradually, the flood rushing to that mighty thing failed.

Stopping it completely was as hard as slamming a vault door. He did it, and lent the closure a deep-throated finality. He tried following through with a bolt of anger, but there was nothing left to throw. He was exhausted.

He collapsed in his sleeping place.

The monster alternately cursed its failure and crowed over its success. It had stolen ten times the strength Ethrian would have delivered willingly.

The boy slept. Time lumbered along. The woman came to him in dreams, again arguing for deliverance. He ignored her, and nurtured his hatreds.

He would shatter the island in the east. He would carry fire and sword through the Dread Empire. His armies would feed on the enemy fallen, and grow fat. They would become invincible. He would take them across the world, to his former homeland, and would avenge his father....

These aren't my thoughts, he told himself. Something is shaping my dreams.

The something left him. His dreams became his own. His strange companions were preoccupied elsewhere.

Often, it seemed, he touched distant minds and unconsciously took from them, adding to his own knowledge and strength. He began to follow his desert companions more exactly.

At first they were delighted with their new strength. As time passed, though, there was a change to consternation which threatened to become fear. Then:

"Deliverer! Wake up!"

A hand rocked his shoulder violently. He ignored it. He clung to his twilight state and drifted out of himself, surveying his surroundings.

The pool had grown again. Water poured out of it now. The moisture ran down into the desert, where it quickly vanished. Plants and creatures crowded the short brook in a dense, intense little life-patch. Life had launched its counterattack against desolation.

This was Sahmanan's doing. She was devoted to restoring

her homeland. Her master simply wanted to extend his rule, to find himself new worshippers.

The shaking became gentler. Ethrian shifted his attention to the body lying between the beast's paws.

It had grown. It was about to become that of a man. A man who would be tall and powerful and dark, like his mother's brothers. The sleeper's face resembled that of his uncle Valther, the one who had married the Shinsaner sorceress. Ethrian and his mother had been living with Valther when Lord Chin's agents had spirited them away.

He considered the woman trying to waken him. She had substance now. She appeared to be in her late teens, and of promising beauty.

Only in her eyes was the past of her, the time-depth of her, obvious. Her eyes were older and deader than the desert.

Ethrian permitted himself to be wakened.

"Deliverer! You have to free us, or we're doomed."

What had they contrived now? "Show it to me."

The woman tried to drag him past the pond.

"I gave you power. Reach back. Show me from the beginning."

She made excuses. That would require intercession by the Great One. He was preoccupied.

"Unpreoccupy him. Tell him to make time." How can I have aged in dreams? he wondered.

He had, by drawing on those minds he was not entirely aware of having tapped. He was not the boy who had swum the strait and walked the beaches of Nawami. He was no longer the youth who had flown to witness his father's passing. He had become someone else. Someone more sure of himself and more determined to remain his own creature. He had developed an arrogant face. He now had eyes like a snake.

"Please!"

"Show me. From the beginning."

A savage bellow raged across his mind as the stone beast

responded. It flung images at him like a barrage of angry spears.

They were coming. Shinsan was in the desert. The stone beast was animating a handful of its soldiers in waiting. They were out there now, overwhelming Shinsan's reconnaissance parties.

Ethrian saw it through, to the moment, and wondered if anything could stop the Dread Empire. What drove it so? Did it feel compelled to conquer even lifeless lands?

He yielded no more power. The beast was trying to panic him.

Its soldiers obliterated a half-dozen patrols. The explorers stopped coming.

"Deliver us!" the woman begged, her soft eyes filled with water. "They'll come again, and they'll destroy us."

"They might. That's their nature. Who is master here?"

"The Great One."

"Then you get no help from me. I won't bend the knee to him." Ethrian turned away, stripped himself, waded into the cool of the pool. Fish brushed his legs. Waterfowl chivied their young into the reeds. Sahmanan pursued him along the pond's edge, begging from beyond the vegetation.

"You've made a work of art of this," he told her. "Why not confine yourself to this? The patrols are gone."

Would they give up? Of course not. Shinsan did not accept defeat. Her soldiers would try an alternate approach. It would have more weight behind it.

What would they do if they caught him?

A slow smile crossed his lips. Shinsan might provide the leverage needed to best the stone beast. He would play the wronged prisoner welcoming liberation. Why should they know whom he was... ? If he did not free it, the Tervola would dispatch this trifling godlet before noticing an ordinary boy.

He was living on borrowed time anyway. He could lay his bet with little to lose. The beast would accept his demands or perish.

Perhaps it discerned the trend of his thoughts. It growled. It threatened him. It pleaded. He ignored it, except to say, "When you're ready to pledge yourself my slave."

Hellish laughter rolled across the desert. It was the great jest of the godling's lifetime.

Question, Ethrian said to himself. How do you force a god to keep his word after you strong-arm him into giving it?

He climbed out of the pool and returned to his resting place. The desert air dried him quickly. "Sahmanan, come here. Sit. Tell me about yourself."

She started talking, and casting frightened glances upward.

"No. Tell me about the child. About the little girl who grew up to become a priestess. About her mother and father and sisters and brothers. Tell me what games she liked, and what songs her friends sang when they played."

Black, brooding disapproval drifted down from above. The beast knew what seeds he was planting.

"Tell me your story. I'll tell you mine."

"Why?"

"Because we were all children before we became whatever we became. In the child is the understanding."

"Where did you get that idea?"

"From an enemy. Lord Chin, of the Tervola. A man with a black heart, but brilliant even so. One of my grandfather's master teachers."

"Your grandfather?"

"Varthlokkur. They called him the Empire Destroyer. The most terrible wizard ever to tread this earth."

"I don't know the name." She seemed taken aback.

"He's one of the great old wickednesses of the world. You could've seen him if you'd waited a second longer out west. He showed up just after you charged into the wall." Ethrian laughed a soft, wicked little laugh. "He might have seen you. I'm sure he saw me."

Her eyes widened. She glanced up, momentarily worried.

The stone beast ignored her. It was too busy with its patrols.

Ethrian toyed with Sahmanan for weeks, prospecting for a vein of humanity. It was there. He knew it with a certainty that was absolute. It compelled her to "waste" her strength on her restoration hobby.

He had few successes. That vein lay deep, like a diamond seam. Layers lay over its top. The meek, innocent ingenue with empty eyes. The creature older than the stone beast itself, that had built itself a heart of steel. The priestess....

Ethrian resumed a normal cycle of sleep and waking, doing his sleeping during the fury of the day.

He wakened one afternoon, suddenly. Instinct made him leap into the air. Terror wriggled down into the core of him. The stone beast had flung out a tremendous bolt of power. The surge left a bleak, hungry vacuum behind. He shuffled this way, then that, moving aimlessly while trying to assemble his wits.

"They came back!" Sahmanan wailed. "They're going to destroy us!"

He felt the stone beast's fear. It had fought, and had lost, and in its despair had flung everything in one great black hammer stroke. If that blow failed, doom was upon Nawami.

Ethrian raced around the beast's paw. He clambered up its back. Sahmanan followed. At the base of the thing's neck, she gasped, "Get down! He failed!"

Ethrian flung himself against weathered stone. Something tortured the air. He heard the crackle of bacon frying magnified ten thousand times. A titan's drumstick hammered out one mighty beat. Ethrian turned his head warily. He saw an iridescent dust tower hundreds of yards high, settling back to earth. A thousand diabolic faces leered out, laughed, faded as an unseasonal breeze dispersed the dust.

The stone beast whined. Sahmanan begged. Ethrian

ignored them. He scrambled to the peak of the monster's head, sat cross-legged, faced west. He let his being slip its moorings and drift toward the grey mountains.

He halted when he spied something atop a long, dusty dune, facing the stone beast. Another joined it, then another. Their shapes seemed to waver.

Ethrian drifted closer. It wasn't just the heat making their edges raggedy. Their cloaks of office rippled in the breeze. There were six of them now. No: seven. The one in the middle was shorter and wider. They wore grotesque masks. Their jeweled eyepieces glistened in the desert sun.

Tervola, he thought. They've stopped playing. They've come to see for themselves.

Soldiers of the Dread Empire joined their captains. A dozen. A score. A hundred. They stared at the stone beast.

The short one spoke. He made a slight gesture, then descended the back of the dune. One Tervola and a handful of men started forward. The others settled down as if for a long wait.

Ethrian fled toward his body.

6

S HIH-KA'I CLAMBERED TO the top of the grey
dune. His legs ached. He was soaked with perspiration.
He felt greasy inside his field gear. He was tired and
short on patience. What am I doing out here? he wondered.
I belong with the Fourth Demonstration.

He stopped. The breeze felt good, though it had to work
to penetrate his field dress. He surveyed the tower of dust
still falling in the distance. Other dusts piled up around his
boots, gently driven by the wind.

"Very spectacular, Lord."

"Thank you, Pan ku. I thought it might say something to
our friends over there." He stared at the solitary mountain.
Other Tervola joined him. "Am I seeing things?" he asked.
"Or is that a creature carved out of stone?"

"I believe so, Lord," said a Tervola named Meng Chiao.
"It looks old."

"Perhaps. But it's alive. It's the source of our trouble. Set
up a transfer behind the dune. I'm returning to the fortress.

I'll be right back."

"As you wish, Lord."

Shih-ka'i slid and scrambled down the west face of the dune, began trudging toward the nearest active portal. "I'm too old for this," he grumbled.

"Lord?"

"Talking to myself, Pan ku. Ignore me."

He wondered why he needed to be here on the line. He was no field officer. The novelty? He had never served with a combat legion.

He stopped. "Pan ku, there's no need for you to dog me. I'm coming back. Why don't you wait here?"

"If you command me to, Lord. Otherwise, I wouldn't feel right."

"All right. If you don't mind the exercise and the sun." The man's devotion gave Shih-ka'i a small, pleasant feeling of worthiness. Rare were the Tervola who inspired the personal affection of their men.

"I don't mind, Lord."

Shih-ka'i transferred to the Seventeenth's headquarters. Had he become too dependent on that one sorcery? It had its limits, and he dared not lose them in the bigger picture. His brethren had learned that the hard way during the last war. A large force could not be supported through transfers alone. They were too slow. They had too small a capacity. Their lifespans were limited. Only a few could operate within a small area. More began interfering with one another. Still, they were superb backing for small tactical operations. To move and supply a legion, old-fashioned boot leather and wagon wheels remained the most practical approach.

Portals had their dangers, too. Sometimes people disappeared. That had happened too often during the western war. The wizard Varthlokkur had learned to tamper with the transfer stream.

Shih-ka'i shuddered.

Easy, he told himself. It's just weariness working on your nerves.

Nerves were not the whole problem. He was apprehensive about that stone thing. Caution was indicated. It was a complete unknown.

Tasi-feng greeted him. "What's happening out there, Lord?"

"We found the center of it. Giant artifact shaped like an animal. Looks like it was carved from a mountain. I sent Hsu Shen to take a closer look. Are the ballistae ready?"

"They're waiting, Lord. I inspected them myself. The Candidates did a good job. Every shaft was properly impressed and ranged. All we need is someone to target up front."

"I'll do that. How many shafts?"

"Twelve were all we had, Lord. Six in the trough, six standing by."

"Should be adequate. The damned thing will look like the moths have been after it before we're done. Let's look them over."

The ballista battery waited in a field outside the fortress. At first glance the engines looked like common siege equipment. The frames, troughs, and cranks were of standard imperial design. The specialized pieces were the bows and strings. Those had been prepared in a thaumaturgical arsenal hidden deep in the heart of Shinsan. Not even Lord Ssu-ma knew its location.

The shafts, too, had come out of that arsenal. They were of a very dark, hard, and heavy material. Inlaid into them were traceries of silver, gold, and a dull greyish metal. The heads were crystals in spearhead shape. They glowed with a fierce inner fire.

Shih-ka'i thumbed one, asked, "Ever wonder what one of these costs?"

"A small fortune," Tasi-feng guessed.

"I'm sure. Crank one back. And set me a portal here so I can jump back and forth."

"I arranged a portal earlier, Lord. Over here. I thought you'd want to range them yourself."

Shih-ka'i scowled. Lord Lun-yu was too damned efficient. Or he himself was too predictable. "First three at two-minute intervals. I'll come back if I want more." He surveyed the crews. Candidates all. Ordinary soldiers were not permitted to operate specialized equipment. It became dangerous in the hands of the untrained.

"You. Go ahead and shoot."

A ballista string whipped forward. There was a tremendous crack. A shaft hurtled into the air, a quicksilver sliver slicing into the distance. It did not follow a normal, gravity-defeated arc. It was still climbing when last it caught the sun.

"Two-minute intervals," Shih-ka'i reminded. He entered the ready portal. Pan ku followed as soon as the portal permitted.

A minute later Shih-ka'i topped the dusty dune in the far desert. He faced westward, waiting for a silver sparkle to appear over the mountains. "Hsu Shen run into anything yet?" he asked.

"No, Lord. He's halfway there."

"Signal him to take a position where we can see him, then to wait. I don't want him too close to target. Ah. Here it comes."

He sealed his eyes, reached with Tervola-trained senses, touched the hurtling shaft. Another part of his mind found the stone thing. He etched a mental line from spear to target. "Coming down, men. Shield your eyes."

The shaft hurtled toward the earth. Impact! Light-balls swarmed the touchdown point like a hundred round lightning flashes blasting away in rapid succession.

Shih-ka'i opened his eyes. "I'll be damned," he murmured. He had missed by two hundred yards.

Roaring, rising heat sucked up dust from hundreds of feet around the impact point. A pool fifty feet in diameter bubbled and splashed like overheated water. "Warm your hands around that," Shih-ka'i said. But his cockiness had fled.

He had missed. That could be no accident. He faced west again, watching for the next flash of silver.

He concentrated harder this time. He retained control till the moment of impact. And this time he felt the will resisting his own.

He opened his eyes. "Another miss!" But this time the first great upwelling of molten earth splashed the flank of the stone thing. He had brought the weapon in close.

"More power on the impression?" he asked the other Tervola.

One of the oldest, exiled by Lord Kuo, replied, "No, Lord. Range and impression felt perfect. It's the targeting. Something is resisting."

"Then I didn't imagine that."

"No, Lord. I suggest we all target the next one."

"Absolutely," Shih-ka'i said. "I want to see what happens when we get a direct hit."

"It's coming, Lord."

Shih-ka'i felt for the shaft and found it. He drew his targeting line. His brethren came in. They made of the line a tube from which the missile could not escape.

The missile hurtled down. The will trying to shunt it aside failed. It struck. Shih-ka'i opened his eyes.

Gouts of molten rock had blown out of the stone thing's haunch. "Dead on," he crowed. "Dead on. Now we wait."

They did not wait long.

"Is that someone standing on its head?" Shih-ka'i asked. He squinted, could not be sure. His eyes weren't what they had been.

"Looks like two of them, Lord."

"Curious. Can you tell what they're doing?"

"No, Lord."

A great angry bellow shook the desert. It filled the universe and rattled Shih-ka'i's teeth in his jaws. Dust devils raced across the barrens, circling in panic. Shih-ka'i pictured this as the flight of frightened ghosts. He smiled at his own imagination. "Prepare to defend yourselves," he ordered.

Something had changed. The feel of the situation was different. One of the Tervola said, "Something is happening around the thing's forelegs, Lord."

Shih-ka'i squinted again. "Tell Hsu Shen to get back here now!" he snapped.

Soldiers were pouring into the desert! Out of nowhere. Horsemen. Infantry. Battalion after battalion....

"Form line of battle, gentlemen. Meng Chiao. Prepare portals for an emergency withdrawal. Gentlemen, I'm returning to the fortress. I'll make my arrangements there and come right back."

He descended the rear of the dune, slipping and sliding in his haste. Pan ku was a step behind him. He hoped the others did not think he was fleeing. They might lose heart.

If there was a flaw in Shinsan's military structure, it was the failure of the Tervola to meet the high personal standards they set for their men. They themselves sometimes yielded to emotion on the battlefield.

Tasi-feng was surprised to see him back so soon. "Lord Ssu-ma. Did something go wrong?"

"Not at this end. I may have made a poor decision up there. We've awakened something very old and very nasty. Nine shafts left? I want the first six at thirty-second intervals. Portals are to be arranged to allow the forward group to be evacuated in a hurry if necessary. Inform all legion commanders that Seventeenth is combat operational. They're to be ready to march on short notice. Contact Northern Army. Tell them I may invoke my right to demand reinforcements."

"Lord, we're concentrating too many portals in too small an area."

"I'm aware of the risks, Lord Lun-yu. I'm also certain we've grabbed a monster by the tail. It might not let us turn loose." Shih-ka'i turned to the Candidates manning the ballistae. "Thirty-second intervals. Loose the first shaft."

He watched silver flicker up and into the east, then strode through the portal.

The situation had worsened in his absence. A sea of warriors surrounded the stone thing. A soldier-river swept toward the dune. Hsu Shen's men were kicking up clouds of dust in their race to rejoin their comrades.

Flying things swarmed over the lonely mountain like clouds of gnats. "What are they?" Shih-ka'i asked.

"Dragons with riders, Lord Ssu-ma. Small dragons, probably specially bred. It's impossible to be sure from here, but the riders seem to be nonhuman. Ou-yan is trying to get a better look, but something keeps interfering."

Shih-ka'i moved to where a Tervola sat cross-legged before a wide silver bowl pushed deep into the sand. The man kept chanting the same cantrips over and over. Cloudy pictures would form in the water in the bowl. Then something would interfere and they would fade away.

"Shaft coming, Lord," Pan ku said.

Shih-ka'i turned, caught it, drew a line connected with the flood chasing Hsu Shen. He brought it down perfectly. Whole platoons vaporized. Companies were decimated by splashes of molten stone.

"Shaft, Lord."

Shih-ka'i flung that and the next into the rapidly expanding horde around the stone thing. Huge, steaming holes appeared amidst the darkness of them.

That desert-shaking roar came again.

"I think somebody's mad, Lord," said Pan ku. Shih-ka'i glanced at his batman. Pan ku wore a straight face.

"I think so, yes."

"The flyers, Lord."

The gnat-swarms hurtled toward the dune. "Stand by!" Shih-ka'i ordered. "They could be dangerous."

"Shaft, Lord."

Shih-ka'i drew a line between the shaft and a flyer bobbing in the heart of the swarm. When the flash faded, he saw several objects falling in flames. Two split up as riders separated from their mounts.

The others came on. They bobbed too much for accurate counting, though Shih-ka'i decided there were at least fifty. More were gathering above the stone thing.

He put another shaft in. It was more effective. At least six flyers went down. The last shaft took out another four.

Their weaving and bobbing ceased. They peeled off in twos and threes to streak toward the dune. "Spell of concealment," Shih-ka'i called. "Spell of visual dislocation."

A blackness covered the dune. No one appeared to be where he had stood a moment earlier. The first flyers streaked over so low their passage stirred the dust. The riders struck with shafts of light.

"Casualties?" Shih-ka'i demanded.

"None, Lord."

"If anyone should be injured, send him through the portal immediately. We don't leave anyone they can use against us. Same with any of their people we capture. Through the portal. Does anyone own access to an aerial demon? Meng Chiao? What are you waiting for? Get it up there."

Bolts of power pounded the dune. The Tervola turned most of them aside. They flung back whatever sorceries they commanded. Few had any effect.

"Hsu Shen won't make it, Lord."

Shih-ka'i could see that. He was considering the problem already. He had three shafts left at the fortress. He wanted to use them against the thing of stone. Should he sacrifice Hsu Shen? No. "Pan ku. Come with me. I'll return shortly, gentlemen."

He did not return as quickly as he anticipated. He paused to give the big map a look and to leave Tasi-feng with fresh instructions.

"We've lost control out there," he said. "They've got too much and we've got too little. We'll stall them as long as we can. Here." He indicated a position on the map. "The most likely place for them to come westward. Move a brigade out now. Have them march light. The heat out there is murderous. We'll use portals as much as we can."

"Lord, we don't have enough of them."

"Take them away from the other patrols. Tell them to march to that pass and start digging in. Orders to all legions. Start marching here immediately. Begin reinforcing with their ready units now. Take whatever initiatives you deem necessary. As soon as you man this place with their people, send out the other brigade. I've got to get back. Hsu Shen is in trouble. I want those last three shafts at one-minute intervals."

"As you command, Lord."

Shih-ka'i trotted out to the transfer portal. "Pan ku," he panted, "I don't think I'm young enough anymore."

"If I might be so bold, Lord. Why don't you stay at the heart of the web and let your officers do the running?"

"You make perfect sense. I don't know why. I just want to be on the scene. Maybe because I've never been there before."

They passed through the portal and climbed the dune.

Hsu Shen was in big trouble. He was close now, but horsemen were about to split around him and cut him off. Shih-ka'i checked the sky. The dragon riders were engaged in complex aerobatics, trying to vanquish Meng Chiao's demon. The demon had left his mark. Their numbers had been reduced.

"They're very clumsily controlled, Lord," the demon's master observed.

"They're like the men we met in the mountains?"

"Dead? Yes, Lord. However, the riders aren't human. We obtained a specimen and sent it through for examination."

"Good. Good. Casualties?"

"Only two men so far, Lord."

"Excellent."

"Shaft, Lord," Pan ku said.

"Thank you." Shih-ka'i took another look at Hsu Shen's situation. He would have to spend at least one shaft to salvage the advance party. He caught the weapon, imagined the line. The missile came down. It shattered the pursuing riders.

"Begin evacuating the troops," Shih-ka'i ordered. "We don't have much more time."

"Perhaps not enough to get us all out, Lord."

Shih-ka'i considered the size of the approaching horde. "We'll form around the portal. Send the men through first."

Meng Chiao trembled. "As you command, Lord."

"Shaft, Lord."

"Thank you, Pan ku." Shih-ka'i continued to study the enemy. Hsu Shen was safe for the moment. Should he drop the weapon into the crowd surrounding the stone thing? Those two figures atop its head....

He targeted, connecting shaft and stone head.

The line bent immediately. "I need help, gentlemen. Targeting on the idol's head."

Slowly, slowly, the foot of the line crawled back toward the great beast's head....

The shaft arrived too soon. Shih-ka'i could not bring it down where he wanted. It hit the beast's shoulder. Tons of molten rock blew away, showering the soldiers swarming below.

"I think you did more damage that way than you would have with a direct shot," Meng Chiao observed. "Look at the swath that cut."

Shih-ka'i did not respond. He was watching the minute dots scamper down the monster's back. Too late to get them now. "Meng Chiao. Pass the word. After we bring the next shaft down, everyone who can should call up a demon and turn it loose."

"The thing controlling them is crazy-angry, Lord," Meng Chiao observed. "It's not doing well at all. Minds me of a spiteful child breaking its toys."

"Uhm. Keep it angry."

"Shaft, Lord."

"Aye." Shih-ka'i glanced at Hsu Shen. He would make it with less dramatic help. "Help me, gentlemen. I'm going to bring this one down across its snout."

He imagined a hard, iron arc. His companions added their wills to his. This time there was less resistance. The enemy mind remained distracted by anger.

An instant after the last shaft struck, the desert again reverberated to a great angry roar. "That one hit a nerve," Pan ku remarked.

"So it seems. Get those demons up, gentlemen. Centurion! Can't you move those men into the portal faster?"

"No, Lord."

"Very well. Don't slack off." Shih-ka'i turned to watch Hsu Shen finish his last hundred yards.

Hsu Shen's men ran lightly and well, in good order, as befit soldiers of Shinsan. They did not cast fearful glances over their shoulders. The only gear they had abandoned was that which their commander had told them to drop. They retained their shields and weapons. "Good men," Shih-ka'i observed.

Meng Chiao responded, "This is the Seventeenth, Lord. This was Lord Wu's legion."

Shih-ka'i smiled within his mask. "I see." The man spoke as if his remark explained everything there was to know about the legion.

Lord Wu, in his time, had been one of the great Tervola, but he had been one of those unfortunates seduced by recent politics. He had died mysteriously in Lioantung when that city had been the seat of Eastern Army.

A demon appeared. It howled grotesquely. It stood fourteen feet tall and had a half-dozen arms. It pranced around cursing the man who had summoned it. After receiving orders, it whirled, estimated the enemy force, changed shape.

Shih-ka'i watched it become a copper rhinoceros of epic proportions. It galloped toward the enemy. He loosed a sigh of disgust. "Someone isn't taking this seriously."

The shiny rhino trundled past Hsu Shen. It bellowed heartily and charged the nearest horsemen. It rumbled around in circles, flipping its nose horns this way and that. It overwhelmed opponents by virtue of sheer mass.

"A clown thing with a certain effectiveness," Shih-ka'i admitted grudgingly. He did not feel a demon of that temper befit the dignity of a Tervola.

The demon shifted shape again, became octopod. It armed six tentacles with swords seized from its victims.

A dragon rider came out of the sun. It put a spear-bolt through the demon. The thing did not approve. It yelped like an injured puppy, faded away.

A dozen more Outside monsters joined the fray. They stopped the riders briefly. Hsu Shen and his men came puffing up the dune.

"Centurion, put these men through first. They're exhausted."

"Yes, Lord."

Shih-ka'i examined the progress of the evacuation. It looked too slow. Too damned slow.

The riders pushed forward despite heavy casualties. They surrounded Shih-ka'i's dune-walled position, then waited at a respectful distance. Lord Ssu-ma laughed. "You've got us now, don't you? No chance for us to get away, eh? All you have to do is bring up the infantry and finish us, eh?" He directed his Tervola to concentrate on the nearest foot soldiers.

He stared at the stone thing. Was it stupid? If it kept on this way, its entire army would be destroyed before it broke out of the desert. Not many of the fallen remained in condition for reanimation.

That pleased Shih-ka'i.

Sure as he lived, he knew the master of the dead meant to march across the world. And once his armies broke out of the wasteland they would begin to swell. That explained why the thing was squandering manpower now. It anticipated no difficulty acquiring replacements.

The enemy infantry came on in such numbers that the demons, under constant attack from above, were swamped.

Shih-ka'i glanced back. The evacuation was going well. A man every ten seconds. Six a minute. Sixty every ten minutes. Three quarters of the force had gone. The others had formed round the portal. The maneuver was a tactical success already.

Give me a little luck, he thought. Let the portals remain useful a few minutes more. Let the stone thing persist in its profligate stupidity.

He did gloom about his minor exploratory thrust having become an embattled retreat which threatened to embroil the entire Eastern Army in an unexpected war. A big war. At a critical juncture in Shinsan's history. He guessed there were fifty thousand enemy soldiers scattered around the desert. They seemed to have stopped coming from their place of hiding.

They did him a favor, did the foe's infantry. They followed the example of the cavalry. They elected to surround him before making their attack. Shih-ka'i stepped into the portal just before their charge began. There was but one man behind him, his faithful Pan ku. They came over the dunes and found a whole lot of nothing. The Tervola had pulled their bolt hole in after them.

"What are they waiting for, Lord?" Tasi-feng asked. Four days had passed. The foe had not come west. Recon reports painted a portrait of confusion on a Brobdingnagian scale.

"I don't know. Maybe we got our bluff in on them. Maybe they won't come at all."

"Do you think so, Lord?"

"Not really. But a daydream doesn't hurt if you don't put much faith in it. Anyway, let's not be ungrateful for the gift of time." Shih-ka'i had not expected to have time to move people into the mountains and get them dug in. He would not have given an opponent that edge.

He had gotten what he needed and more. The Seventeenth's two field brigades were in place and waiting. Elements of the rest of Eastern Army were assembling at the fortress. If he were given another week, he thought, transfers would bring in enough people and thaumaturgic equipment to destroy thrice the number of zombies he had seen near the lonely mountain.

He had stripped his army of Tervola. The troops were coming overland under the command of their noncommissioned officers, with some units transferring in as opportunity arose. He was drawing Tervola and equipment from Northern Army, too, pushing his writ from Lord Kuo to its limit. He had ignored the predictable outrage of the Commander, Northern Army.

Northern Army was also on the march, but there was no way it could contribute troops here. Shih-ka'i had directed its three legions to assume a defensive posture along the west bank of the Tusghus, a broad river lying roughly midway between the Seventeenth's old headquarters at Lioantung and the fortress on the edge of the desert.

The transfer streams were being pushed to their limits within Eastern Army's territories. Too many miles lay between the fortress and even the closest of the legionary main forces.

"Hsu Shen," Shih-ka'i called. "Evacuation report."

The Tervola scuttled over. He had developed an obsequious manner since his rescue. "Finally getting some cooperation, Lord Ssu-ma. They believe our activity more than our word." He was speaking of the native tribes. Shih-ka'i had ordered them evacuated beyond his third defensive line, the Tusghus. In the absence of orders to the contrary, he meant to make the foe pay for every mile of advance, and to deny him any opportunity to strengthen himself with local bodies.

His legion commanders believed he was overreacting. He argued that only overreaction had salvaged the earlier probe into the desert.

"Lord Chang. Have you found Lord Kuo?" Shih-ka'i desperately wanted to confer with his superior. He was considering asking permission to commandeer additional Tervola should the fortress be lost.

In private even Pan ku chided him for anticipating such an extremity.

Chang Sheng commanded the Twenty-Third, the legion stationed immediately south of the Seventeenth. He was another of the dozens of Tervola banished to Eastern Army. He had held a seat on the Council of Tervola before his rustication. He resented Lord Kuo, resented his fall, and resented serving under a pig-farmer's son. He was not a happy man.

Before all that, though, he was a soldier of the Dread Empire. His army was at war. "No, Lord. He's gone to ground. There isn't a trace of him. I'd guess he doesn't want to be found."

"So be it. Get some sleep." Chang Sheng had been searching for Lord Kuo more than thirty hours. "He'll know we're hunting him. He'll have a reason for remaining silent. I'll accept it as tacit approval of my request for permission to act in accordance with our needs."

"Lord, I'd say it means the Matayangan situation is ready to blow up."

"Probably so. Worse luck."

Meng Chiao strode in. He was supposed to be in the mountains. He saluted Lord Lun-yu. "The enemy are moving up now, Lord."

"Be there in a few minutes. Their strength?"

"Thirty thousand plus, Lord. All infantry."

Tasi-feng glanced at Lord Ssu-ma. Shih-ka'i kept his mouth shut. He had assigned the mountain operation to Tasi-feng and the Seventeenth. He had assumed the larger task of directing the movements of the army. He could not run out and check the disposition of every century. He nodded at Tasi-feng.

Lord Lun-yu asked, "Are the men clear on the rules? Injured to transfer immediately. Enemy casualties to transfer if portal time is available. To be dismembered otherwise. We have ten to fifteen minutes to incapacitate a body before shock terminates and it can be animated again."

"They've been advised, Lord."

"Good. Remind them not to turn their backs on enemies who are down. They might get up again."

Shih-ka'i smiled into his mask. He wasn't the only mother hen.

"As you command, Lord." Meng Chiao departed.

Tasi-feng asked Shih-ka'i, "Will you be coming through, Lord?"

"Later, maybe. Just for a minute, to get an idea of their strength and tactics. I'll be too busy here to interfere much."

Tasi-feng bowed slightly. "I'd better double-check my signals with the batteries before I leave."

"Go easy on the shafts if you can." Shih-ka'i had been able to gather just forty-nine. Tasi-feng had explained that most of the thaumaturgic arsenal had been transferred to Southern Army.

"I intend to, Lord."

"And watch the flyers. The air is our weak flank."

"Yes, Lord." Tasi-feng bowed slightly and departed before Shih-ka'i could fuss any more.

I'm as antsy as an old maid, Shih-ka'i thought. Let be, Ssu-ma. These are good men. They have millennia of experience between them. Field experience. Their soldiers are the best. If they can't stop this army of the dead, it can't be stopped.

Why was he so terribly nervous?

Because of the dragon riders? The autopsy hadn't told him anything good. They were nine feet tall. They were immensely strong. They were partially immune to attack by the Power. In all probability, in life, they had been smart, quick, and deadly, and had wielded the Power in their own right. A demand upon the libraries of Shinsan had produced no knowledge of any such creature having existed within the era of reliable historical records.

Shih-ka'i could not discover what had caused the desert, nor who had built the cities lying in ruins in the forests facing it. A search of the oldest legend-histories had produced only a passing reference to a great stone god of the east, a guardian facing an endless sea. Cautious, daring reconnaissance had confirmed that the continent ended not far east of the solitary mountain. Beyond lay nothing but an island and ocean.

The description of that island piqued Shih-ka'i's curiosity. In Ko Feng's reports on the Pracchia conspiracy he had referred to an island in the east. It had sheltered the laboratories of the conspiracy and the headquarters of its mastermind. This island fit Ko Feng's description. He wondered if these armies of the undead were another Pracchia gambit... How could that be? All the High Nine but Ko Feng had been killed at the Battle of Palmisano, or earlier. Both the west and Shinsan had made every effort to eradicate subsidiary nines following the war.

Lord Ssu-ma thought he would very much like to land a force on that island and see what had been left behind. The Pracchia conspirators had controlled some interesting sorceries. Lord Ko had been unable to salvage any. Most had been under the aegis of one Magden Norath, a renegade Escalonian who had guarded his secrets well.

Shih-ka'i made a quick inspection circuit of the fortress. Preparations were proceeding perfectly, if too slowly to soothe his nerves. He took a deep breath. "Pan ku, let's see what's happening in the mountains."

7

YEAR 1016 AFE

CONSPIRACIES

IST WAS ABOUT to retire when a nervous servant announced that the King wanted to see her. "He's here?" she asked, startled.

"We had him wait in the library, My Lady." The woman's tone conveyed a plea for understanding. The monarch could not be told to come back when his visit would be more convenient. Astounding enough that he should just drop in off the street, though this King was uniquely plebeian in his habits.

"What does he want?"

"He wouldn't say, My Lady."

Moths gamboled about in Mist's stomach. This had a bad smell. "Tell him I'll be right down. See if he'll take some brandy."

"Certainly, My Lady. Shall I waken Marta?"

"I'll dress myself." She took her time, composing herself by chanting verses from the Soldier's Ritual used by the warriors of her homeland. She did not leave her bedchamber till she was convinced that she was in complete self-control.

"You're out late," she observed as she entered the library. A tic of irritation pulled at one eye. Her warmth sounded false in her own ears.

The King scanned her quickly, his gaze impersonal. He was unimpressed by her beauty. She always felt inadequate in his presence: felt like she had a great hairy mole on the end of her nose or a livid scar across her cheek. He and Michael Trebilcock and Varthlokkur were all immune to her carefully crafted looks. Weird and frightening that so many such men should surround her, making treacherous the ground on which she was accustomed to operate, leaving her uncertain and inclined to become flustered....

"I was over at my house. I wanted to see you. Thought I'd save a trip and do it now."

"You look exhausted."

"I had a rough day. Excuse my manners. They may not be what they should."

Her preparations were inadequate. Already she was growing flustered. She gobbled, "What's on your mind?" and was immediately dismayed. She hadn't wanted to be so direct.

"Just call me curious about what you and Aral are up to."

Damn, she thought. She managed to mask her surprise. "Up to? What do you mean?"

"Let's say I've noticed the coming together of what appear to be the elements of a 'situation.' I always try to be reasonable. Thought I'd give you a chance to explain before I got excited."

"So?" The moths were back. Brandishing tusks dripping venom. Suddenly, she understood why Varthlokkur was in town. If Bragi thought he needed his back covered, he was *sure*....

"These are the ingredients: One exiled Princess of Shinsan, minus the tempering influence of a good man who fell at

Palmisano. One young merchant of considerable wealth and influence, perhaps bedazzled. From the staff of Lord Hsung's Western Army, Tervola who remain secret supporters of the Princess in exile."

Mist held her breath. How could he know that? That damned Trebilcock! He really did have somebody inside Lord Hsung's headquarters. She'd hoped she was wrong about that.

"Interestingly enough, these ingredients have come together just when my spies tell me Shinsan has been caught with what looks like an explosive crisis on its Matayangan frontier."

Gods! Did he know everything? Did Trebilcock have an agent here in the house?

"A handy distraction," the King continued. "Now, if you were me, wouldn't all those things make you wonder?"

He spoke with an odd formality. Rather like a magistrate, she thought. His voice was tight. His gaze wandered nervously, but she was too distracted to seize and use his discomfort. She drifted away inside herself, trying to select a response which would not compromise her ambitions. Finally, "You're right. I was approached by people inside Shinsan. By a traditionalist faction opposed to Lord Kuo's penchant for change, and disturbed by the empire's increasing instability. I'm the last living descendant of the founder, Tuan Hua. I was shaped during the Dual Principiate of the Princes Thaumaturge. They think I could reimpose old-fashioned stability and values, given a chance. So far it's just been talk. I don't think anything will come of it."

"Why not?"

"I've been approached before. These groups never have enough power or influence. And what they really want, instead of what they say they want, is a figurehead. A legitimate pretender who can assume their sins after they're in power. A scapegoat, really." Was he listening? Accepting?

His face remained as impassive as a gambler's.

"And you wouldn't settle for that."

"No. You know me that well."

The King steepled his fingers under his nose. For a moment he seemed to be praying. "Where does Aral fit?"

"He's a merchant. The trading climate would improve if a friend of Kavelin ruled Shinsan. He's been trying to assemble financial backing for a coup. I haven't had the heart to shatter his hopes."

The King examined the spines of her books. She hoped she sounded plausible. She had rehearsed for this interview countless times, knowing it to be inevitable, but it had come early. All her planning had toppled around her. She could not recall her lines. She could but tell most of the truth and hope that it would be enough.

He took a deep breath, decided not to say whatever was in his mind. She was sure he had been about to bring up his secretary's embassy to Lord Hsung. Were it as successful as it sounded likely to be, it would rob her of all hope of enlisting the support of Kavelin's mercantile community. Her only real option was to sabotage Prataxis's efforts. She hadn't yet crossed that bridge. And now she knew she didn't dare. Surely he'd just caught a glimmer of the possibilities. If anything happened now, the blame would be laid at her feet.

He was playing his old, old game of giving the villain all the rope he wanted.

"Sounds good," he said at last. "Kavelin would benefit. Assuming Shinsan's historical inertia could be altered. Otherwise what damned difference does it make who's in power?"

What? He wasn't going to raise hell? He was going to agree with her? Despite Prataxis? She let him sit through an extended silence while she marshalled her composure. He didn't seem to notice. She asked, "What are you saying?"

"That I wouldn't be averse to a scheme. But I'm not too excited about you involving my people without you and me having an understanding up front. Also, right now *you* are one of my people. You're Chatelaine of Maisak. My first line of defense against Shinsan. We have here what Derel would call a potential conflict of interest. I wouldn't want to find myself worried about my hold on the Savernake Gap."

Mist's heart fluttered. How could he know so much? Did he? Was he shooting in the dark? Was he giving her more rope? Using his well-known obsession with the eastern peril as a tool? "I see. You want guarantees. What did you have in mind?"

The King smiled thinly.

She had made a tactical error. He *had* been fishing this time. And he'd caught her. Damn! Why did he have to be so astute?

"Not now. Not here," he said. "We both need time to think it over. And I'll want witnesses. Varthlokkur and the Unborn should do."

She pretended amusement. "You don't trust anybody, do you?"

"Not now. Not anymore. Why should I? Your scheme is only one of my problems. I mean to walk light and careful till it's all under control."

She laughed a genuine laugh. Her confidence began to return. He responded with a smile. She said, "You should have been born an easterner. You would've made a great Tervola."

"Maybe. My mother was a witch."

She had heard it before, of course, but still she was startled. Was that it? Was he doing a little magical snooping? Perhaps with Varthlokkur showing the way? She started to ask, was interrupted by a servant who said, "My Lady, there's a gentleman here looking for His Majesty."

Mist looked at Bragi. He shrugged. "Send him in," she said.

The King's adjutant bustled in. "Sire, I've been looking all over. We need you back at the palace." The man looked grim.

"What is it, Dahl?"

"An emergency, sire. Please?" The young officer gave Mist a glance so melodramatic she was tempted to laugh.

"We'll talk later," the King told her. His look said as much as all of his conversation.

She would have to walk very carefully for a while. Matters had reached a stage too delicate for risk-taking. All her fault, of course. She had gotten too eager, had begun looking too far ahead, to deal properly with all the little things cropping up now. "Overconfidence, get thee behind me," she murmured.

The hour was late. The King and Varthlokkur were seated on steps in a dark and otherwise deserted courtyard. Neither man was wholly awake or alert. Ostensibly, they had come out to watch a spectacular meteor shower. "There goes a big one," the wizard said. "All the way down past the wall."

"I saw one one time that broke up in about twenty pieces. Really something. There's another one." After a few seconds, "I saw Mist. She was too evasive. Made me more suspicious."

"So?"

"So she's into some scheme to get her throne back. In a lot deeper than she'll admit."

"And?"

"Damnit, you're not contributing a whole lot here."

"What do you want me to say?"

"Give me a guess. Am I wrong? Is she really involved in something?"

"Hell, you know the answer to that. Why ask? Of course she is. Once you attain a throne, you don't give it up without a fight. Consider her viewpoint. There isn't much here for her since Valther was killed. Her children, of course, but she isn't the maternal sort. She once had something big in Shinsan. Now she wants it back."

"She's vulnerable, though. Through the children."

"Aren't we all." The wizard turned bitter. "They're hostages to fortune."

"Can she make the comeback?"

"I wouldn't know. I don't know what's happening in Shinsan's politics. And I don't want to know. I just want to ignore them, and have them ignore me."

"But they won't."

"No. They won't. Not forever."

They watched shooting stars for a while. Then Varthlokkur said, "It won't matter if she does win, you know. Shinsan is Shinsan."

"You don't think she'd change anything?"

"She couldn't if she wanted. She wouldn't be allowed. You and I and Kavelin have earned their special attention. Someday they'll come again."

"Look at that one! Almost like a comet for a second."

"Uhm." Musingly, the wizard continued, "It should be a while coming. They've had some bad years, and they're staring trouble in the eye in Matayanga. They haven't fully pacified the territories they occupied during the war. Right now they're hopping like the one-legged whore the day the fleet came in."

Bragi chuckled and looked the wizard askance. That was not a Varthlokkur figure of speech. "If they'll give me a decade, or even another year, I'll be grateful. I'll take it and be happy because I don't think we can turn them back again. I think having Mist in charge might set the day of reckoning back a little, and soften the blow when it falls."

"It's your choice. Just don't forget O Shing."

"O Shing?" O Shing was the prince who had overthrown Mist and driven her out of the empire, only to be overthrown himself.

"He didn't want to come west. He fought it all the way. And that's why he's no longer with us."

"I know. But the people who pushed him out are gone now too. Holy...! Did you see the size of that one? All right. I'll take a few days to poke around and to think about it.

Then I'll get Gjerdrum and you and a couple others together and we'll decide whether we should help her. And if we do, how visible our help should be."

"It's your choice, as I say, but you're just asking for grief if you do it. You have problems enough at home. Problems more deserving of your attention. Also, watch who you include in your 'we.' I have no intention of getting involved with the Dread Empire again. Unless they come after me first."

"Pardon me for jumping to conclusions. I thought it might be a way for you to make contacts who could check out your Ethrian questions for you."

The wizard stiffened. He turned slowly, gazed at the King. After a moment, he nodded and said, "Maybe it would, at that."

Three men had gathered in Mist's library. Two leaned over her silver divining bowl. Her bowl did not contain the common water. She was wealthy. She could afford the far more expensive and reliable quicksilver coveted by every seer.

Aral Dantice shifted restlessly, nervous as a youth on the brink of losing his virginity. Mist watched him as closely as she did her bowl. She had made a mistake, telling him how much the King suspected. He had the Michael Trebilcock shakes. If this went the wrong way, he might crack... She did not want to think about that. Heroic measures might be required.

Cham Mundwiller filled the air with clouds from his pipe. The third man occupied a chair against one wall. His eyes were halfway closed. Neither his stance nor expression betrayed any emotion. He was as patient as a snake.

His coloring and mien matched Mist's. His clothing was western. He seemed uncomfortable with it. Though duskier than Dantice or Mundwiller, his face had a pallid look. He was accustomed to wearing a mask.

Mist's breath caught, sounding a little gasp. The easterner's eyelids twitched. "Aral!" Mist said. "Come here."

Dantice stared down into the bowl, at four minute human shapes seated round a table. For a long time now the four had been arguing, pounding the table, pushing bits of documentary evidence at one another. Nothing seemed changed. "What?" he asked.

"It's going our way." She grinned at herself. Her voice had picked up a high, musical squeak of excitement.

"How can you tell when we can't hear what they're saying?"

"Hush. Just hush and watch."

They watched the figures argue. Suddenly, Mist leapt away from the table. She yelped happily and threw her arms around Dantice. "It's official. The King got his way. We don't have to hide and sneak anymore." She kissed him.

He responded with a vigorous male salute. Mist stepped back. Head tilted, unable to control a lopsided smile, she said, "That might be nice too, Aral."

He blushed. He stammered.

Mundwiller exhaled a blue cloud and smiled knowingly. Aral turned redder still.

The third man saved him. He rose, stared into the bowl. His face remained arctically cool. He nodded once, returned to his chair. "It's good."

Dantice shuddered. Mist smiled, mildly amused. Lord Ch'ien Kao E always got that reaction when first he spoke. His throat had been injured long ago. He retained just a ghost of a voice, a dry husk that grated like salt in a raw wound.

Mist asked, "What troubles you, Lord Ch'ien?"

The man steepled thin fingers before his narrow chin. "The move suggests acceptance of the inevitable. It suggests that your King is well aware of what we're doing. It suggests that our secrets aren't nearly as secure as they should be." His obsidian eyes met theirs in turn.

I'm losing control, Mist thought. If I don't grab it back I'll soon be a spectator in this game.

"There haven't been any leaks at this end," Aral declared. He met that snakelike gaze without wavering. He was not intimidated by Ch'ien Kao E the man, only by what the man symbolized. He had met Tervola during the Great Eastern Wars. Aral Dantice, the caravan outfitter's son, was still alive.

"You're sure?"

"Absolutely. Wait. I do know one roundabout way for there to be a leak. Through my friend Michael Trebilcock. It's more circumstantial than deliberate. We share a few couriers."

"Smugglers."

Aral bowed slightly. "Sometimes they tell me what they think Michael is doing. I imagine they tell him what they think I'm up to. Lately, they've hinted that he may have developed an agent inside Lord Hsung's headquarters. It looks like he has. The King's actions make me think that agent might be aware of us."

Damn your eyes, Aral, Mist thought. Why did you have to tell him that?

"I see." Kao E turned her way. His reptilian eyes narrowed. "Princess?"

"You have some idea whom such a man might be?"

"I believe so."

"Does a weak link matter at this point?"

"Trebilcock obtained leverage. A lever is a tool any hand may wield."

She nodded. "Too true. Speak to him. Find out what the leverage was, and the extent of the compromise. Use your own judgment afterward."

"As you wish, Princess."

Dantice got a cold, pale look. He stared at the bookshelves, shuddered.

Cham Mundwiller sucked on his pipe and said nothing.

His face remained a mask of stone.

Mist glared at Aral and tried to force a thought into his mind. *This isn't a game, Aral. We're playing for an empire.*

"Where is this Trebilcock?" Kao E asked. "His testimony might be enlightening."

"Nobody knows," Aral replied. "He disappeared a while back. Somebody attacked General Liakopulos one night. Hurt him bad. Next day Michael was gone. Nobody knows if there's a connection."

That was the night the King visited me, Mist reflected. *The night that Haas creature dragged him away, acting like he thought I was the villain of the day.* "I've looked for him," she said. "I like to keep track of him. He's a dangerous man. I can't find a trace." She frowned at Aral, who could not conceal his distress. She wondered how he had become professionally successful with so little aptitude for conspiracy.

Aral asked, "Do you think he's dead? That maybe he found something and it was too much for him to handle?"

Not a good conspirator at all. He let his concern for his friend distract him completely.

"I wouldn't know, Aral. Lord Ch'ien, don't interfere with Trebilcock. The King and Varthlokkur are much too fond of him."

Kao E rose, nodded. "As you will. I'd best return. I do have my duties. And I have to relay the news to our friends."

"By all means," Mist said, concealing her delight at his going.

Kao E strode toward one corner of the room. He vanished as he was about to collide with the bookshelves. A column of air coruscated momentarily.

"That's one spooky critter," Aral said. "I don't like him at all."

"Don't let him put you off," Mist replied. "He's stuck with me a long time. He's one of the few Tervola I trust."

"You know your own people." And, "What he is to you

and what he is to me aren't necessarily the same thing. He probably thinks of me as a useful trained dog."

Mist turned quickly, hoping he missed her surprise. That was exactly the way Lord Ch'ien would view a western collaborator. "Master Mundwiller. You haven't said a word since you got here."

Mundwiller looked down at the silver bowl. The scene therein continued, mouse-sized players arguing in silence. He harrumphed. "I'll say good-bye, then. I'm not needed here." His eyes twinkled.

Aral started to say something, thought better of it. Mist, too, found herself short on words.

Mundwiller paused at the library door. "I'll leave you with a thought. My friends and I will be more comfortable knowing you're working with the King."

"What did he mean by that?" Aral asked once the door closed.

Mist smiled. She ran her tonguetip along the edges of her perfect teeth. "I don't know. I'm not sure I care." But she did, of course. Those old moths tumbled and giggled in her stomach. She had dodged fate's hammer today. Obviously, Mundwiller had allowed himself to be drawn in only so he could apprise the King of the course of her plot. She shivered and concentrated on Aral.

He took a backward step, then retreated round the table. Sudden sweat moistened his face. He looked like a man running from a dream.

He did not escape.

Mist smiled wickedly. From this dream he would never recover. Nor would he want to. She would see to that.

Varthlokkur glanced up as the King stepped into the small room where he held his most private conferences. Bragi seemed smugly pleased. He said, "Mist will be here in a few minutes."

The woman arrived ten minutes later, ushered in by Dahl Haas. Aral Dantice ran at her heel like a faithful pup. The wizard observed through hooded eyes. Something had changed. There was a new shyness between them. He looked over at the King, who had been acting that way himself. Over a bit of fluff young enough to be his daughter. Must be something going around, he thought.

"Sit down," the King suggested. "Let's get to it. I've been cooped up in the castle all day, so I don't feel like arguing. We made a decision. You already know what it was. Now we implement it, Mist. But first, I want to know who the Tervola was and what he was doing in Kavelin without my permission."

Even Varthlokkur was startled. And a little disgusted. This young man had started with such promise. Now he had spies everywhere, like the worst tyrant.

If he was startled, Dantice was stricken. He made a sound, half belch and half mouse squeak. His eyes widened. And Mist, for one of the few times Varthlokkur could recall, was taken completely off guard.

That amused him. He enjoyed watching a colleague caught short.

"I have my resources too," the King said. "The Tervola is important to me. Call it a gesture of good faith."

Mist recovered. She spoke honestly and, Varthlokkur noted, said a few things which surprised Dantice.

The King glanced at the wizard, soliciting an opinion. Varthlokkur had detected no outright falsehood. He nodded. Bragi said, "It sounds good. Assuming Kuo isn't in on the planning from the other end. What's your timetable?"

"It's still iffy. We move when Lord Ch'ien thinks the Matayangan attack has peaked. We seize the key points of the empire. We don't bother Southern Army till the Matayangan attack ebbs. Only then do we replace Lord Kuo."

"Right. If he lets you. What if he negotiates his way out of trouble with Matayanga? If he doesn't attack?"

"The plan isn't perfect. I'd lose."

"You wouldn't try to force that war, would you?"

"No! No more than Lord Kuo is. Shinsan can't stand much more warfare."

The King glanced at Varthlokkur once more. Again he could only indicate that he believed she was telling the truth.

The King nodded. "All right, Mist. What can I contribute?"

"You're doing it. Giving us a safe springboard. The only other thing might be the loan of a few shock troops for the strike itself."

Varthlokkur studied Dantice, and in his little twitches read what his part in the plot was to have been—before the King had become involved. He was to have gathered the financing for mercenary forces meant to do the job now in the hands of royal soldiery. The lad is a fool, the wizard thought. But this is a woman who can make fools of men far wiser.

The King said, "Sir Gjerdrum, put together the forces she needs. And keep it quiet."

Varthlokkur turned to the young knight. Poor Gjerdrum. He was bitterly opposed to this venture. None of the King's arguments had swayed him the least. Yet he was going along, because it was the King's will.

He's probably right, Varthlokkur reflected. When you come right down to it, we're all going along because that's easier than arguing. And chances are Bragi is being a damned fool. He can't separate his private feelings from what is politic. If he doesn't learn soon, Kavelin is in for hard times.

Nepanthe stalked the bounds of her apartment like a thing caged. She was tormented by a diffuse, unconquerable certainty that her world had shifted around her, that suddenly she was a foreigner in her own time. Nothing seemed quite real anymore.

She knew why. All her lost anchors, all the missing friends

and loves. She had no more family, and few friends—just no anchor left. Except her husband, and hers was a marriage of convenience, from her viewpoint. She needed a protector. She had accepted the protection of a man who wanted her. Any romance existed only in Varthlokkur's imagination.

These days she just drifted above and away from everything. Her lack of touching points ached. Sometimes she wondered if she were quite sane.

Her life was one long necklace pearled with dissatisfaction and unhappy moments. There had been good times, but those she had to struggle to remember. She had no trouble recalling the misery. Indeed, she dwelt upon it.

She paused to stare out her window. The sky was a heavy grey. More bad weather? It seemed the sun had vanished with their arrival. Did gloom follow her like a doleful hound?

"Maybe it's just being pregnant," she murmured. "I can't be this way all the time. Right now even I can't stand me." A weak, mocking smile toyed with her lips. "I *have* had friends."

The baby kicked. She rested her hands upon her stomach, tried to guess if she were feeling an arm or a leg. "Guess you're going to be a boy. They say boys are more active."

The baby kicked again. She gasped. It was strong. "Varth?" But he wasn't there. Out with the King again, probably. What were they up to, anyway? She still didn't know why Bragi wanted Varth here. Not really. He had his tale to tell, but he was tricky. You never knew. Even Varth might not know.

She hadn't gotten out of the apartment much, but still had sensed the deep currents twisting through Castle Krief. Servants chattered and speculated. There was trouble with the succession. Bragi had been chosen King, but his family hadn't been made hereditary custodians of Kavelin. The crown would be up for grabs if he died. Several parties wanted control of the succession.

Then there was the eastern situation, and the sporadic

civil war in neighboring Hammad al Nakir, which could have considerable impact here.

And, of course, there were the traditional ethnic frictions within Kavelin itself, frictions three enlightened monarchs had been able to ameliorate only slightly.

She stared out her window and thought of her distant mountain home. She had been no more happy at Fangdred. Each day had witnessed its prayer that the outside would call them forth. Now they were free of that isolation, and she only longed to retreat to the safety of her mountain fastness.

"I must be mad. I can't even be satisfied when my prayers are answered." The baby moved again. "What are you doing in there? Jumping rope?" She tried to relax. There was surcease in sleep, sometimes.

Sleep was slow coming. Her back ached. Her legs and feet hurt. Her mind would not abandon its neurotic harping despite her efforts to silence it. And the baby would not lie still.

But sleep of a sort did come, and with it visions as disquieting as anything her mind threw up while awake.

They belonged to a family of dreams she had begun to know well. She dreamed about Ethrian, a desert, and a great, frightening shadow. Her son was calling for help. His voice was weak and remote. The shadow was amused. It lashed out at her child, inflicting intolerable torment. She reached out for Ethrian, but he couldn't tell she was there.

She had had a lot of Ethrian dreams lately, mainly when she wasn't too deeply asleep. They varied, yet always showed her son alive, trying to evade some shadowy peril.

Varth claimed it was just pregnancy doing strange things, that her dreams had no parallel in the real world. But she had been through this before, several years ago. She hadn't been pregnant then.

She believed cluster dreams reflected truth. There was great magic in dreams, though she hadn't the knowledge to interpret them. Her own touch of magic was severely diminished now she no longer had brothers. Their grasp of the Power had always required the concentration of the entire family....

Varth was no expert, either, but he should know enough to realize her dreams had significance... or did they? Suppose he was right? Suppose they were manifestations of her fears and insecurities?

She was coming out of the twilight into which she'd fallen. She wasn't chasing every will-o'-the-wisp notion. She was trying to think linearly... And she was disappointed. For an instant she'd felt she'd reached a half-open door, about to capture an unsuspected glimpse of the truth.

She heard a soft rustle, quiet footsteps. She recognized the maid's step. "I'm awake, Margo."

"Ah, Lady. I didn't want to interrupt your nap. Your husband asked me to check."

"Tell him to come in."

Varthlokkur seated himself on the edge of her bed, held her hands. "How are you feeling?"

"Pretty good. What's happening in the rest of the world?"

"The usual. They're being born, they're dying, and generally acting silly in between. Four hundred years I've watched them and they haven't changed. They keep right on doing the same stupid things."

Disappointment trickled through Nepanthe. There would be no discussing her dream while he was like this. "You're in that mood again?"

"What mood?"

"All is vanity and chasing after the wind."

"Hunh! Sometimes it's the only realistic philosophy."

He was just within the penumbra of melancholy. He would be unfit to live with if his mood deepened. But he was salvageable now, if she kept him from losing himself inside. "What set you off?" Let him roll it out. Let him look at it and get mad. That would break the chain.

"It's Bragi. He's changing. A few years ago his eyes were wide open. Nothing got by him. Nobody fooled him. And he never fooled himself."

"What are you talking about?"

"He isn't that way anymore. There are intrigues here in Kavelin. Conspiracies about to explode. And he won't see what's happening. He goes off and plays Captures or plots against Shinsan. While the real danger grows like a cancer, right behind him."

Victory! He was angry. "Why do you care? Kavelin isn't your home. And you'll outlive its troubles."

"I don't know. You're right. Since Ilkazar fell I haven't been attached to any particular place. But maybe I like what the old King, Queen Fiana, and Bragi wanted to do here. Maybe I like the promise of their dream, if it succeeds. Maybe I'm aggravated because Bragi has gotten distracted from the real issues. Maybe he's changing into somebody I don't like."

"And maybe you're misjudging him, Varth. He's tricky. You never know what he's doing. He might have his thumb on the pulse of whatever it is that's worrying you. You can't ever forget that he's got Michael Trebilcock. The way people talk, Michael is everywhere and nowhere, and not a whisper of intrigue gets past him. My maids say the nobles are scared to death of him."

"Uhm. Bragi does have good help. But what happens if he gets so weird they stop agreeing with what he does? Never mind. It's beyond my influence. I shouldn't worry. How was your day?"

He had slipped into a more pliable mood. Not a good mood, but the best she would see. "I had another dream. Ethrian was calling for help again."

Varthlokkur's face folded into a dark scowl, like a savage old thunderhead. She half expected lightning to prance across his brow.

She chose her words carefully. "I don't think this is just

pregnancy and wishful thinking, Varth. There's something touching me. I'm not saying it's Ethrian. Probably it isn't. But I think you should take me seriously and try to get to the bottom of it. It might be important in some way neither of us can see right now."

"All right. I'll do that." His voice was cool, unhappy. "I'll let you know if there's anything to it." He rose. "I have to go out. I shouldn't be long."

She watched him leave. Run, she thought at his back. Get away. Why do you get so upset when I talk about Ethrian?

Several days had passed. Varthlokkur encountered the King in a hallway. Amidst the dancing shadows cast by oil lamps, they paused. Varthlokkur asked, "Any word on Michael yet?"

"Aral found a cold trail. A friend of his saw Michael in Delhagen a few days after the attack on Liakopulos."

"Strange."

"Everything is, these days. How long till Nepanthe's time?"

"Two weeks. Three."

"Nervous?"

"Very." The wizard's smile felt weak. He was beginning to worry. He was getting tied up here, and he had promised Nepanthe that he would take her home before the birthing.

"Nothing to worry about. She didn't have trouble with Ethrian."

"Do me a favor? Don't mention that name. She's got a bee in her bonnet about him lately. She's decided he's still alive. Thinks we should try finding him."

"Is he?"

"I don't know."

"A couple weeks ago you said…"

"I know what I said. This isn't the time to worry about it. We've got a baby to get born." He was surprised at himself. He was snarling. Did the possible survival of the boy so threaten him?

"I'll check back later, in case something turns up."

"It won't." He watched the King depart. The man's shoulders were stiff in a carrying-the-weight-of-the-world fashion. "My friend, you're going to have to learn to mind your own business at least some of the time." He wheeled and stalked toward his apartment.

8

THIS ONE IS coming right at us!" Ethrian shouted. "Let's get out of here!" Sahmanan ran down the stone beast's neck. Ethrian pursued her.

A flash of silver plunged out of the blue. The beast shunted it slightly. It hit his side. He responded with a great bellow of rage.

"What are they?" Sahmanan asked, rising from the beast's back.

"I don't know." Ethrian surveyed the destruction wrought among the beast's soldiers. "But they're effective. Let's get down from here before one of them gets us." He gave her a gentle shove.

He looked out across the desert. The Tervola remained standing atop their dune. They did not seem dismayed by the advance of the armies of the dead.

Ethrian and Sahmanan were almost to ground level when another shaft arrived. It plunged almost straight down, in front of the beast's nose. It released its energy in Sahmanan's pond.

Huge gouts of steam flung skyward. Chunks of stone fell out of the beast's forelegs. The paving blocks between them churned and tossed. The exit from the caverns collapsed.

Sahmanan wept for her shattered project.

"Your Great One isn't doing so hot," Ethrian observed. "They're cutting us to ribbons. Maybe I made a mistake, giving him the power to defend us. He's just wasting the armies."

"He can get more."

"Really? You think the Tervola will let us out of the desert? That's just an exploration party. What happens when they get mad? They know what's going on now. They know what they have to do. Your Great One keeps on, we'll be dead by the end of the week. Him included."

Sahmanan cocked her head. "The silver things. They've stopped."

She was right. The bombardment had ended. Ethrian examined the damage the last shaft had done. "Going to take a lot of work to clear this." He walked on round to where he could see what was happening at the dune.

Nothing was happening. The stone beast's soldiers were standing around. "What now?" Ethrian demanded.

"They're gone. He can't figure it out. They walked down the back of the dune and disappeared."

Ethrian spat in disgust. "A transfer portal. I swear, I could do better than this so-called god if..."

"Don't talk like that!"

"I'll talk any way I want. Incompetence is incompetence. I want out of this place. I won't make it if this keeps on."

The stone beast growled something about not yet being in possession of his full might. Ethrian snarled that he had misused what he had been given. The argument persisted throughout the four days it took to clear the exit from the caverns. Ethrian insisted that the beast become his slave. The beast refused.

Sahmanan usually spoke for the godling. Now she remained quiet and thoughtful. She pottered round her pool like a child trying to find all the pieces of a broken china doll.

"They're waiting in the mountains," Ethrian told the woman. "A full legion, ready for battle. I suppose your Great One will waste the rest of his manpower there."

"He doesn't take defeat lightly, Ethrian."

He glanced at her. That was the first time she had used his name. "Neither do they, friend. Neither do they. In fact, they've been defeated only once. By my grandfather, my uncles, my aunt, and the man who killed my father. They were trying to avenge that when I was captured."

As if hoping the stone beast would not hear her, Sahmanan whispered, "I believe you. I'm afraid of them. But how do we get Him to listen? It isn't like it was. He doesn't give me my share anymore. In the wars with Nahaman I did most of the fighting."

"Maybe he blames you for losing."

"But I…"

"Whose fault it was wouldn't matter. He wouldn't admit it if it were his. He's supposed to be a god. Gods are supposed to be omnipotent and infallible."

"What should we do?"

"Follow the army. Be ready to help. We'll share its fate whether we do or not. The Tervola aren't merciful."

Sahmanan nodded. "Wait here."

She went down between the stone beast's legs, bucking the flood pouring from the caverns. For a long time Ethrian watched the soldiers march out, form units, and head toward the mountains. There seemed no end to the hidden horde.

Maybe the beast needed no finesse. Maybe it could accept the ridiculous casualties indefinitely.

Sahmanan returned as the sun was setting. She led two

small dragons. "They lost their riders. The Great One has no use for them."

The thought of flying startled butterflies in Ethrian's stomach. "I don't know...."

"There's nothing to fear. It's like riding a horse. Just tell it what to do. They were as intelligent as us when they were alive."

"They aren't alive now." He meant they had to be animated by the stone beast. Riding them, they were at his mercy.

He smiled suddenly. He had nothing to fear. Did he? The godlet would preserve him till it acquired everything he had to give.

"Just do what I do," Sahmanan said. "Up!" Her mount hurled itself into the air. Its wings pounded like brazen gongs. She circled a hundred feet overhead.

Ethrian took a deep breath. "Up, you devil."

The dragon's back slammed against his behind. He wobbled, held on. The ground sank away. His heart hammered. He closed his eyes.

When he opened them his mount was circling behind Sahmanan's. They were a few yards above the stone beast's head. The change in vantage made the desert look ten times more vast. "I don't think I was meant for this," he shouted.

The woman glanced over her shoulder, said something to her mount. It peeled off the circle and streaked westward.

"Follow," Ethrian croaked.

He soon got the hang of flying, and knew he would never enjoy it. The fall was too long. Sahmanan, though, seemed born for wings. While he plodded along, inexpertly enduring, she hurtled high and low, exulting in aerobatics. He became queasy just watching.

Finally, she glided as close as the monsters' wings permitted. "We're almost there." The mountains loomed ahead. Barren foothills climbed below. Her right hand thrust out. Ethrian spied a notch marked with patterned lines. The lines swelled into defensive works.

Sahmanan dropped like a stone. Her wild plunge broke only yards above the lifeless mountainside. Her dragon banked and slid off into a side canyon which expanded into what had been a broad meadow in olden times. Ethrian followed at a higher altitude, and descended only when there were no mountains to crowd him.

The one-time meadow boasted rank upon rank of undead soldiery, arrayed as they had been beneath the earth. He counted, and counted, and counted some more, and scanned the column still winding across the desert. He could not calculate the number of them.

"How many soldiers?" he asked as his feet hit the ground. He sat down immediately. His nerves were raw.

"We had a hundred-fifty thousand. All he could control, plus a margin for replacement."

"What do you mean, all he could control?"

"He can only animate so many. About a hundred thousand right outside the mountain. Out here... Well...."

"Hmm." This bore closer scrutiny. "You'd better explain. If he's got weaknesses besides stupidity..."

"The farther from the mountain, the fewer bodies he can control. Inside five miles he can handle a hundred thousand. You couldn't tell them from live soldiers, except they'd keep getting up. Out here he can't control more than fifty thousand, and those clumsily. That's why these are just standing around. He has thirty thousand up in the pass."

"And if we go to the edge of the desert?"

"Ten or fifteen thousand. At a thousand miles he couldn't animate more than four or five."

Ethrian surveyed the ranks. "How did he plan to go anywhere? He has big ideas. Looks like a penny-farthing empire to me. It'll never get out of the desert."

"That's why we're important."

"How so?"

"Later." She would answer no more questions. It was not

yet time, she insisted. First the beast had to avenge himself on the men in the pass.

Ethrian found some shade. After a time he decided he had it reasoned out.

The beast meant him to yield fully. It thought it could trick him into slavery. Then it would transfer its ability to manipulate the dead. Mobile, he would create the new empire.

He took his speculations to Sahmanan. She merely nodded.

He was smiling when he returned to his patch of shade. His position was stronger than he had anticipated. Smug, he dozed off.

He did not go into a deep sleep, only into a twilight state. He controlled his thinking. The moment was too good to waste.

Gently, gently, with little tugs at stubborn folds, he pulled himself free of his body. He floated over the army of the dead, unafraid of falling. He rejoiced in his freedom. There was no pain here.

He noted a darkness clinging to the mountains where the legion lay. He let himself sense, felt the edge of the stone beast's power. It was driving its hordes against Shinsan's earthworks.

Ethrian willed himself westward, was not pleased with what he found. The beast had hurled thirty thousand men at the defenses. Silver missiles slashed huge gaps in their ranks. Dead soldiers who got close enough to fight were overwhelmed immediately. The darkness was the smoke of fires burning the captured dead.

The beast's army was doing little damage in return. Shinsan's few casualties went out through the transfers before the beast could seize them.

Ethrian was disgusted. He drifted away to the west. He moved swiftly, covering a wide region. He became awed by the mind directing the legions.

The Tervola were three or four jumps ahead. He saw no hope of escaping the desert. The stone beast would squander his strength in that pass, send a trickle against the enemy fortress, and there it would end. A year hence the Tervola would chuckle over the great war in the desert, and marvel at the stupidity of the enemy they had defeated.

He fluttered back to his body.

"Have a nice nap?" Sahmanan asked.

"No." He told her what he had done and seen, and how little had remained of the beast's assault force on his return.

"Will he just keep on? There're only five thousand men up there. But they've got ten times that many coming to help. And behind those is the strength of Shinsan. Sahmanan, he's stubborn and stupid, but you've got to make him see what he's doing."

"I don't think he'd listen. He's angry. Maybe when he calms down."

"Calm him down. Do something. He's destroying us."

For a moment Sahmanan looked both vulnerable and winsome. She nodded once, violently, and mounted her dragon. The thing jumped into the air and sped eastward.

Ethrian considered the sun. It would set in another hour. He should rest. Sahmanan might be successful. He returned to his shady rock.

There was a little twilight left when Sahmanan awakened him. "Back already?"

"He wants you."

"He's willing to talk?"

She nodded. "He saw things today... He's very calm, very rational, and very worried. Their counterattack shook him."

"Counterattack?"

"They let him spend most of his strength, then surrounded what was left. He didn't save a single soldier. They didn't lose five hundred men. He learned a lesson."

"He's willing to listen!" Ethrian grinned. "Let's go."

They flew. Sahmanan set a vicious pace. The wind whipped round Ethrian. He kept his eyes closed half the time. They reached the stone beast in half an hour.

The youth felt the change immediately. The rage and arrogance had gone out of the monster. It felt like a child who had planned to show off and had fallen on its face.

Ethrian took a stance in the rubble and shouted, "Sahmanan says you're ready to talk." His father had taught him to be bold, observing that the gods had given men gall for a purpose.

The beast was deflated, but not crushed. It responded with mild amusement.

Ethrian called up, "I know your limits. I know your weaknesses. I know what you need. And you have no one else."

The beast's amusement grew. "I now have the strength to find someone else."

Ethrian glanced at Sahmanan. She nodded. "But he doesn't have the time."

"Know what you're up against now?" Ethrian shouted.

"If you mean our opponents, yes. I underestimated them. The world has changed. Man's power has waxed. That of the gods has declined. Deliverer, I'll offer an alliance. The three of us as partners, against the world. You free us and guide our armies. Sahmanan will wield the weapons of Power. I'll channel my strength to you."

Ethrian turned to the woman. "I'm not sure I follow him."

"It's a troika offer. You deliver us, he gives you the armies and myself the power to battle the Tervola. We work together to build an empire."

"What does he get?"

"You might have to be a god to understand."

"Try me. Otherwise, I can only judge him by human standards."

"He wants to be the god of our empire. He wants us to

create a new Nawami. After we do, we can move him to its capital, as patron deity."

"That's all?"

"All? That's everything, Ethrian. He's awake now. He can't survive without worshippers. You look west and think of revenge. He looks and sees survival. Today's defeat showed him how fragile our chances are."

"How long before he would fade, or whatever happens?"

"Maybe centuries. Gods don't die fast. But the time of decision is now. We have to crush those people. We're doomed if we don't. You were right. They won't accept defeat."

The youth looked up. His old hatreds smouldered on. "If we make this compact, how do we guarantee it? How do you make a god keep his word?"

The beast snapped, "Time binds me, Deliverer. I can't stay here much longer. If I fail you, you can leave me to die."

"Your word is good till you have someone to worship you."

"For that long at least. There's no reason we shouldn't stand together afterward. Ask Sahmanan if I haven't treated her well. Even when it was not in my immediate interest."

Sahmanan agreed. "He stands by those who stand by him. I wouldn't be here if he didn't."

"All right. We're on the right road. Let's test it. Godling, invest me first."

The beast said nothing. Ethrian felt its displeasure and uncertainty. Sahmanan asked, "What do you mean?"

"What I said. If he gives me the power to control the dead, I'll believe him. I'll give him what he needs." He studied the woman carefully, saw no sly smirk of victory.

"Lie down," the beast told him. "When you waken, you will go test yourself against our enemies. We can take care of my needs later."

Ethrian told Sahmanan, "There has been a change."

"I told you. Don't think he likes it. But there's a realist under that arrogance and bluster."

"Stand watch?"

"Of course."

The youth settled himself. He could not sleep! His mind kept pursuing visions of what he might do once this power was his.

He wakened suddenly, unsure where he was or what had happened. The woman in white stood above him. He lurched up, looking for crabs.

"It's all right. It's all right. It's over, Ethrian."

"Over? What?... I don't feel any different. Didn't it work?"

"It worked fine."

It seemed no time had passed. "How long was I out?"

"All night and all day. It's night again."

"That long? Really? We'd better do something. The Tervola..."

"They're still up there. The Great One says they're restless. They're ready to come see what we're doing."

Ethrian became filled with all the things that needed doing. "Where are those dragons?" The two beasts dropped from the sky. "Did I do that?"

"No. The Great One brought them. From now on, though, I'll manage them. You concentrate on the soldiers."

Ethrian frowned. The beast was not totally stupid. "All right." He hoisted himself onto a scaly back. In a moment he and Sahmanan were airborne.

As they sped westward he wondered what he would do. He really felt no different.

He felt it when he glided toward his waiting army. It was a vacuum that consisted of tens of thousands of vacuums waiting to be filled. Visions fluttered through his mind: The mountains as seen through countless pairs of dead eyes. He was disoriented for a moment. Then he began seeing with all those eyes at once. He felt the cord of power reaching back to the stone beast. His power. Power he could use any way he wanted.

The dragons landed. Ethrian peered over his mount's

head. His silent army had turned to face him.

"I'll be damned," he said. "I don't have to do much, do I?"

"You have to decide who does what, when, and where. The rest is unconscious."

"I just tell so many to go attack and they will?"

"Yes. You have to tell them how and where."

He closed everything out and went out of his body. Eagerly, he swept up the mountains. He studied the enemy position, and returned. "I'm ready to start," he announced, and heard the amazement in his own voice.

"What should I do?"

"Just wait right now. Let me find the men I need."

In the heart of the night, when life was at its lowest ebb, the army of the dead returned to the attack. They went in silence. They did not move in massed formations as before; they were scattered all over the slopes. A fall of shafts would harm only a few.

The first ten thousand bore bows or crossbows. They did not try to close with the soldiers of the Dread Empire. They stayed out and sniped.

"That looks good," Ethrian said. "Sahmanan, take your dragon up. Distract the Tervola."

In moments she was speeding toward the pass, a spear of light preceding her.

Now the spearmen and javelineers, Ethrian thought, and another ten thousand men went in.

The mountains flickered under the fury of an exchange between Sahmanan and the Tervola. Lances of fire scored the underbelly of the sky. Ethrian mounted his dragon. He lifted the monster till he could see the battle's shape.

The spearmen were advancing perfectly, widely spaced. They passed the snipers and began skirmishing with troops the enemy had sent to rout the bowmen. They did not do well, one on one, but were having more effect than had the masses in the stone beast's assault. They were more supple and quicker under Ethrian's more immediate control. Shinsan's skirmish line fell back. The spearmen reached the earthworks. Snipers kept hurling darts into the fray.

Ethrian brought up ten thousand swordsmen, also in scattered array, and behind them wave after wave from the horde in waiting.

Or half-horde. The stone beast had squandered sixty thousand before relinquishing control.

Ethrian found it hard to believe that all those bodies were moving simply because he willed it. He had only to imagine a movement, and the men he wanted making it, and it happened. A hundred men to storm a knoll where an arrow engine was taking his main thrust in enfilade? There they were, scrambling uphill, falling, lying still for ten or fifteen minutes, then rising to charge again. It was like daydreaming with the daydreams coming true.

He had the Seventeenth completely engaged. Sahmanan kept the Tervola occupied. Only a few demons roamed the contested slopes, and they had little effect.

He had thought-space left for other maneuvers. Ten thousand tireless soldiers marched southward, to pass round the legion, form smaller units, and head west. When they left the desert they would begin "recruiting." Perfection, Ethrian thought. Sheer perfection.

He banked his mount and dropped lower, passing above the battle at a hundred feet. "Spooky," he thought aloud.

The battle was so quiet! Machines might have been fighting down there. He heard only the movement of feet and the clang of weapons. The dead had nothing to say. The soldiers of Shinsan were schooled to fight in silence. Few would cry out even when mortally wounded. Their sole voluntary sound was the rumble of signal drums.

A ballista shaft screamed up. It ripped a hole through his mount's wing. "Hey!" he said, more surprised than frightened. "That was too close."

They might not throw their magical shafts at his scattered men, but they would target him if they realized that he controlled their attackers. If he perished, the dead army would collapse. There might be nothing left when the stone beast reanimated.

He wished he controlled the flyers. Now would be a good time to commit them. Bring them swooping in, blasting away, and scrub the Tervola before they could defend themselves.

He thought at his snipers, telling them to take higher ground and concentrate on enemy commanders. They were no longer needed to cover the assault itself.

He was losing men, but it looked good. Already several hundred of the enemy were out. The defense had begun to fray. Several strong points had yielded. His own fallen were rising again.

They were worth ten live soldiers. They could rise and rise again… Omnipotence engulfed him. For a moment he knew how it felt to be a god.

He felt for the enemy dead, tried to raise them, to confuse the legionnaires by making them fight among themselves. He found nothing. Dead men, yes, but none ready for his command. They were passing through the transfers before they cooled.

Just for an instant he had forgotten that he battled the Dread Empire. There was no confusion on their side of the line. They would not lose sight of their mission. They would not panic. They were, as always, the best. He might end up taking but a single body into his own force, that of the last man guarding the last portal while the last corpse went through.

Ethrian reached into the Seventeenth's fortress, trying to find dead men there. He sensed bodies, but none he could touch. He would have to put his own warriors inside first. The enemy were too much in control right now.

He was not disappointed. His strategy was working. The pass would be his. He laughed. Most of his soldiers had gone down at least once, but few had been badly mauled. They rose again and again.

His laughter rang across the night. Sahmanan heard it. She called back, her voice merry with imminent victory. The Tervola heard it as well. They responded defiantly. The Seventeenth's battle drums roared.

The drums. Those infernal drums. He had heard his father tell of their endless, terrifying rumble, but never had he heard them before. Chills crept down his spine. Fear hit him. He began to doubt.

Those were the drums of the Dread Empire, drums of promise, drums which proclaimed, "We of the Seventeenth do not stand alone. We of the Seventeenth know no fear. A hundred legions will rally behind us. Come find your doom, enemy of the empire."

Though his blood ran hot with the joy of victory, Ethrian could not help but hear the drums.

He was winning. The mountains would be his. He would travel on and meet Shinsan again, round the fortress beyond desolation's edge....

There were other legions and other armies. A hundred legions might be an exaggeration, but, for certain, this victory would be a small one. A minor incident on the road. The great battles were yet to come.

He had heard his uncle Valther describe the battles in Escalon, when Mist and O Shing had taken war to that once mighty kingdom. Compared to those this was a skirmish. For battles of that epic stature he would need all the might of his stone godling, and more.

The moon was a sickle that night, and rose just an hour before dawn. Its wan silver light splashed the concluding movements of a battle determined and grim, clearly lost and won, yet still as vicious as when it had begun.

The Dread Empire did not yield. Not a step. Before the last of her defenders fell, Ethrian lost forever his twenty-thousandth man.

And yet he was joyful. He had seventy thousand left, and was knocking on the doors of lands where others could be conscripted into his cause.

The last few drums spoke their defiance. He thought to his dead battalions. The dead gave voice to a battle cry. "Deliverer!" they rasped. All together, like a hellish choir. "Deliverer!"

He smiled as they completed the demolition of Shinsan's fabled Seventeenth Legion.

9

YEAR 1016 AFE

THE FORTRESS IN THE BORDERLAND

LORD LUN-YU SENT the message via Meng Chiao. "Lord Ssu-ma, they're attacking again. And there's a new mind in control."

"Oh?" Shih-ka'i had a cold feeling. "What makes you think that?"

"Their effectiveness. Their tactics. Perhaps you should come see what we mean, Lord."

Shih-ka'i considered the Tervola. Chiao was disturbed. His stance and little fidgety movements betrayed his inner turmoil. "All right. Pan ku. We're going to the mountains." He glanced at the big map. Everything was shaping up nicely. Eastern Army was coalescing. Should the dead break through the pass, they would find a hard knot blocking their path here.

A few days more would help. Yes. Every minute would help.

Shih-ka'i followed Meng Chiao through the transfer. He sensed the new mind immediately. He said, "We're in trouble."

"Yes, Lord," Tasi-feng agreed. "We won't be able to hold them."

"I didn't expect to. This was a delaying tactic. Stall them as long as you can." He glanced skyward, where a woman in white circled on a small dragon. "Is she good?"

"The best, Lord. Nearly as powerful as the Princess Mist. She's given us no chance to support the men, so they're not having much luck capturing enemy casualties."

Shih-ka'i glimpsed a second dragon. "Who's that?"

"We don't know, Lord. Possibly the new control."

There had been two people atop the thing in the desert. "I don't want to waste shafts, Lord Lun-yu, but if you get a good shot, call for one."

"As you command, Lord."

"I'll return to the fortress. Guard your portals carefully."

"We're shifting them now, Lord. We'll fall back on them as they force us."

"Very well." Shih-ka'i walked toward the nearest transfer. He told Pan ku, "This new mind is a dangerous one. I sense a whole different outlook."

"I felt it too, Lord."

"I think we can expect a siege."

The Seventeenth remained rooted longer than Shih-ka'i expected. A day passed and another night came before the last soldier retired.

"How many did we lose?" Lord Ssu-ma demanded.

"Less than a hundred, Lord," Tasi-feng replied. "Permanently, that is. I assume that's what you meant. Six hundred dead we got out."

"Good. Excellent. I want you to transfer your wounded again, once new portals are set. To Lioantung. We won't have to worry about them again unless the enemy breaks through both us and Northern Army."

Tasi-feng no longer believed his commander was overreacting to an insignificant threat. He tried to buoy his own spirits by saying, "We estimate another twenty thousand bodies permanently destroyed, Lord."

"Any idea what they have left?"

"Not reliably, Lord. At least fifty thousand. Plus the flyers."

"Plus the flyers. We may end up wishing we had our own flyers. Chang Sheng! Any luck enlisting the dragons?"

"None, Lord. They won't explain, but their elders claim they know this evil of old. They won't face it again."

"That's it?"

"That's all they'll say."

"Curious," Shih-ka'i said. "That's not like them. They've never been afraid of anything."

"They're scared of this, Lord. It looked like they were ready to abandon their breeding caves."

"Ah? Where could they go?"

"I couldn't say, Lord."

Shih-ka'i moved to the map. "Gentlemen, I've placed scouting parties along this arc. We should know their intentions soon."

Tasi-feng indicated a red arrow. It humped over the area of confrontation to spear the eastern shore. "What's this, Lord?"

"Don't worry about it. Just a job I gave Hsu Shen."

Had Hsu Shen gotten his boats assembled yet? The man's last report placed him on the coast, preparing to cross to the island. Shih-ka'i was eager to place a portal there. He wanted to know if it were indeed the former headquarters of the Pracchia, wanted to see if anything interesting had been left behind.

A Tervola named Yen Teh, from one of the southern legions, ran toward Shih-ka'i's group. He was without his mask. His face was pallid. "Lord," he gasped. "Lord, I've just heard… Matayanga… They attacked. With two million men."

"Two million?" Shih-ka'i murmured. He could not

encompass the number. There was no way to support an army that size.

The Matayangan strategy must be predicated on an expectation that heavy casualties early would reduce their forces to manageable size. He peered at his map. "Two million? Gentlemen, we're on our own. There won't be anyone to help us."

The hall became very still. No one had believed the southern situation could deteriorate this far, that the Matayangans would dare attack. For centuries no nation had been that foolish. But two million men? Inconceivable. The Matayangans were risking everything on one pass of the dice. Their losses would cripple them for generations, considering what would happen after Southern Army assumed the offensive.

"Trying to swamp us with the first rush," Shih-ka'i observed. "And they might do it. But that's not our problem. Ours is out there. Lord Lun-yu, take charge of the recon patrols. I want to know exactly when they're going to attack."

"As you command, Lord."

The enemy again baffled Shih-ka'i. He did not pursue a rational strategy and immediately assault the fortress. He came from the desert, but in no rush. He gave Shih-ka'i four more days to prepare. Shih-ka'i assembled the bulk of Eastern Army. Those on the march elsewhere would arrive within days. So many men were on hand, in fact, that most had to remain in fortified encampments outside the fortress. Eastern Army would provide a hell of a fight. Northern Army would have ample time to prepare positions along the Tusghus, against possible failure here.

During the respite Shih-ka'i visited the island in the east. He and Hsu Shen wandered long-abandoned halls. Nothing of value remained, though there was adequate evidence that this was indeed the island of Lord Ko Feng's memoirs.

"Someone stripped the place," Shih-ka'i said.

"So it seems, Lord."

"Curious. Most curious."

"Lord?"

"Ko Feng says they left in a hurry, planning to return later. When later came, he was the only conspirator left. He never came back. So who stripped the place? Can you suggest a culprit?"

"I'd suggest Lord Ko, Lord. After he was banished."

"I don't think so. I'd try a divination if our stone friend weren't right over there." The thing could be seen from the ramparts, if one had Hsu Shen's eyes. Shih-ka'i could see nothing but rusty vistas.

Pan ku came galloping up. He gasped, "Lord, the legion commanders request your presence."

"Very well. Hsu Shen, sit tight. I'll give you a century. I may want you to hit the stone thing from here."

Hsu Shen appeared distrait. "As you command, Lord."

Shih-ka'i chuckled. "Of course. Pan ku. Let's see what they want."

In minutes he entered his map room. He scanned the big picture. An arc of enemy markers glared in from the desert. "Lot of them out there now, eh?"

"Fifty thousand, Lord," Tasi-feng replied.

"Still showing no inclination to attack?"

"None, Lord."

"That's odd."

"Lord, we have a few matters to bring to your attention," Chang Sheng said.

Shih-ka'i turned. His legion commanders faced him, standing shoulder to shoulder. Their underlings had stopped work. "Yes?"

"Uh..." Tasi-feng stammered. "We had a report from fifth cohort, Twenty-Seventh." Tasi-feng moved to the map, indicated a position four hundred miles south. "They encountered an enemy force shortly after dawn, here." The point was well behind the desert line. "One thousand dead soldiers, accompanied by several hundred tribesmen, both living and dead."

"A recruiting force?"

"Apparently. Leading Centurion Pai Mo-Jo engaged immediately and destroyed all but a handful. The escapees were all live tribesmen."

Shih-ka'i listened patiently while Tasi-feng appended the required report on casualties and equipment losses. Then he said, "An outstanding accomplishment, considering the man was outnumbered and had no wizardry of his own. Send my personal commendation. Recommend him for decoration. I applaud initiative in the ranks, Lord Yuan."

The Twenty-Seventh's commander bowed slightly. "Mo-Jo is one of my best, Lord."

Shih-ka'i drew himself into the stiff parade-ground stance he had used to intimidate the Fourth Demonstration. "What did you really want to discuss?"

Tasi-feng exchanged glances with his fellows. The others were not forthcoming. He said, "Though it may be premature to mention this, Lord, we felt you should be informed."

"Informed? Please inform me, Lord Lun-yu."

"Sometime soon, Lord Kuo will be unseated. We legion commanders and our senior deputies intend to support his successor. Likewise, our brethren of Northern Army."

"I see." Shih-ka'i's stomach tightened into a hard little knot. Politics had caught him after all. He was considered beholden to Lord Kuo. He remained stiffly erect. "What does that have to do with the business at hand? We're an army at war. Consider the situation map. We're nearly surrounded. Southern Army's situation is worse. The empire is in dire peril. What the hell do you think you're doing? Silence! For me, it's a matter of supreme indifference who sits the imperial throne. I'm Tervola! I am an officer of the imperial army. My sole function is to defend, preserve, expand. *Your* function is to help me fulfill mine. It's neither my right nor yours to crown or uncrown emperors. It is of no moment who sits a damned throne four thousand miles away. Even so, the games you play on your own time are yours. Make kings if you like. But on my time you make war. And, gentlemen, when Lord Ssu-ma Shih-ka'i makes war, he does so every second of the day. Resume your posts."

He thought that would do it. He had allowed emotion full vent, and they had quaked before its gale.

Lord Chang responded, "Admirably spoken, Lord Ssu-ma. We hear the voice of an elder age. It tells us what we need to know."

Pan ku's sword whispered from its scabbard behind Shih-ka'i. Shih-ka'i glared at Lord Chang. Sheng stared back. Shih-ka'i thought, I should've known they wouldn't bend. They're not recruits. They're veteran intriguers.

Sheng said, "I suggest we carry out Lord Ssu-ma's instructions. The Deliverer cares naught for our aspirations, either."

The legion commanders turned away. Their underlings resumed work. Shih-ka'i allowed himself a moment to relax. Then, "Lord Chang."

Sheng turned. "Lord?"

"You said 'Deliverer.' What did you mean?"

"Lord Yuan's man Mo-Jo took live captives. They called the leader of the dead Deliverer. They claimed that was because he came from the land where gods dwelt in the age before the desert. They think he'll restore a lost paradise."

"Does the idea have currency with the tribes?"

"No, Lord. The majority are fleeing across the Tusghus. They have a full measure of the savage's fear of the dead."

"Good. I'll be in my quarters." He whispered, "Pan ku, put that ridiculous toad-stabber away." He did not wait to see if his directive were accepted. He knew Pan ku.

He slept for a few hours, then wakened suddenly. Something

had disturbed him. For a moment he thought it was concern about his commanders. But no, that was settled. They had spoken their pieces. A decision had been reached. He commanded Eastern Army. His writ stemmed from the empire, not its ruler. They would follow him while he remained faithful to that ideal.

No political concern had wakened him. Was it a prescient flash? Were the dead about to begin battering the next obstacle blocking their westward path? He stared at the ceiling, allowed his Tervola-trained senses to roam.

He could detect nothing.

Pan ku burst in. He did not apologize for his presumption. "Flyers, Lord." He snatched up Shih-ka'i's mask and stationed himself by his master's armor.

"They're attacking?"

"Yes, Lord."

In minutes Shih-ka'i stood on a balcony overlooking one of the drillyards.

The night was full of dragons; he guessed at least five hundred. The waning moon illuminated them perfectly. They dropped to deposit riders. There were two aboard each, the usual skullface and another behind. Most of the skullfaces remained mounted, urging their beasts back into the air while hurling bolts of power into the fortress. They took no particular aim.

The dead warriors rushed here and there without apparent purpose. When they encountered members of the garrison, they fought.

Chaos ruled. Shih-ka'i spotted a half-dozen fires.

The dragons raced back to the desert to collect another wave of invaders.

"We'll go to the map room," Shih-ka'i said. "We'll organize from the heart outward." He scanned the east wall. The men were holding their posts. Good. There would be an attack when the Deliverer believed he had created enough confusion.

They had to cross a court to reach the building where the

map room lay. Raiders caught them there.

They came out of the darkness, in total silence. Shih-ka'i was uncertain how many there were. One skullface, for sure, and at least six of the pudgy warriors. They flung themselves forward as if recognizing him. He blasted two with a small spell. Pan ku separated another from his head. Then blades were flashing in Shih-ka'i's face, and for the first time in a long life, he was wielding a sword in his own defense.

He had drilled a thousand times, as training demanded, and had performed well, but had always wondered how he would do against a deadly opponent. He was not sure he could kill a man.

The training took over: He did not think, he acted. His blade became a spider weaving a web of protection. The shortsword in his left hand darted like a serpent's tongue, making the deadly strikes from dangerous angles. Pan ku guarded his back for the few seconds it took to even the odds.

Then Shih-ka'i faced no one but the skullface. Bodies lay scattered about them. Would he have the stomach to dismember them? He couldn't leave them lie....

The dragon rider bore a sword in keeping with its size. It was a good six feet long. The creature swung it in great screaming arcs. Shih-ka'i reeled each time he turned a stroke. Fear knotted his stomach.

There was an astonishingly loud clang. The skullface staggered forward, fell to one knee. Shih-ka'i found its eye with his shortsword, then followed with a vicious overhand chop with his longsword. Pan ku struck another two-handed blow.

And the damned monster tried to rise!

They hacked away till it surrendered its unnatural life.

Panting, Shih-ka'i and Pan ku considered one another over the body. Pan ku grinned. "He was a tough one, Lord."

"That he was. Let's get them carved up. We've wasted too much time already."

Shih-ka'i had seen any number of corpses dismembered, but there was a difference between observing and doing. His gorge threatened to rise. He wondered if that happened to the men. The world saw them as battalions of heartless torturers... They were men. Mere men, superbly trained and superbly in command of themselves. They had pride....

I have to be as strong as that centurion Mo-Jo, he told himself. I am the leader. I have to be the toughest and best.

"Finished, Lord," Pan ku said.

"Let's go."

"Grim work, eh?"

"Indeed. I had less stomach for it than I expected."

"This will be a grisly campaign, won't it, Lord?"

"We've never seen its like, Pan ku."

As they entered the map room from one end, a doorway at the other exploded. The planks of it flew about like autumn leaves in a gale. A dozen dead warriors burst through, spearheaded by three skullfaces.

Tasi-feng met them with a burst of power which flung the smaller warriors round like ragdolls in the jaws of mastiffs. The skullfaces were unaffected. The other Tervola hit them with as many killing spells as there were spellcasters. Noxious clouds boiled off the collapsing bodies. For a time it was difficult to breathe.

Shih-ka'i joined Chang Sheng over a map of the fortress and its environs. Sheng said, "They're attacking here and here, into the joints between the encampments and the fortress."

The palisades and trenches surrounding the camps were puny compared to the defenses of the fortress itself. Sheng continued, "Their assault hasn't developed sufficiently to betray their intent. Their logical course would be to encircle and reduce the encampments. But they're concentrating their dragons and wizardry on us."

"Trying to keep us pinned down."

A Tervola approached. Shih-ka'i remembered him from

the deep probe into the desert. "Yes, Ou-yan?"

"Message from Lord Shih-mihn, Lord. They've launched human wave assaults. They've broken through in three places. He thinks they want to force a melee."

"There's your main thrust, Lord Chang. North camp. Melee. We can't permit that."

The price would be defeat. Should the enemy break Shih-ka'i's formations and force his men to fight individually, few would have time to salvage legion dead or destroy enemy fallen. Those would keep coming back into the fray. They would grow more numerous, rather than fewer.

"Lord Chang?"

"Doesn't sound good, Lord. But I suggest we wait before we jump. The men won't fold."

Sheng was right. The defense stiffened under pressure, Shih-ka'i mounted an observation tower to study the north camp.

Huge, stinking fires burned there. His soldiers flung ever more bodies upon them.

The dragons continued to drop warriors into the fortress. The garrison was dealing with them now. Many flyers never left. Their riders were cut down as their feet touched the ground.

Shih-ka'i was pleased.

"Lord." Pan ku pointed. Squinting, Shih-ka'i found the two dragons circling high overhead.

"The white one is their sorceress. Lord Lun-yu says the other commands the dead."

The woman suddenly glowed a brilliant blue. A blue egg formed between her outstretched hands. It tumbled toward the earth. It was a yard thick when it ploughed into the roof of a barracks.

That roof caught fire, though it was made of clay tile.

More eggs fell. Soon there were a dozen witchfires burning. How long would their witchery keep them going?

That didn't matter. The woman could drop more.

She threw a score into the northern camp, where they did more damage.

His Tervola had to stop her. He rushed to the map room… The place was a shambles. Fighting continued in one corner, where a pair of skullfaces exchanged minor sorceries with Tasi-feng's underlings.

"What happened?" Shih-ka'i demanded. "Never mind. I can see. Get some men in to clean up before these bodies reanimate."

Tasi-feng said, "Lord, some of our dead weren't properly disposed. They're roaming the fortress. The men can't tell friend from foe."

"You can, can't you?"

"Yes, Lord."

"We all can." Shih-ka'i clipped a quick series of orders. "Let's get out there. We're useless here now, anyway. Give the witch all the attention you can. Throw up a shaft barrage. That southern attack looks like a feint."

Two hours passed. They left Shih-ka'i perplexed. The witch had been driven from the sky, yet the situation had worsened. A stream of blue balls sailed out of the desert, into the north camp. The camp's defenses had been breached in a dozen places. The dreaded melee threatened.

At least the flyers and skullfaces had been beaten away from the fortress.

Shih-ka'i assembled his officers. "We're going to lose the north camp," he told them. "They're reanimating too many of their men, and we haven't provided an adequate defense against the woman's witchery. Let's review their dispositions."

Shih-ka'i was convinced the enemy was concentrating on the one camp, betting the defense would collapse suddenly, giving him an opportunity to recoup his losses. He would then aim the tireless dead at the south camp, then the fortress.

"We'll give them a surprise," Shih-ka'i said. "Tell Lord

Shih-mihn he has to hold till dawn."

In the bloody, smoky dawn troops from the south camp cut through the screen surrounding them and attacked the enemy army. The Tervola harried the witch from one hiding place to another. The dead fought stubbornly. Not till noon was the north camp finally relieved. Shih-ka'i immediately ordered the troops outside to withdraw to the Tusghus River.

"We surprised them this time," he said. "We won't again." Then, "The fortress can stand alone." He surveyed the cables and nets being rigged over areas where flyers might land.

"Suppose they pursue, Lord?" Tasi-feng asked.

"I wish they would. I'd bring up Northern Army and play hammer and anvil."

The Deliverer disappointed Shih-ka'i. For three days he attacked the fortress, scoring only local successes. Stubborn Shih-ka'i always overcame. Undying pyres burned in the drillyards, day and night.

That third day Lord Shih-mihn sent a message saying he was embattled with a horde of natives. Young, old, women, children, armed and unarmed, dead and living. They had swarmed out of the forests screaming, "Deliverer!" The legionnaires were destroying large numbers, but could not continue their withdrawal while the battle lasted.

Shih-ka'i stared out at the ragged thousands surrounding the fortress. "This Deliverer can't be everywhere at once." The enemy stood frozen, in ranks of motionless, slowly corrupting flesh. Something had been lost in the transfer of power. The Deliverer's host was rotting slowly. The stench of corruption had joined that of burning flesh. Before long the Deliverer would need a whole new army. He could not make skeletons walk. "Lord Lun-yu. Take a brigade and sortie. They won't put up much of a fight."

Tasi-feng destroyed thousands of listless besiegers before the air suddenly became angry and the rest returned to life.

He withdrew. Shih-mihn reported that the horde attacking him had collapsed.

"Gentlemen," Shih-ka'i said to his Tervola, "if this Deliverer makes one more mistake, we'll destroy him."

No one asked what he meant. He told them without being asked. "One, he could expose himself to injury. Two, he could let us get his witch. Three, he could get too eager and stop recruiting savages. Or let us stop him from recruiting."

Still no response.

"Anyone want to be a hero?"

There was another message from Shih-mihn. His attackers had fled into the forest. He was moving toward the Tusghus again.

"Shall I sortie again, Lord?" Tasi-feng asked.

"No. He'll bring those poor creatures here now, to finish us. We taught him a lesson today. Now he knows he can't bypass us."

The assault began during the night, spearheaded by children and women. It never let up. More natives came out of the wilderness, some having walked a thousand miles. Shih-ka'i cursed them for not having had the sense to stay under the empire's protection. And congratulated himself for having had the foresight to get the majority moved.

Shih-ka'i destroyed them by the tens of thousands, and still they came. And the transfers kept sending casualties to Lioantung. Sections of fortress fell. The courts and cellars and barracks filled with dismembered corpses awaiting destruction. The stench was as wearing as the interminable attack.

"Lord Lun-yu, what kind of monster is this Deliverer? What mad creature depopulates half a million square miles to take one fortress? Is he some demon who's slipped his master's leash?"

"He's just a boy, Lord. Seventeen or eighteen. Normal in most respects. With a big grudge against the empire."

"A grudge!"

"Live prisoners say he's vowed to destroy us."

"You think he will?"

"No, Lord."

"He's made an impressive start, hasn't he? How long can we hold out?"

"Two days, surely. He's short of draftees."

"I'll leave it with you. Keep buying time. We bought enough for Northern Army. Now I'm afraid we're buying it for Lioantung."

Tasi-feng sighed and stared at the floor. "As you command, Lord. Lord... maybe you can contact Lord Kuo now."

"Lord Kuo? I thought he was being retired."

Tasi-feng shrugged. "I don't know. Maybe he has been. We haven't been in touch."

Shih-ka'i made a last inspection of the fortress. It was in abominable shape. The witch still lobbed in the occasional blue egg. He suspected Tasi-feng was too optimistic, claiming they could hold two more days.

He and Pan ku went down to the deep cellar where the portals were massed. As always, casualties were passing through. "At least they'll get out," he observed. "This is the last place the Deliverer will reach. The men won't have to make a pointless last stand."

Pan ku replied, "I hope not, Lord. I'd feel bad if we lost them. The Seventeenth is a good legion."

10

YEAR 1016 AFE

FIRE IN THE EAST

ΠEPANTHE SAT AT her window, staring without
seeing. The extreme end of pregnancy had worsened
all her tendencies toward alienation, introversion,
and brooding. She cried a lot. She snapped at people for
no good reason. She considered the gross swollenness of
her belly and loathed herself for being ugly, hated herself
for bringing another child into a pitiless world. There
were irrational moments when she hated the little parasite
growing inside her. She spent much of her time feeling
sorry for herself, or, gradually, adding to her obsession with
her lost son.

She had little spirit or volition now. She did what her
husband told her, what her maids asked. Her great initiatives
consisted of starting the occasional conversation.

She had been listless, most of the time, since her first
husband's death, not long after they had lost their son. She'd
always been susceptible to mood swings, into this grey state
and out. Since Mocker's death the downs had grown longer

every year. She had tried to fake the highs and had failed. She now just stayed out of the way and tried not to complicate her second husband's life.

Varthlokkur had pursued a hundred wild goose trails in his efforts to quicken her soul. She was aware of his attempts, and only wished he wouldn't bother. She didn't think she was worth the trouble.

The most potent draughts and magicks worked only for a short time. Varthlokkur had concluded that only that supreme medicine, time, would cure her. He now left her to haunt her inner landscapes as she would.

She sensed that he had come to stand behind her. She turned. "You look tired, dear."

"I was up all night. Michael Trebilcock was away on a mission and ran into trouble. I had to send Radeachar to get him out. He's safely home now."

"Michael? Isn't he the one who took Valther's place?" Thus far had she slipped. Sometimes she couldn't remember.

"Yes."

She resumed staring out the window, no longer interested. She had lost six brothers as well as her husband and son. Well, five. Luxos was alive, living in the Kratchnodian Mountains like some crazy old hermit. Crazy like me, she thought. We both might as well be dead.

The world had taken everything. Everything but Varthlokkur and this child as yet unborn.

She could not care about them. She didn't dare. Fate would punish her if she did. They would be taken too.

"Varth?"

"Yes, dear?"

"I really do feel Ethrian sometimes. I still don't know what it means. Can't you find out for sure?"

Varthlokkur sighed. "I've tried, dear. There's just nothing there. I'm sorry. I truly wish there were. It's just your heart trying to turn back the sands of time."

He's probably right, she thought. He's so seldom wrong. But... there was some doubt. No one had ever actually seen Ethrian dead.... "It's not imagination, Varth. It can't be. He's there. I know it."

"Then why can't I find him? Why can't I find one shred of evidence that he survived? Why do I find so much that says he's not? Stop tormenting yourself. Please. It's not healthy."

True concern edged his words. She sensed it and shied away. "It's not false hope!" Emotion began to flavor her voice. It grew stronger as she shouted, "He's alive and I know it! Why are you lying to me?"

"I'm not." He spoke gently, as if to an injured, retarded child. "You're lying to yourself. Please don't. It's not healthy."

"Not healthy! Not healthy! Stop it!" She surged out of her chair. "It's because he's Mocker's son, isn't it? That's why you want me to forget him." Her reasoning was insane and she knew it, but the words just would not stop. She wanted to hurt someone, to give some of the pain away.

Agony tightened his features. He calmed himself before responding, "That isn't so. And you know it. He was my grandson. My only. I loved him too. I would have done anything for him. But he's gone now, Nepanthe. It's time to accept that. Please. This is starting to tear us apart." He took her into his arms.

She pounded fists against his chest, the irrational words exploding forth. "You're lying! He's alive. I know he's alive. He's in trouble, and you won't help him."

"Dear, this isn't good for the baby."

She kept hitting, weeping. Finally, she sagged against him. "I'm sorry. I don't know... Oh!"

"What? What happened?"

"I think my water broke. That shouldn't happen yet... Oh! Yes. It did. I can feel it." Her mind became very clear. Not here! Not now! Please... Everything else fled. "Get a doctor. Wachtel if he's still Royal Physician. Help me to the bed."

Her voice had changed dramatically, had become all business.

Varthlokkur guided her across the room, turned her so he could help her lie down.

"No. Undress me first. This was an expensive dress. Mustn't ruin it. Then find Mary and Margo. Tell them to get everything ready."

"Shouldn't I get the doctor first?"

"I don't need him right this minute. Ethrian was twelve hours coming. Elana said he was easy. We've got time. Just warn him that it's coming."

"It's too early."

"Maybe. Maybe I figured it wrong. Nothing we can do about it now." She was half undressed. She saw how nervous he was. "Let me finish this. You get the maids, tell Wachtel, then come back and get some sleep."

"Sleep? How could I sleep?"

"You'd better. You won't be any help at all if you don't. You're too tired to think straight now." She was amazed at herself. She seemed to have changed personalities like changing shoes. The whiner had vanished the instant she found herself faced by a situation wherein she had some control.

"Okay. Sure you'll be okay if I leave?"

She touched his cheek tenderly. "Of course. Silly man. Old as the world, you are. A destroyer of empires. Creator of a monster like Radeachar. And you're as nervous as an eighteen-year-old awaiting the birth of his firstborn. And I love you for it. I love you for caring."

"I'm worried for you."

"Stop. This isn't anything a million other women haven't survived. Just do what I told you. Here. Wait. Help me lie down."

He looked down at her distended belly and its fiery stretch marks, at breasts swollen to twice their normal size. Nepanthe flinched. She knew she was not attractive this way.

"You're beautiful," he said.

Tears sprang into her eyes. "Pull the sheet over me and go. Please."

"What's the matter?"

"Just do it. Please?"

He did.

Nepanthe broke into wild tears after the door closed. She could not decide whether they were tears of joy or of disappointment.

The wizard moved through the palace with a fast, jerky step, like a marionette manipulated by a drunken puppeteer. Puzzled eyes followed his progress. He didn't notice. He went directly to the suite occupied by the Royal Physician.

That Doctor Wachtel was held in high regard was evidenced by the fact his personal suite was outshone only by the Queen's. King Bragi himself occupied only two small rooms. The doctor had five.

Wachtel and the wizard were old philosophical adversaries. The doctor received him with ill-concealed glee, yet did not crow about his having come to petition aid. He asked the pertinent questions, reiterated Nepanthe's advice. "Get what sleep you can. It'll be a long time yet. I'll just check in occasionally till the pains get closer together."

The wizard grumbled and babbled and asked foolish questions, and the doctor humored him. Only mildly reassured, Varthlokkur returned to his apartment. He went in and held Nepanthe's hands till the maids ran him out. He tried to rest, without much success.

Varthlokkur was pacing, oblivious to his companions. The King stepped into the wizard's sitting room, watched him for half a minute. "You've got a classic gait," he observed, chuckling, "Get any sleep?"

"A little." As if only suddenly aware of location and

situation, he asked, "Shouldn't I be in there?"

"Does she want you?"

"I don't know. Wachtel doesn't."

"I see his point. Made a nuisance of myself at a few birthings. Fathers may be good for the mother's morale, but they're hell on doctors and midwives. At least till they've had enough kids to know when to keep their mouths shut."

"I could help. I have skills...."

"I think the main help Wachtel wants is a closed mouth. He needs you, he'll ask."

"I'm well aware of his opinion of me."

"How's she doing?"

"All right, they say."

As if on cue, the doctor came from the bedroom. He was drying his hands.

"Well?" Varthlokkur demanded. "Is it here?"

"Take it easy. No. She has a long way to go. It'll come around midnight, I'd guess."

"Guess? What do you mean, guess?"

The old doctor scowled. "I meant what I said. I don't have your faculty for seeing the future. All I can do is go by past experience."

"The future? My heavens. I forgot to cast horoscopes for the child." In moments he was furiously busy. He flung charts and books, pens and inkwells onto a table. "Guess I'd better do both today and tomorrow," he muttered. "Midnight. Damned."

The King grinned at the doctor. "That'll keep him out of your hair. See you all later. Duty calls."

Pink ripped the night above Castle Krief. Bold letters formed: IT IS A GIRL. People were amused. The King was heard to say, "Wizard, that's carrying the Proud Papa routine a little far."

Grinning, Varthlokkur accepted congratulations from a horde of well-wishers. He sprinkled silver. He filled the castle halls with diminutive magical delights. Imps dashed about singing silvery hosannahs. The wizard's joy was contagious. He shook hands with people who never had dared approach him before. They contracted the joy-fever and carried it to others. It spread out of the castle and caught on in the town. Winecasks rolled out. Kegs were bunged. For a while it seemed one birth, and one man's pleasure in it, would write the end of an era, would put paid to the long, grim, sober struggle for survival which had ground the nation since the war's end.

"Eat! Drink!" Varthlokkur urged, pushing people toward the groaning tables he'd set out. "Come on, everyone."

"Make way for the King!"

The noise died a bit. King Bragi pushed through the crowd and thrust out a meaty hand. "It was a long time coming, wasn't it? How's Nepanthe?"

"Perfect. Came through beautifully. Happy as anyone can be."

"Good. Good. Can I see my wife now?" He had sent Queen Inger to hold Nepanthe's hand during the delivery, the only meaningful gesture that had occurred to him.

"If you can find her." The crowd swirled and whirled and swept them apart. When next the wizard spied the King he was forehead to forehead with Dahl Haas, trying to hear over the merriment. Bragi grew pale as Haas talked.

Varthlokkur's joy evaporated. He felt it now. The east was a-boil, roaring, raging. A great typhoon of magical energy had been released there... He should have sensed it earlier. He was getting old, letting one part of life distract him from another this way. He pushed through the crowd, feeling grimmer by the moment. He ignored the startled looks caused by his rudeness. He seized the King's hand, yanked, did not let go till he had dragged the man to the castle's eastern ramparts.

Horrendous flashes backlighted the Mountains of

M'Hand. Their peaks stood forth like rotten, jagged teeth. He hadn't ever seen anything like it. The barrage rolled on and on and on, like endless summer lightning playing mutiny beyond the horizon.

"What is it?" the King whispered.

Varthlokkur did not reply. He sealed his eyes and let the indirect might of it touch him. He grunted. Even here, so far away, the psychic impact was like the blow of a mailed fist.

There wasn't a cloud in the sky. A billion stars watched with cold indifference as the two tiny creatures on the stone barrier stood with faces continuously splashed by evil light.

"What the hell is it?" the King demanded, voice scarcely more than a breath. There was no sound in the east, yet the very roots of the walls seemed aquiver.

Varthlokkur stared, ignoring his companion. The signal fires which carried messages from Fortress Maisak and the Savernake Gap were all ablaze. He barely heard the King ask, "Is Hsung attacking Maisak?"

"It's begun. Matayanga is attacking Shinsan. Lord Kuo was waiting. A god wouldn't dare those battlefields now."

The flash and fury went on. "I wonder," Bragi said. "Did Baxendala and Palmisano look that hairy from this far away?"

"Maybe. Though Lord Kuo has mustered more power than we ever saw during the Great Eastern Wars. What can Matayanga throw at him? Besides numbers? They're not much in a thaumaturgic way."

More and more people came to watch the display. There wasn't an ounce of joy left. Varthlokkur spared them hardly a glance. He did not want to see them. They looked like refugees, all huddled and silent.

Bragi said, "I suppose the Tervola will have a taste of that for us someday."

"Shinsan is an empire unaccustomed to defeat," Varthlokkur replied. "We'll see them again. If they survive this."

"If?"

"Would Matayanga have attacked if its kings believed defeat inevitable?"

Horns sounded outside the castle. "That's Mist," Varthlokkur said. "She'll have been alerted before we were."

The woman joined them shortly. "It's begun. First reports came in last night. Southern Army detected the Matayangans moving up. With two million men. Just for the first attack. They've conscripted everyone over fifteen."

"Human waves," Varthlokkur said. "Will they break through?"

"Southern Army is outnumbered twenty to one. There'll be other waves. Lord Kuo is trying to assemble a reserve, but he might not have gotten started in time."

"When do you make your move?" the King asked.

"It's too early to worry about that." Concern creased Mist's perfect brow. "We have to find out what's happening first. If it gets too bad out there we'll drop it."

"What the hell for?" the King demanded.

"You forget she isn't interested in destroying the Dread Empire," Varthlokkur said. He eyed his friend. There was a touch of monomania in the man these days. "Only in seizing control."

"Yeah. Well. Let's set up in the War Room. Looks like we'll be busy for a while."

Mist said, "My place would be better. I'm already in touch with my people out there."

The King looked at Varthlokkur. The wizard nodded. The King said, "In two hours, then."

Varthlokkur turned and took another look at the fire-gutted sky. Worms writhed in his guts. What bold fools we are, challenging the man who has that dancing at his fingertips.

Once Mist was out of earshot, the King whispered, "Are we backing the wrong horse?"

"We? This was your idea."

"Uhm. So it was." Bragi made a sour face.

Lord Ch'ien made a small gesture. Mist glanced up. The King was standing in the doorway, agog. It had been years since he had been here on the top floor of her home. She had made changes.

He strode over. "How about I replace your sentries with mine? We'll draw enough attention without having orientals standing around."

"Right." She beckoned an Aspirator from the runner pool, gave him his orders. Taking the King's arm, she indicated a bank of seats which had been constructed along the nearer and side walls of the room. The entire third floor had been stripped of partitions. The windows were heavily curtained. The far wall was bare and shadowed. A huge table occupied the center of the room.

"Ask your staff to sit and stay put," she said. "And tell them to stay away from the south wall. They could get us killed if they stumbled through a portal."

A man stepped out of thin air. He reported to the gentleman in charge of the room's centerpiece. Mist listened with one ear. A routine report.

"I'd about give my left arm for a map like that in my War Room," the King murmured. The map atop the table was thirty feet long and fifteen wide. It represented Shinsan and the empire's tributaries. Every city of significance was noted, as were all major geographical features. The whereabouts and movements of the empire's many legions were marked in bright colors.

Another messenger popped into the room. A tableman listened, began spreading red sand.

Mist told Bragi, "Sit down." Then, "My people are doing better than I expected. I'm getting first-rate information. Probably because Lord Kuo is keeping his head down."

No probably about it, she thought. Lord Kuo was laying low somewhere, letting the thing take shape. She rose, took a pointer, tapped the map. "Somewhere in all this blank space he's hidden his reserve army. In a few days he'll drop a big hammer on the Matayangans."

"How is Southern Army doing?"

She kept her opinion to herself. "You see the map. It's maintaining the integrity of its lines. Against the odds, that's all you could ask of any army. Just a minute."

A messenger had appeared. She moved round to where she could catch snippets of his report. "Damn!" she said, though softly.

The table chief moved small, numbered black markers into a cluster at the map's easternmost edge. He moved others to a riverbank two hundred miles behind the cluster.

"What's all that?" the King asked.

She told the whole truth when she replied, "We're not sure. Communications are muddled. Eastern Army is under attack."

"Matayanga caught them with a surprise ally?"

"This started before the southern thing. It's been on more than a week."

"There's a whole second war there?"

"Something awful is happening..." She controlled herself. Bragi might be an old friend, and an old fighting companion, but he wasn't part of the family. One did not show one's fears to the outside world. "Before he disappeared, Lord Kuo gave Eastern Army a new commander. Lord Ssu-ma Shih-ka'i. He's an old peasant who came up the hard way. Goes way back. Very capable, and stubborn as hell."

"Uhm."

She sighed. Good. He wasn't interested in the east.

"Any notion when you want to move?"

"Not before Lord Kuo comes out of hiding. I don't want to jump in blind."

"If we're going to be a while, I'd better make arrangements for my people." The King rose, grunting as he did so. Mist watched him go. He was feeling very tired, very old. She felt a moment of empathy. She, too, felt tired and old. And she'd feel much more so before this was done. The danger would mount by the minute, and every minute would increase the odds against the coup attempt remaining secret. "Wen-chin," she murmured, "please don't waste any time."

The interminable wait became a deathwatch. The Matayangan attack went on and on and on, and still the time did not ripen. Tempers began to flare.

"Lord Kuo must have nerves of stone," Mist opined to Lord Ch'ien. "I don't think I could have held off this long."

Lord Ch'ien tapped the map with the tip of his pointer, sketching the outline of the bloody stain of Matayangan advance. His hand quivered. The red sand thrust deep into Shinsan. Mist's informants said the original Southern Army hardly existed anymore. Some hard-hit legions had been disbanded and their survivors distributed as replacements. There was a huge gap in the army's line. Matayangans were pouring through.

Lord Ch'ien said, "My limit has been surpassed. Maybe that's why Lord Kuo is in command."

"Tut-tut. No second-guessing at this stage of the game."

The King appeared. He scanned the map. "It's been two days," he said. "All this courier traffic has to leave traces. How long before somebody starts adding things up?"

"I know! I know!" Mist snapped. "Pretty soon we'll *have* to assume they know. Damn the man! Lord Kuo, I mean. Why doesn't he move?"

"He hasn't got them where he wants them yet," Bragi observed laconically. He considered the map again. "But if he waits much longer, there won't be anything left for you to take over."

"Compare the size of the cancer with the whole," she snarled. Then, "Lord Ch'ien. The time. If he hasn't moved within fifty hours, I'll do so myself."

"In the dark?" the King asked.

"If I have to. I won't be able to trust my people much longer than that. By then if one defected they'd all stampede." Wearily, she added, "It would take ten years to put it all together again."

Aral seated himself beside her while she was talking. He said something meant to be soothing. He tried to take her hand. In front of Lord Ch'ien. She pulled away.

It was time to put paid to this nonsense. She shouldn't have started it. Fool. Man-weak fool. She'd lost the Tervola once because of Valther. She wouldn't make that mistake again.

She ignored Aral's look of pain.

Lord Ch'ien hadn't caught the byplay, she saw, but Bragi had. He was nodding to himself. She felt her cheeks reddening. He didn't comment, though. He said, "It's late. I'm going to get some sleep."

She watched him speak with his captains before leaving. Their continuous presence irked her. They had eyes like hawks. She had to keep them in mind every instant. Damn this having to depend on outsiders!

Her irritation mounted as the hours passed. Her men, too, were tense. They couldn't speak without snapping at one another. The conspiracy was about to shake itself apart. And still time twisted the springs of tension tighter.

The night churned slowly onward. The red stain of Matayangan invasion seeped across the table. Confused messengers arrived from the far east, their reports only further obscuring the situation there.

"Lord Ch'ien."

"Princess?"

She tapped the map with the pointer. "Do we dare move while this is happening?"

Lord Ch'ien eyed the east briefly. "I think we can discount

it. For the moment. Our people there will keep those forces uninvolved." The weariness edging his voice made it more husky and hollow than normal. Mist shuddered.

Lord Ch'ien volunteered, "Western Army will be the real worry. I've heard that Lord Hsung has an agent in the palace here. By now everybody in this squalid village knows something is happening. The stupidest spy would have sent a message mentioning it."

"Time. The invincible enemy. Are we going to manage it, old friend? Or will time do us in?"

"I couldn't say, Princess. But I do have a feeling we're close to the moment of decision. There's a new tension in the blanklands there."

Mist stared at the unmarked portion of the map, closing out all else. And, yes, Lord Ch'ien was right. She could feel a great something flexing its muscles there, tensing, like a serpent coiling to strike. So. It wouldn't be much longer.

"Princess?"

"Lord?"

"The moment approaches. And still we haven't decided what to do with these people once they've served their purpose."

This was a discussion she had hoped to avoid, and yet had known to be inevitable. "I don't follow you."

"You know who they are and what they've done, Princess. This petty King. This sorcerer Varthlokkur. These carrion-eaters who orbit them." He indicated several of the King's men. "We have to decide what to do if we're successful."

Mist sighed. "They've dealt honorably with us, Lord Ch'ien." She couldn't tell him that they were her friends. A princess of the Dread Empire did not have friends. Not foreign friends.

"For their own ends. They hope to weaken the empire, to delay the inevitable day of reckoning. The King... He would destroy us if he could."

She could not deny that. She didn't try.

"Who knows what treacheries they have afoot, planned for the moment of our success."

Serpents wrestled in her bowels. She'd been too long in the west. She'd become infected with its softnesses. Damn that villain Valther! If he hadn't insinuated himself through the walls surrounding her emotions....

"You're in charge, Lord Ch'ien. Do whatever seems appropriate." She fixed her gaze on the map and tried not to think about what she had done. Moral abdication was as great a sin as any. After a time she left her seat and went downstairs, hoping a meal would ease her tension and soften her self-disgust.

One of the King's men dragged Mist out of her kitchen. He gobbled incoherently and pointed. Baffled, she allowed herself to be pulled to a window.

The east was afire again. Lord Kuo had begun moving. And she had been so tired, so dispirited, so self-involved that she hadn't felt it start. "Thank you." She hurried upstairs.

The air had changed. The old stink of fear and tension was gone. Now a different tenseness filled the place, the tension that develops just before the battle. The eager, wary tension of soldiers about to strike. Everyone was moving faster now, more crisply, with a bounce in their steps. They had forgotten their weariness. They paused when she entered the room. She waved them back to work.

"Reports are beginning to come in already," Lord Ch'ien said. "The indications are favorable."

"Good." She turned to one of Bragi's men. "Will you get the King?" She turned back. "What do we know?"

Some time later she glanced up from her ongoing conference and discovered that Varthlokkur had arrived. The wizard was surveying the room from a high seat against the north wall. He looked rested and alert. He would miss nothing.

The King arrived moments later. He spoke with several of his men. She watched him listen and nod, question, listen, and nod. He paused longest with the wizard. Then he came to her, and led her to the eastern end of the table. "Mist, do you know anything more about this business here?"

She felt almost relieved. About this she could speak the whole truth, could speak without having to worry about choosing each word. "We don't know. We've had one garbled message this morning. It said Northern and Eastern Armies still support us, but that they're too busy with the Deliverer to become directly involved."

"The Deliverer?"

She glanced up, startled. Varthlokkur had come over, as sudden as a surprise thunderstorm.

"The enemy chieftain out there. They call him the Deliverer. Some kind of prodigy, apparently. He's decimated Eastern Army. Northern Army and Eastern Army have decided to make a stand on the Tusghus."

"Uhm." Bragi studied the map, then glanced at Varthlokkur. "How come you're so interested?"

"Ethrian. He's out there somewhere."

"He's alive, then?"

Sweat sequined the wizard's forehead. He rubbed it away. Mist watched him closely. There was something here she hadn't been aware of before, some strain between the two men. Varthlokkur said, "I'm not sure. Intuition says yes."

"Maybe we can bring him home. Great for Nepanthe. A new daughter, then her lost son restored."

"I don't think so. This isn't the son she lost. If it is Ethrian, she won't want him back."

"You don't know her very well, then."

Mist became very attentive. Ethrian? Not dead? What?... She examined the wizard. Never had she seen him so bleak.

"What is it?" the King demanded.

"I'll never tell her about this—if it's what I suspect. Forget I mentioned his name. She's had enough hurt from life."

Mist frowned. The man wasn't making sense.

"But—" the King said.

Varthlokkur interrupted. "She doesn't need the pain. All right? I don't want her to see her child grown into a monster. I warn you. Tell her and you've lost my help forever."

"Take it easy, man. I don't even know what you're talking about. Do you, Mist? What are you trying to do, Varthlokkur?"

Mist drifted over to Lord Ch'ien and related what she had heard. "I think you'd better send someone to see what's happening out there," she said. "This could be important."

Lord Ch'ien nodded, beckoned a reliable man from the messenger pool.

Mist turned back to the wizard and King just as Michael Trebilcock came into the room.

She'd never learned the details of Trebilcock's disappearance and sudden return. Evidently he had gone into the desert kingdom of Hammad al Nakir and found evidence linking the attack on General Liakopulos with the regime there.

The King waved to her. She went over. Bragi said, "Michael says there was an uprising in Throyes. Hsung put it down."

"I know."

"He says Hsung is going to deploy the Argonese army in his flanking counterattack against the Matayangans."

She was surprised. "Is that reliable news, Michael?"

"No. A rumor out of the Throyen command. But it's certainly his style."

"It is that. I'll accept it as fact." She stepped away. That wasn't good news. If Lord Hsung deployed the Argonese, then he would have troops of his own still free to resist her stroke. "Lord Ch'ien?" She explained. He looked grim.

She backed away to one of the chairs, sat watching the map. The long red arm thrusting into the empire's underbelly had begun to develop a waist near its root. Lord Kuo was going to amputate it, going to isolate a huge army in enemy territory. The Matayangans could not endure being cut off long.

"Will it work?" she asked Lord Ch'ien, pointing.

"Depends on how much Lord Kuo has to work with," he replied. "It's a bold stroke, certainly. Deserving of honor even if it fails. The impression we get from the reports is that the reserve was stronger than Southern Army itself was."

"Any problems in that for us?"

"We won't know till we jump in. His security has been superb."

Mist chewed a thumbnail and studied the map. Her eyes kept drifting to the mystery war in the east. Her nephew Ethrian was there? Part of that? How? Why?... She forced her attention back to the main show.

The moment of decision came. Go or abort. Attack and risk shattering the hope of saving the empire from these southern barbarians? Stand fast and surrender all hope of ever recovering her throne? It would be never if she didn't grab it now. If Lord Kuo pulled this out, he would become untouchable....

She decided, looked up. "The King," she said. "Where is the King?"

Someone said, "He just left, ma'am."

"Get him. I need him here. Now."

Bragi clomped back into the room a few minutes later. Mist guided him to the map, indicated the pincers nipping the Matayangan arm. "We're going to go. When the heads of these prongs are ten miles apart. Lord Kuo will be completely preoccupied. Lord Ch'ien estimates that will be four hours from now. We're alerting my people. I'll need three of your assault teams. My people will take over everywhere else while yours are hitting Lord Kuo's headquarters and arresting him." She indicated her people. "Most of my Tervola will go with you. They'll sort out the confusion for you."

The King's eyes narrowed. A subtle something entered his face. She didn't identify it until he replied. "You ain't number one yet, Mist. You're Chatelaine of Maisak till the dust settles." He glanced at Varthlokkur. The wizard remained seated, watching blandly.

She stamped a foot irritably. These damned touchy barbarians. Had to remind you where the power lay.... She forced an apologetic smile, softened her features. Just a few hours more. Then she would be dependent upon no one.

"I'll start assembling them now." The King turned away, gathered his captains.

Mist returned to Lord Ch'ien's side. She glanced back once, found the wizard Varthlokkur gazing her way. His face was expressionless, yet she had the feeling he was amused. She shivered.

She hadn't been paying him enough attention. He was the real threat here in the west. Without him Bragi could not have survived the Great Eastern Wars. Without him the Dual Principiate would never have fallen, and none of this would have come to pass.... He seemed so inefficacious in person you forgot just how deadly he could be... Now, more than ever, she'd best remember. He hated the Dread Empire. This might be his moment to enter a silent dagger and accelerate the destabilization begun with the deaths of her father and uncle... It hardly seemed possible that less than two decades had passed since the fall of the Princes Thaumaturge. The empire had had more masters and mistresses since than during all the centuries that had gone before.

Is the empire dying? she wondered. Is it an empire embarking on an era of decadence?

"Three and a half hours," Lord Ch'ien said. "The indications remain positive."

"Thank you. What're the reports from our people in Western Army? I have a feeling Hsung is going to be trouble."

Nepanthe lay with the baby at her breast. Outside, fell witchlight tumbled around the mountaintops like a playful litter of kittens. "Maggie," she called softly. "Maggie?"

"Yes, My Lady?" The servant girl rose from where she had been dozing over her knitting.

"Where is Varthlokkur? Has he sent a message?"

"I'm sorry, Mistress. There's been no word at all. Even the Queen is upset, they say. She hasn't heard from the King in days."

Slowly, Nepanthe turned her head till she could see the witchfire again. A deep sorrow possessed her. "What is that? Does anyone know?"

"They do say it's the Dread Empire at war, Mistress. But not with us. No. Not this time. This time darkness stalks one of those faraway kingdoms you only hear about in stories."

Nepanthe did not reply. She was no longer listening.

She was alone and scared. The presence of the serving girl did nothing to comfort her. Maggie wasn't someone she knew, someone she could open her heart to, someone who wouldn't laugh at her fears... Varth had promised that the baby wouldn't be born here... Be reasonable, she told herself. The child wasn't due for weeks.

She looked down at the hairless, wrinkled, red, tiny head. As if sensing her scrutiny, the baby wriggled, began nursing again. Nepanthe watched the little cheeks move and smiled.

Then she realized that the maid was still talking. Her question was getting far more answer than she cared to hear. "Maggie? Would you see if Queen Inger can come in?" She needed someone, and didn't know anyone... She would have called for Mist, but her brother's wife would be in the thick of whatever the men were doing. That woman only pretended to her sex. Inside that gorgeous body she was just another man.

Queen Inger came in a few minutes later. "Thank you for

coming," Nepanthe gasped. "I didn't really expect you to. You have your own things to do."

"I'm probably as desperate to talk as you are, honey." The Queen was cool and blonde, tall and elegant. Truly regal, Nepanthe thought. Always in command of herself and her surroundings. "I haven't seen Bragi for days."

"Varth has been gone since the baby was born. I know he has things to do, but he could at least stop and say hello."

"What're they up to? Do you have any idea?"

"I don't even know where Varth is, let alone what he's doing."

"They're at the Chatelaine Mist's house. Them and their cohorts. I know that much. What they're doing is anybody's guess. They won't talk to anyone. Won't even answer my messages."

"You can bet it has something to do with *that*." Nepanthe levered herself out of bed, went and leaned on her windowsill. The Queen watched over her shoulder. "It never ends, Inger. I wish... No offense to you, understand. I wish Bragi had never come to Kavelin. We had nice homes in Itaskia. We weren't important and we weren't wealthy, and life was hard, but our families were all together and we were mostly happy. That damned Haroun bin Yousif... I hope he's burning in Hell. If he hadn't gotten Bragi and Mocker involved...."

"You can't change anything. I think it was fated. If it hadn't been Haroun, something else would have driven you out."

Nepanthe turned, her eyes suddenly narrow. "That's right. Duke Greyfells was your uncle or something, wasn't he?" The Duke of Greyfells had been a mortal enemy of her first husband and the King when Bragi was just a mercenary.

"Another branch of the family entirely, dear. Our side never got involved in politics. I wish Bragi wasn't now."

"You don't like being Queen?"

"I love being Queen. I just hate all the trouble and pain and conspiring and responsibility that goes along with it."

Nepanthe turned and stared into the distance once more. The sorcery-storm had developed a bilious, lime-colored tint. Sorcery. That too had dogged her all her days. It had claimed Ethrian. It devoured the innocent.

"Does Bragi ever talk about what happened? With Mocker?"

"No. He doesn't want to remember. And he can't forget. He's haunted by it. Sometimes he wakes up in the night crying. Or shouting. He can't convince himself that he had no choice. And he didn't, you know."

"I know. I don't hold it against him. I'm saving my hatred for the people who made Mocker try to murder his best friend. I wish they weren't all dead. If they were alive, I could dream about torturing and killing them."

"He'd do anything to make it up to you, Nepanthe. He still feels that badly."

"I don't want anything, Inger. I have Varth and the baby. The only thing would be… Ethrian. I wish I could know for sure. If he's dead or alive."

"I thought they killed him after Mocker failed. That's what everyone says."

"Everybody thinks they did. But nobody saw it happen. And I keep getting this feeling that he's out there somewhere, and he needs help." She stared into the violent sky, began shivering. She didn't mention her dreams. Varth always laughed at them. Inger might too. "Sometimes… sometimes I think Bragi and Varth know and they just won't tell me."

"Bragi hasn't ever said anything to me."

"I just wish I *knew*. If you hear anything… Tell me. Please?"

Inger patted her shoulder. "Of course. Of course. What are friends for?"

I don't know, Nepanthe thought. I've never had enough to find out.

The sky raged and swirled.

11

THE STONE BEAST SPEAKS

ETHRIAN AND SAHMANAN stood atop a hill. The broad expanse of the Tusghus rolled away below them. Ethrian squeezed a dagger so hard his knuckles whitened. "Damn!" He hurled the blade at the ground. It skittered into the brush. He could not find it again.

"What's the matter?"

"We're winning the battles and losing the war," he snarled. "They're eating us up. How do we get across this? There're as many of them as there are of us. There isn't anybody left for me to recruit."

"Take them alive. You did that with some of the natives."

"I can't."

"Why not?"

"They won't let me. Their armor has spells that stop me."

The earth shook. A column of fire rose a few hundred yards behind them. Trees smouldered.

Ethrian muttered, "Another three hundred men gone. Why do they clump up? I can't keep them spread out unless

178

I think about it every minute."

"They still have memories. They don't like what they've become. They huddle because it comforts them. Reach across the river. Find people who aren't soldiers."

"I've tried. There aren't any. They've emptied the whole damned countryside."

Fighting broke out south of the hill. The uproar approached, then drifted away.

The enemy no longer needed his transfers to shuttle his legions. He was using them tactically, launching small surprise attacks. Ethrian hadn't the skill to detect portals left hidden on this side of the river.

"We can't sit here forever," Sahmanan complained. "We have to break loose and start recruiting."

Ethrian's hatred flared. It had grown geometrically since his assumption of the beast's power. He marveled at himself. Sometimes he thought he had become quite mad.

Maybe the stone beast did beat me, he thought. I'm becoming the beast, hungry for destruction, hungry for human fear, impatient when I'm balked.

The beast hadn't surrendered everything. It had given him nothing but its power over the dead. Its Word it had retained. Ethrian now coveted that.

Sahmanan suggested, "We could use flyers to drop men in the woods behind them. Pick off soldiers one at a time. Send them back to their units...."

"They can tell the difference. Nor could we move enough men quickly enough. We've got to try something new. Anything in your bag of tricks?"

"Nothing I haven't already used. I have to keep my head down anyway. They're getting me figured. I won't survive another battle like the one at their fort."

"Go get the Great One, then."

"What?"

"Get the Great One. Go pry him out of his rockpile." He

looked across the river. What would the Word do to those earthworks?

He grinned as wicked a grin as any a madman ever produced.

Darkness wears a thousand masks, evil a thousand shapes.

He did not think himself changed. Outwardly, he resembled every youth his age. But the dark rot was spreading within. The cancer had grown from the seed planted by the Pracchia and fertilized by the stone beast.

They called him Deliverer, those whom he drove to their deaths again and again and again. He was on the brink of becoming the thing they proclaimed. Deliverer of Darkness. Messiah of Evil. Prince of the Left Hand Trail.

But no, he would protest. I'm just Ethrian, requiting evils done me and mine.

Sahmanan sensed the cancer. She understood its depth. A mistress of wickedness herself, she was appalled by its potential. She knew his ancestry. His grandfather was the wizard who had destroyed Ilkazar. His mother was a woman of the Power. The same blood had run in his father's veins. He might become the greatest disciple darkness had known.

"Go get the Great One," he told her.

She looked round with furtive glances, as if expecting the beast to be peeping from the brush. "Don't ask me to return to slavery."

Ethrian studied the river's far bank. "Do we have a choice? We're dead if we stand still."

"Take a different path. Send the dead over till they're destroyed. Go with me somewhere. We can start over. Let the Great One rot. Let him slide back to the hell where Nahaman and I found him." Her passion amazed them both. She meant what she said. Like her sister, she had rebelled.

"So. You're turning on me." Ethrian's words were as chill as the corridors of time. "I thought it would be the Great One who betrayed me."

"Ethrian..."

"Get him. Or we fight amongst ourselves."

Sahmanan looked past him. Dead soldiers were coming out of the woods. He meant it.

"You idiot!" She flung herself forward. Her impetus smashed him against a prehistoric granite monolith. He kicked her....

She sang a spell.

The world went white. Heat blistered Ethrian's skin. He felt a big vacant place in his mind. Hundreds of soldiers had ceased to exist... He bellowed in rage. He had come close to killing himself.

The boulder and Sahmanan's spell shielded them. He cursed, said, "One of us was thinking. Thank you." Then, "I'm blind!"

"Your sight will return. Ethrian, don't let hatred control you like that."

After a time, he said, "All right. It won't happen again. Sahmanan?"

"Yes?"

"I'm sorry. You still have to bring the Great One."

She sighed. "All right. When the ground cools and we can leave the protection of the spell."

Ethrian stood on the hill alone. A scimitar of moon rose behind him. He leaned on a spear, staring at the fires on the distant shore. Soon now, Lord Ssu-ma, he thought. I'll break your will, you stubborn pig. I'll carve the heart out of your empire. I'll make it my own. I'll find my father's murderer....

But first he had to use the stone beast without falling under its control. And Sahmanan. What of her? How strange she had been this afternoon. What was that natter about escaping slavery?

She didn't add up. She sang too many conflicting songs.

The air behind him whispered to the approach of vast

wings. The sound waxed. Soon it filled the night. A swarm of shafts streaked across the water. The sky burned behind Ethrian. A dozen shadows of him reached toward the river. He raised one hand, thought, This is me, Shinsan: A clawed shadow reaching for your heart.

The shafts dropped dragons and riders, though these were not the shafts of the desert battles. These hadn't a tenth of the power of those. They had a homemade feel, as though his enemies had exhausted the real thing and were making do with what they could concoct themselves.

He smiled. "The thing you fear pursues you. The thing you dread is upon you. Your time has come."

A dragon smacked down behind him. Sahmanan called a question. He did not turn.

She was beside him in a moment. He felt the immense presence of the Great One. "I brought him, Ethrian."

"And what does he think?"

He didn't have to ask. He felt the beast's joy, its eagerness, its lust for a chance to embarrass an enemy it hated because it refused to bend or be conquered, or even to fear.

The stone beast wanted to be taken seriously. These Lords of the Dread Empire no longer did so. They knew the situation as well as did Ethrian. They now perceived the Deliverer and his godling as fading nuisances they would eliminate within days.

Ethrian had drifted across the river and had seen the confidence there. They *knew* they would break him this time. They were abiding his attack, expecting him to destroy himself.

The stone beast said, "You did well to summon me, Deliverer. You had no other hope. Together, now, we will crush them. But I ask you, how do you plan to cross the river?"

Ethrian had given that no thought. He was worried about smashing his enemies, not about getting to them. He did not have a single boat. His troops hadn't built rafts or pontoons. The legions had destroyed all local craft during their retreat.

He cursed himself for being a fool.

"Not much of a general, are you, Deliverer?"

The stone beast's sarcasm stung. His own accusation had come home to roost.

"What would you suggest, Great One?" He tried for sarcasm himself. He glanced to the east, where the sun was about to rise.

"Sahmanan. I'll feed you strength. Freeze the river."

Ethrian gaped. "Freeze it?"

The beast laughed. And the youth shivered, knowing he had best take care.

Sahmanan performed some lengthy, darkness-hidden ritual. After a time, she said, "Aid me, Great One."

Ethrian felt the cold grow. It taunted his burned skin. It rolled down the hill. The woods became so chill that branches snapped. He closed his eyes, drifted out of his body.

There were scums of ice on the river already. The cold swept toward the nether shore. Over there they had begun to respond, ere ever the chill reached them. Their fires grew higher. Their drums hammered rhythms of warning.

Frost formed. The air grew misty. Snowflakes trickled down. Shinsan's soldiers calmly manned their earthworks.

If I had soldiers like these... Being the best would avail them not. A man's skill meant nothing once he heard the stone beast's Word. Ethrian knew. He had seen Sahmanan's visions of the war with Nahaman.

His spirits rose. Soon he would stand on the western shore, its master. The legion dead would rise around him, ready to move on... In a flash of whimsy he flung himself westward, through the wild forests, hunting the place they would try stopping him next.

It was a venerable city, an interesting city. It would delight him. He looked forward to taking it. He loved cities.

Refugees swarmed outside this one.

Here were the hordes that had escaped him earlier. He harangued them with a silent scream: I'm coming for you! There's nowhere you can run!

His anger faded. He was too far from his flesh to sustain an emotion long. He looked within himself, and was disturbed by what he saw. He was too attached to this idea of being Deliverer.

He sped back to the river and battle that would be Shinsan's last hurrah.

Dawn had come to the Tusghus. There was ice enough for men to cross. Sahmanan was spreading it up and down the stream, providing a broader avenue for attack.

Ethrian passed among his enemies, and grew nervous as he did so. They were not afraid. Their wizard-captains had convened no panicky conferences. They had their first and second and third lines set, their pyres ready to burn, their portals ready to evacuate their dead. Their commander was taking breakfast with his legion commanders, indifferent to events on the river.

Fear me, damn you! the youth raged. But, of course, they could not hear him. And that was just as well. They might have mocked him in their arrogance.

He thought, You'll see. When the stone beast speaks, you'll see. Then you'll show a righteous fear.

He returned to his body. He found Sahmanan now seated on the earth, eyes closed, face pruny with concentration. A black box, ten by six by five inches, lay in her lap. "That's a god?" It seemed bigger in the woman's visions.

The sun was several diameters above the horizon when her eyes clicked open and she said, "It's done."

Ethrian started his forces moving to the river's edge. They would strike when the beast Spoke.

It whispered in his mind, "I can't speak without a mouth, Deliverer. Lend me yours."

Again Ethrian chastised himself for lack of foresight. And not in respect to traps. "Use Sahmanan."

"Impossible. She's no more corporeal than I."

"You could have fooled me." He summoned a soldier.

The beast said, "I can't use the dead."

"Then we're wasting our time." How stupid did the beast think he was? "Sahmanan, let the river melt."

"I forbid it."

The woman hesitated.

Ethrian knew the instant she chose her ancient master.

"Lend me your mouth, Deliverer."

"No."

The beast's rage hammered him. He endured it more easily than he endured his own.

"Don't fight," Sahmanan pleaded. "Ethrian, call an animal out of the forest. Anything large will do."

He reached out, found a she-bear immediately. He brought her shambling to the hilltop, trailed by baffled cubs.

"Send her to the river," the beast snapped. His rage continued unabated.

Ethrian drove the bear, and followed himself. Sahmanan brought the box. Deep inside him the youth felt the Great One probing, trying to insinuate a tentacle or two, trying to take over. There would be a showdown. He or this dark godlet would bend the knee....

The beast's anger boiled. It fumed and smouldered and spread. Ethrian felt it touch the baffled she-bear as she started across the ice. Her cubs skittered and whimpered behind her. She ignored their snuffling and whining.

Ethrian smiled. What were they thinking over there? All this great sorcery, the freezing of the river in summer, so a bear and her cubs could cross?

Maybe they wouldn't connect her. They might think her just a poor creature wandering on the ice....

They weren't deceived. Ethrian felt the shaft barrage

screaming down the sky. He felt the beast's rage crest, then explode. The bear's mouth opened, then Spoke.

The youth reeled as the Great One shifted his attack, trying to take him by surprise.

The Word rolled across the ice. It fell on the might of Shinsan.

Ethrian's universe went dark.

He wakened to find Sahmanan leaning over him. "Are you all right?" she demanded.

He searched his mind. "Yes." He was surprised. "How long was I out? Where's the Great One?"

"Twenty minutes. I took him back uphill. He's still out. He didn't expect you to hit back."

"You left him?"

"We don't need him now, do we?"

He examined her closely. She meant it. "Then take him back to the desert."

"All right." She donned a conspiratorial smile. "He won't be happy about it."

"Do I care?" He faced the far bank of the river. They were stirring over there! He left his body, fluttered over, flew back. Distracted, the stone beast had done only half a job. "I'm wasting time," he muttered.

The army of the dead marched onto the ice. It was a pathetic assemblage of stiff-legged men, slipping and falling and rising to try again. The ice had developed a water film. The beast's strength had gone out of Sahmanan.

Will it last? Ethrian wondered. Faster! Faster!

Groggy legionnaires were at work over there. Six unconscious men into every portal every minute... They were escaping! "Faster!" he shrieked.

The first clash of arms echoed across the ice.

The least stunned of his foes responded to his attack. They rekindled their fires and remanned their breastworks. And the ice kept melting.

It was the shortest and most profitable of his battles. It lasted only an hour. He gained eight thousand recruits. The legions fell back, almost in disorder.

His gains barely replaced his losses. The ice broke up too fast. Some of his creatures were caught on floes that swifted away on the flood. They fell into the water. Fish got some. Others became entangled in the roots of trees growing along the banks. Or they raced on toward the distant sea, ever farther from his control.

The Tervola blasted away as they withdrew. They salvaged the bulk of their army. He tried to pursue them, but each mile they covered lessened his control of his warriors.

It wasn't till the last redoubt had fallen that he flew over to join his army.

Sahmanan returned from the desert. "He's back in his temple. I can feel his rage and fear from here."

"He shouldn't have tried to trick me. Look here. We've won. They can't stop us now. There aren't any more big barriers."

"What happens when you destroy them? Go on till the only people left are the dead you command?"

He looked at her, and sensed a touch of loathing, of incipient hatred. "Let me be, woman. I have only one goal. The eradication of Shinsan. We'll worry about what's next when that's done."

"I thought you'd say that."

"What do you mean? Never mind. Let's go. We have an appointment at a city west of here. If we move fast they won't have time to prepare. And we can catch up with the refugees."

Sahmanan shook her head dolefully, led him to their dragons.

For two days Ethrian patrolled the remote flanks of his host, seeking recruits. His efforts were hardly worthwhile. Only the very old, lame, and weak had stayed behind.

He recruited them. He took anything that would move.

The third morning after the Tusghus crossing Ethrian departed a wood and found himself facing Northern Army across a small plain. "I don't believe it. Where do they get the nerve? After what we did at the river."

Sahmanan laughed. "You said they were the best. You said they don't frighten. You said they wouldn't have time to prepare that city. What else could you expect?"

"I don't know."

This time the enemy came to him. They cut their way through the recruits. They slashed deep into his better soldiers, whose efficiency suffered from continued decay. They went after legion dead incorporated into his army. They brought with them portals mounted on wagons. The fighting continued till it seemed both armies must be destroyed. Then the legions withdrew.

Ethrian wept in rage.

They had taken back their dead. They had robbed him of the seed of a new host. They had left him with fewer than twenty thousand bodies able to hobble or crawl.

He reviewed them in the dawn. They were gaunt, stinking, horrible things all, clad in rags, with limbs lost, chunks torn from their flesh, missing ears or noses or eyes. Maggots crawled in their flesh. "Looks like the earth opened up and a battlefield yielded its ancient dead."

"And you want to go on?" Sahmanan demanded.

"I intend to destroy them. I'll find a way."

"They bought another day. They'll be another day ready."

"So be it." He marched westward, leading his shambling, dragging parody of an army. "It doesn't matter," he said. "Destiny rides with me. I know. I hear its voice. I was chosen. I was anointed. I am the Deliverer."

Sahmanan stared at him, aghast. The madness had enslaved him. "I don't want to die," she whispered. "Not for your nightmare *or* the Great One's."

Next day they came to the city called Lioantung.

Ethrian had made a spirit-visit by night. He had seen the panic-stricken mobs streaming westward, leaving the city to the army. He had had an inspiration for his attack.

It would take time, but time he had. He had been into the minds of those legionnaires who had served him briefly. He now knew that stubborn pig of a Lord Ssu-ma would get no help. Shinsan had bigger troubles on another frontier.

He was in a gay mood as he surveyed the city walls.

12

"I DON'T LIKE THIS, Bragi," Varthlokkur whispered. "I've never liked transfers." Serpents the size of anacondas were at play inside him. He borrowed a trick from the enemy and began silently chanting the Soldier's Ritual.

"What?" The King thumbed the edge of his sword. "Why not? What's wrong?"

"They scare me," Varthlokkur admitted. "There's something that lives in the transfer stream... I detected it way back when I was a student. Something huge and shadowy, that snaps up the unwary traveler." Varthlokkur scratched his forehead. His skin was wet and cool. Was he pale as well?

Bragi looked at him oddly. "How often does it happen? Can't be too often or Shinsan wouldn't use them all the time."

"Seldom," Varthlokkur admitted. "Once in ten thousand times. And I haven't heard of anyone disappearing in the last four or five years."

"Those are pretty damned good odds. Whoa! There's the

190

signal, Ch'ien says. Ready?"

Varthlokkur nodded reluctantly. He did not want to make the transfer, but a man had to do what he had to do. He gathered himself together.

Bragi sprang at the waiting portal. The wizard heard an echo of curse and metallic clash, cut off suddenly. Then he was through and in the midst of it himself. He unleashed a spell meant to blind the defenders. The King howled.

"Damn it, I told you to keep your eyes shut!" Varthlokkur roared.

The King shouted, "The doors! Grab the doors!" They were in a great hall of some sort, rather like the ground floor of a public building.

The wizard had no time to sightsee. He applied the flat of his blade to the behinds of soldiers stumbling out of the portal. "Move it!" he shouted. "Over there. Block that hearing charm."

Wild spells ranged the eastern headquarters, caring nothing for allegiances. Priceless tapestries went up in flames. Works of art wrinkled and blackened, or sagged and began to run like wax in the sun.

Lord Ch'ien arrived and took charge of the friendly Tervola. In fifteen minutes the inner headquarters was secure. In five more Lord Ch'ien had made peace with the garrison outside. Shinsan's soldiers avoided becoming involved in the squabbles of their nobility. These men just needed assurance that the headquarters hadn't been invaded by Matayangans.

"All secure here," Varthlokkur said. Lord Ch'ien agreed.

"For now," the King said. "Better see how the other groups did. Varthlokkur, send some messengers."

The wizard grabbed one of Lord Ch'ien's assistants and quickly adjusted several portals. He chose soldiers and sent them through. They were back in seconds.

"Baron Hardle has taken his objective," Varthlokkur told the King. "But Colonel Abaca is in trouble. He dropped right into Lord Kuo's lap."

"We'd better get there before Kuo closes the portals."

"It could be too late already," Lord Ch'ien said.

"The more we talk, the worse our chances." The King charged the portal Varthlokkur had reset. The wizard followed as closely as he dared, the snakes in his gut coiling and writhing once more.

They exited into a vast cavern. The nether end was a den of chaos. Abaca was cornered, making a last stand. Varthlokkur hurled a vicious spell of corruption. A dozen eastern soldiers rotted where they stood. Then he was too busy using his sword to loose more than the occasional nuisance spell.

He was cornered, battling an equally inept swordsman, when Lord Ch'ien announced that Lord Kuo's people had decided to surrender. He dropped his guard, sighed, shook his head. His opponent, a mere Aspirator, smiled weakly. "It's over, Lord."

"Aye. Come here. You're as nicked up as I am." They supported one another as they limped over to where Lord Ch'ien and the King were assembling the prisoners.

Baron Hardle, who had led the third assault team, staggered up to the King. "By God, sire, we pulled it off."

"We sure did." Bragi glowed.

"Better get set for the counterattack," Varthlokkur said. The adrenaline was going. He was tired and his wounds were beginning to ache. He would be stiff soon. His temper was turning foul. "Lord Ch'ien, you'd better get those portals secured." Ch'ien nodded, delegated several men.

Tervola spilled from several before they finished. Spell vied with spell. Blade met blade. Blood ran. Varthlokkur ignored the encounter. Lord Ch'ien could handle it. He was more use to the wounded.

One of Lord Ch'ien's men reported, "These men are from Western Army."

The King frowned, asked, "Hsung's gang? Lord Ch'ien,

wasn't Mist supposed to take care of Hsung?"

Lord Ch'ien shrugged. "The best laid plans, and all that, I suppose." And, a few minutes later, after the counterattack had waned, he added, "This doesn't look good. Lord Hsung has recaptured the other two headquarters."

Varthlokkur caught the King's eye. "Careful," he mouthed. Bragi nodded.

"Can we get back into those places?" Bragi asked.

Lord Ch'ien replied, "Not without marching. Across Matayangan ground. They've closed the portals." Then, "Too late anyway. Win or lose, the coup has run its course. We won't waste any more time on it. Matayanga would regain the initiative."

"Damn!" Bragi swore.

Varthlokkur drew him aside. "This stinks of trap. It's all too pat. Lord Hsung knew we were coming. How else could he have been ready to counter? Apparently he couldn't get word to Lord Kuo in time to make the trap work."

The King nodded thoughtfully. "I thought it had an odd smell. Think we're in trouble?"

"I think you'd better send someone to see what Mist is doing. Hardle, perhaps."

"What about you?"

"I have wounded to tend. You want to save Abaca, don't you?"

"Yeah. He's my best soldier. Soldiering-wise."

"Alert the men. Start collecting the wounded near the portals. We may want to disappear in a hurry."

Bragi nodded, went.

Hardle was not gone long. Varthlokkur joined the King when the Baron returned. He reported, "The coup was successful everywhere but where Lord Hsung intervened. Lord Kuo seems to have been killed. Nobody can find him. The Council of Tervola mean to delay taking any position till the war situations stabilize. Lord Hsung is negotiating with

Mist. We've won."

"Does Lord Ch'ien know any of this yet?" Varthlokkur asked.

"I don't think so."

"What's the situation in Kavelin?"

"Crazy. Total confusion."

"Don't tell Lord Ch'ien. Bragi, we've outlived our usefulness. Let's get out of here. And don't turn your back on him till you're gone."

"I won't." The King hurried off to inform his officers.

Am I being paranoid? Varthlokkur wondered. Maybe. But there's no sense in taking chances with officers of the Dread Empire. Especially those of Lord Ch'ien's ilk.

The King began sneaking his wounded through portals reset to carry men back to Kavelin. Lord Ch'ien's people paid no attention. They had their hands full taking control of the Matayangan war.

As the wizard guided the litter cases into a heavy portal, he overheard Baron Hardle telling the King, "You're too trusting, sire. Your friend was Chatelaine of Maisak. Was. Now you're dealing with the mistress of Shinsan."

"He's right, Bragi," Varthlokkur said. "She has to live the role."

The King frowned, grumbled, "She still at her house, Baron?"

"She was when I left. Busy as a one-handed puppeteer, trying to keep hold of all the threads."

"Then her fate isn't out of our hands, is it? Varthlokkur, let's go back. Baron, you get the men home."

The wizard followed the King. He stepped up to the portal, closed his eyes, gritted his teeth, stepped. He sensed nothing as he passed through. No great hungry shadow in the distance. Three times through, and not even a hint of the thing he feared. Was it gone?

He stepped into a situation room which had changed

dramatically. The big map table was gone. Wounded men carpeted the floor. Half were not Kaveliners. Lord Hsung's surprise counterstroke had come near succeeding.

Mist was arguing with several Tervola. Varthlokkur recognized only the one. He eyed the man, then looked for the King.

Bragi was talking to Dahl Haas. "Go downstairs and collect up some good men. Have them slip up here a few at a time. Varthlokkur?"

"I was going to suggest that. We might need them." He watched Mist closely. The woman had just now noticed them. She appeared bewildered by their presence. "Baron Hardle was right. The Princess Mist isn't Kavelin's bosom friend."

"So I see. She looks like she's seeing a couple of ghosts. Figure we're supposed to be spooks by now?" He sent men to guard the portals. "There's a certain value to our controlling her physical whereabouts, wouldn't you say?"

Varthlokkur smiled a thin, evil smile. "Of course. Unless we hang on too long. Then some other opportunist will promote himself number one." He closed his eyes, reached out with his thoughts. He felt the thing. *Come to me, Radeachar. Come to me. Unborn.* It stirred, responding. It moved his way... He opened his eyes, smiled again.

Mist said something to her companions, came toward the wizard and King. "I see you're back." She extended an imperious hand toward the King, as if expecting a bow and kiss. Bragi shook.

"Not all of us, Chatelaine. A lot of good men died out there. Some were captured. Hsung set a trap. We walked in. It almost worked."

"My people were hard hit too. As you can see."

Varthlokkur admired her aplomb. She'd had just the one bad moment when first she had seen them.

She added, "The trickster who did it would like to meet

you."

"Hsung? He's here?"

The wizard had recognized the Tervola immediately but hadn't mentioned him. Bragi was volatile enough without knowing the man he considered his great enemy was here in the room.

"Lord Hsung." Mist's voice was snappy and cold.

"Ain't Lord Nothing to me, woman. Just another beastmask. Don't start taking yourself too seriously. Not here in my territory."

Varthlokkur considered Mist from beneath lowered brows. He couldn't stifle his smile. She saw it and realized what she was doing. She became conciliatory immediately. "Of course. I apologize. It's been an emotional day."

Lord Hsung stepped forward, inclined his head an inch. "Pardon me," he told the King. "I do not yet speak your language well. I wished to make your acquaintance, after our three years of sparring. I had pictured someone smaller and more shifty."

"I learned from a small, shifty guy. Keeping your job? Still going to be boss of the occupation?"

"Her Highness has entrusted me with our western provinces."

"Figured you'd twist her arm. Going to be the same old crap, eh?"

Lord Hsung stiffened, glanced at Mist. Varthlokkur gave the King a warning headshake. It wasn't wise to irritate a Tervola too much. He let his senses drift, thought, *Where are you, Radeachar?*

Here. And a window shattered behind the King. A vast chill filled the room.

The Unborn had come.

It was a thing that looked like a fetus inside a globe of crystal, but no human fetus was ever that big....

Mist squeaked, dismayed. "Do you know how much good

glass costs, Varthlokkur? When you can find a decent glazier? I thought we were on the same side."

"I wasn't the first to forget." He beckoned. The Unborn drifted over and hung behind his left shoulder, its infant eyes open and wise in the ways of evil, filled with malice. "I can't prove anything, of course, but I'm morally certain that the King and I weren't supposed to return from our little jaunt into the east."

"I'll interrogate Lord Ch'ien. Perhaps he exceeded his instructions."

"Perhaps. But I doubt it."

The King said, "When people mess with me I get mean. Mist, you and your friends are going to be my guests for a while."

The Unborn stirred slightly, bobbing behind Varthlokkur's shoulder. Mist glanced at the thing and grimaced. "For how long? I'm involved in two desperate wars."

"Two?" Lord Hsung asked.

"Eastern Army was beaten. Northern Army may not hold. Lord Ssu-ma has performed brilliantly, but even genius has its limits. The eastern front is about to collapse."

Bragi smiled. "Ask me how much I care. The worse the whipping you take, the lighter the weight on my back."

Varthlokkur made another warning gesture. "Not so belligerent, my friend."

Mist said, "This threat has big dreams, Bragi. It won't be satisfied with us. It hates the world."

"Come on."

"These are armies of the dead. They have no love for the living."

Varthlokkur felt the snakes wakening in his belly, felt the color leave his face. The Unborn stirred, disturbed by his emotion. That damned mess out east... It wouldn't go away. Were the gods themselves determined to drag him in?

"Still irrelevant," Bragi said. "I want to know how to get

you to deal straight."

Mist took his hand. "I made some rotten deals to put this over, Bragi. The rottenest was to try trapping you. You refuse to understand what you mean to the Tervola. They want your scalp. Bad. I made it as soft a trap as I could, trusting that you'd have your usual luck. And we all got what we wanted. So let's stay friends."

"Okay. For now."

Varthlokkur smiled again, both at Mist's relief and at this flash of the flexibility of the old Bragi. He sighed, "On your way, Radeachar." And, "Home at last. You realize I haven't seen my daughter since right after she was born?"

"I haven't seen Inger," the King said. "Let's get out of here." But before they departed they reminded their people to keep close watch on Mist and her followers.

"That was close," Mist murmured to Lord Hsung. "Why can't you people be more flexible?"

"We people, Mistress?"

"Tervola. Not one of you learned from the example of O Shing. You forced him to go after Ragnarson because of the defeat at Baxendala. So a lot of great Tervola lost their lives. Whole legions were destroyed. And the balance was not rectified. The ignominy was compounded. And now that same obsession has nearly destroyed *me*...."

Lord Hsung chuckled. "You forget, I was on the other side."

"You represent the sort of thinking that causes the problem. Don't forget, I've been sitting up in Maisak for three years, watching you. You've been conspiring with both sides in the fighting in Hammad al Nakir. You've been sneaking agents into Kavelin. You've been spreading threats and rumors of war just to keep the King on edge. I don't know how much of that I can tolerate. It could come back on us like a bad spell."

"In time, you'll tolerate as much as it takes to destroy the man and his cohorts."

"Perhaps." We'll see, she thought. We'll see. "We'd better move out of here while he's in a mood to let us go. Lord Ch'ien! Where is Lord Ch'ien? Isn't he back yet?"

Varthlokkur encountered the King in the halls of Castle Krief. "How's Nepanthe?" Bragi asked.

"Fine. Just fine." For a woman spoiling for a fight all the time. For a woman barely in touch with her own world.

"What about the baby? Decided on a name yet?"

"She's perfect. No, we haven't."

"Something bothering you? You look distracted."

"A lot of things. But mainly Nepanthe."

"Still nagging you about Ethrian, eh?"

"Mostly." The wizard resumed walking, leaving the King wearing a baffled expression.

Yes, Nepanthe was still nagging about Ethrian. And he was having an ever more difficult time not betraying his suspicions about what was happening in the far east. There was going to be a blowup.... Hell, Bragi wouldn't tell her. He was a politician. He could subvert his friendship for Nepanthe to his need for the aid only a wizard armed with the Unborn could provide.

Couldn't he?

Mist sighed and dragged herself out of the lethargic half-sleep that held her. Gently, she tugged her arm from beneath Aral, sat up, swung her feet to the floor. Dantice snorted, rolled onto his belly. She looked at him fondly.

It had been pleasant while it lasted. Now it had to end. For real. The moment she returned to Venerable Huang Tain she would come under the closest scrutiny, scrutiny unceasing. It would be a long time before she could do anything without first acquiring the approval of the Council of Tervola.

She had few illusions about how much power she had

acquired in the coup. A great deal, to be sure, but nothing like what her father and uncle had commanded in the days of their Dual Principiate. She would rule, but would have to avoid giving offense. She would have to exercise the greatest care, and would be able to eliminate rivals only with the utmost caution. It would be a generation before she consolidated completely.

If she survived the first year. She didn't doubt that there were counterplots afoot already.

What had the empire come to? All this conspiracy, all this grasping after power—there hadn't been any of that in her father's time. He and his brother had ruled for four hundred years and had faced fewer plots than had formed over the two decades since their passing. Was it a sign that the empire was dying? That it was decaying even while it grew?

She left the bed and, without dressing, sat at her writing desk. She wrote a long missive to the King.

She repeated her apologies, telling him he had been a good friend throughout her exile. As a gesture, she was going to leave her children in Kavelin.

She smiled. Crafty witch. Who do you think you're fooling? He knows you. He knows Shinsan. He'll realize they'll be less hostages to fortune if they stay here. He'll know you're trying to shield them from the vicissitudes of Shinsan's politics.

"Aral? Come on. Wake up. It's time."

He sat up, avoided her eye. He had the look of a whipped puppy. He had asked to go with her, and hadn't understood when she explained why he couldn't.

"Up, soldier. Get yourself dressed." She began donning her own clothing. She decided to gather a new wardrobe first thing. She couldn't stroll the places of Venerable Huang Tain clad as Chatelaine of Maisak. Her sojourn in the west, and her having served the western cause during the Great Eastern Wars, would cause her trouble enough. "Here's a letter I want you to take to the King. Okay?"

Aral muttered something she didn't catch. For just a moment she relented. She kissed him. He tried to pull her into the bed. "No. No. Try to understand, dear." She disentangled herself. At the door, she said, "Good-bye, Aral."

It came out sounding more sad than she intended. She wasn't enjoying this parting.

Varthlokkur cradled his daughter with his right forearm. His left hand lay folded between his wife's fingers. He stared out the window at silvery cumulus galleons rushing eastward in ponderous battle array. "Looks like rain tomorrow."

"Something wrong?" Nepanthe asked. "You're pretty remote."

He shifted his attention to the baby's tiny red face. "You thought of a name yet?"

"Yes. I don't know if you'll like it. What about you?"

"No. I've been distracted."

"Distracted? You're always distracted. Lately you've been in another world. What's wrong?"

"Trouble."

"There's always trouble here. Vorgreberg breeds it the way other cities breed cockroaches."

"This is the King's trouble."

"He's always in trouble. How about naming her after your mother?"

"My mother? Smyrena?" That hadn't occurred to him. "Smyrena. It wasn't a lucky name." His mother had been burned at the stake for witchcraft. "I don't know." How much did the King suspect? You couldn't tell a man his wife was behind half his troubles. He might take a poke at you. And the poke Varthlokkur dreaded was a comment about Ethrian to Nepanthe.

And what of Mist? She couldn't ignore the eastern situation....

"There you go again. If you can't talk to Bragi, tell Derel Prataxis. Bragi will put up with anything from him."

"That might do." But he was thinking of telling Michael Trebilcock. He and Michael understood one another. And Michael had the power to *do* something....

"What about the name?" Nepanthe's eyes were heavy. She wanted an answer before sleep took her.

"Smyrena will be fine. Mother would be pleased." He considered the slow cloud castles. "Smyrena it is. Hello, little Smyrena."

The infant seemed to smile.

13

YEAR 1016 AFE

THE FATES OF GODS AND EMPERORS

SHIH-KA'I LIMPED UP the last few steps to the top of Lioantung's wall. Pan ku remained half a step behind, ready to offer support. He avoided suggesting that his master might require it.

Lord Ssu-ma smiled as he leaned against the battlements. Pan ku need not have been concerned. He was, simply, tired and hobbling on an unexpected corn.

The countryside was alive with refugees. The city's civilians were joining them. The air quivered with panic. Shih-ka'i hoped it would not spread to the legions, yet could not banish its touch himself. The disaster on the Tusghus had been more than the loss of a line. It had introduced Shih-ka'i and his officers to real doubt about their ability to defeat the Deliverer.

"Did I make a wise decision, Pan ku?" He stared eastward. Somewhere in those forests Northern Army was on the attack.

"You had no choice, Lord. The men might have lost their confidence."

"And if it's another disaster?"

"Best to find out now. We have to know if it was an isolated incident."

Shih-ka'i did not understand what had happened on the Tusghus. That terrible sound had come thundering from the she-bear, shattering the minds and wills of his legionnaires... He'd never heard anything like it. His secret heart filled with fear when he thought of facing it again. Armed with that weapon, the Deliverer was unstoppable.

It had to be the thing in the desert. Had to be.

"Lord," Pan ku said softly, "Lord Lun-yu."

Shih-ka'i watched Tasi-feng labor up the stair. Lord Lun-yu had less energy than he. "Catch your breath."

"Last civilians cleared out, Lord," Tasi-feng reported. "May have problems later. Some prisoners escaped in the confusion."

"That was to be expected, I suppose. It's the lesser risk. Any word from out there?"

"Still early, Lord, but they seem to be doing well."

"No sign of the problem we had on the Tusghus?"

"None, Lord." Tasi-feng did not conceal his relief. "Maybe they're saving it for Lioantung."

"Maybe." Shih-ka'i had some thoughts on the subject. He meant to pursue them... Well, it had to wait. He was needed here until the Deliverer's intentions became clear.

Nervous, unable to stand still, Shih-ka'i scanned the sky. "Nice day," he observed. It was.

"It's been nice all summer, Lord." Tasi-feng scanned the sky too. Flyers would presage the Deliverer's appearance. Their confidence had been shaken. They had begun to anticipate disaster.

One of Tasi-feng's officers appeared later. "Execution has been perfect, Lord. No sign of the doom of the Tusghus. We have a great tactical victory."

Shih-ka'i grinned into his mask, smacked a fist against the

battlements. "Damn!" he said softly. "By damn! Lord Lun-yu, we'll stop him yet."

Northern Army double-timed through the gates. Their joy was contagious. "They're slipping discipline," Shih-ka'i muttered to Pan ku.

"Justifiable, wouldn't you say, Lord?"

"No doubt. No doubt." Shih-ka'i was elated himself. The battle had gone perfectly. The old confidence had returned. "We'll stop them here."

A messenger approached. "Lord Ssu-ma. Lord Lun-yu begs your presence in the command center."

"Did he say why?"

"No, Lord."

"I'll be there directly." Once the messenger departed, "Any ideas, Pan ku?"

"They've been watching the Matayangan front, Lord. Maybe something's happened there."

Something had. Lord Kuo's hidden armies had taken the offensive. But that was old news. Had Matayanga sprung a surprise of its own?

Shih-ka'i glanced at the handful of flyers circling above. The siege was about to begin.

He looked forward to it. Lioantung would be the rock against which the Deliverer would shatter himself. Or Lord Ssu-ma Shih-ka'i's last battlefield. He had people developing a strategy to pursue should the city fall, but theirs was a half-hearted effort. The country west of Lioantung was dense with refugees. Populations had been compressed too much for further effective removal from the Deliverer's grasp.

The fates of himself, the Deliverer, and quite possibly the empire hung on this old fortress town.

The senior Tervola had assembled in the command center. Their soft talk faded when Shih-ka'i entered. "Politics again, Lord," Pan ku whispered.

"I suspect so."

The Tervola made room for him at the tabletop map of the empire. He and his staff had been following the Matayangan war closely of late. It might affect what they could do here.

The field situation appeared unchanged. "What is it?" he demanded.

Tasi-feng suggested, "Perhaps we could speak in private?"

Shih-ka'i peered into the jeweled eyes of Tasi-feng's mask. "The changing of the guard, eh?"

"Yes, Lord."

"What's to be discussed? Nothing's changed. We have our hands full here. The Deliverer's dragons are overhead."

"Lord..."

"Your games are your games. We have a job. Let's stick to it, eh? What's going on out there can take care of itself. If your candidate wins and doesn't like me, she can send me back to the Fourth Demonstration."

"Lord, we just wanted you to know what was happening. It's not likely to affect us."

"Then talk it out and get back to work. The Deliverer is on his way."

"As you command, Lord." Tasi-feng nodded to someone at the table. The Tervola dispersed.

"I'll be on the wall, watching him come up," Shih-ka'i said. "I don't want to hear any more politics while I'm commander. Understood?"

Tasi-feng bowed slightly. "As you command, Lord. We're perfectly satisfied."

The Deliverer's patrols were encircling the city when Shih-ka'i reached the wall. "What do you think, Pan ku? Send out skirmishers?"

Pan ku shrugged.

"No. Of course not. They're almost done. Make them come to us." The patrols looked like the dead now. "Time is on our side. Another week and he won't have anything left."

The hours rolled. The sun declined. The moon came out. Shih-ka'i remained rooted, watching besiegers who pitched no tents, who lighted no campfires, who merely stood waiting in lines surrounding the city.

"What will he try, Pan ku?"

"That sound again, Lord. Something to shake the walls."

"I'd say so, too. But we can take that away from him."

"Lord?"

"Hsu Shen..."

Pan ku pointed. "Someone coming, Lord."

A shadow flitted toward them, darting from one pool of darkness to another. Pan ku drew his longsword. Shih-ka'i let his senses reach out, felt no danger. "Easy. I think he's friendly."

Pan ku did not relax. He was not that kind of man.

The shadow moved more slowly as it came nearer. Shih-ka'i snorted in surprise. "Put that thing away, Pan ku."

His batman did as he was told. Reluctantly.

Their visitor wore Tervola garb, but no mask. The moonlight illuminated his lean, aristocratic face, exposing weariness and fear. "Lord Ssu-ma."

"Lord Kuo."

"I've suffered a turn of fortunes."

"So I've heard." Shih-ka'i examined his feelings. He wanted no part of Shinsan's tortuous politics. He simply wanted to get on with his job. Yet he owed this man. Lord Kuo had given him his chance at a major command. "We've tried to avoid getting involved."

"Your situation. Is it bad?"

"Looking better today." He explained. Lord Kuo nodded thoughtfully. "What brings you to me?" Shih-ka'i asked.

"I didn't have anywhere else to go." Kuo did not ask for help directly.

"Uhm. My officers aren't your friends."

"That's my own fault."

"The situation being what it is, there's not much I can do."

"I understand."

"There's Hsu Shen's island, Lord," Pan ku said.

"Of course. And we were about to go, weren't we? Lord, I can hide you on the Pracchia's island in the east. Pan ku. Hsu Shen hasn't been in contact, has he? He won't have heard from the plotters?"

"I think not, Lord."

Shih-ka'i had been downplaying Hsu Shen's presence on the island, hoping the Deliverer would miss it. "All right. We'll go now. Pan ku, find My Lord a mask. I saw several in the old Seventeenth museum."

Lord Kuo said, "I should shift to enlisted garb."

"Good idea. Pan ku, assemble a decurion's kit and uniform. Northern Army badges."

Later, in his quarters, Shih-ka'i studied the result. "Pan ku?"

"We need less arrogance, Lord. A soldier doesn't bear himself as if he expects Candidates to throw roses in his path."

"I see what you mean," Wen-chin said. "Drill me."

Shih-ka'i watched the time closely. The night was proceeding. Dawn would reach the island before it arrived here. He wanted to get there before sunrise. He explained, "Hsu Shen and his men should get used to you before daylight begins accenting your little lapses." He examined Lord Kuo's kit with a drillmaster's eyes. "Mask and robes on the bottom? Good. Pan ku, yours is ready?" They would all take kits to make Wen-chin's less conspicuous. His and Pan ku's would remain with Lord Kuo.

Shih-ka'i was a worried man. How long could he shelter Lord Kuo? He owed the man, but how much? Wen-chin's enemies would not see this as a private matter.

Too, Lord Kuo needed a secondary cover if he were to be long exposed to Hsu Shen. That he was Tervola could not be hidden indefinitely. Special investigator? That might do it.

"I think we're as close as we can get on short practice, Lord," Pan ku said.

"Then let's make the transfer. Lord, don't say anything unless you have to. Best they don't notice you. Pan ku, you go through first. Get their attention."

"I'll be invisible," Kuo promised, apparently amused.

Shih-ka'i supposed he was overly worried. Who would be watching for Lord Kuo? The man was believed killed during Mist's attacks on his headquarters.

The Lioantung end of the transfer went perfectly. No one seemed surprised that Shih-ka'i had gotten his man a helper. Other senior Tervola maintained retinues.

Shih-ka'i went through last. He arrived, found Hsu Shen galloping toward him, trying to put his apparel in order. "Lord," he gasped, "you should have warned us. We would've provided a more fitting reception."

"Receptions are of no moment, Hsu Shen. You needn't have interrupted your sleep."

"But..."

"Never mind. It's time to try our luck with the stone thing. They've reached Lioantung. We don't want them doing what they did at the Tusghus."

Hsu Shen nodded. "We've watched as closely as we dared. There's a great rage in the thing. Its servants betrayed it."

"Uhm. Could we enlist it? No. We don't need that kind of ally. Did you find any weaknesses?"

"Have you eaten, Lord? Can we discuss it over breakfast?"

"Fine. We've been up all night, and had nothing since yesterday noon."

Over the meal, Hsu Shen said, "We observed what happened both before and after the battle on the Tusghus." He explained how the woman in white had removed and returned the godling to its home.

"Very good," Shih-ka'i said. "I appreciate it, Hsu Shen.

I'll remember you. How dangerous is it in its current circumstances? Can it stop us?"

"I don't know, Lord. When the woman removed it, it seemed happy. No reason to dispute what was happening. When she returned it, it was unconscious. It awakened furious."

"And now?"

"Angry somnolence? Yes. It's in a dreaming rage. But we're really too far away to tell anything for sure."

"I understand." After a few minutes, Shih-ka'i said, "We'll go over tonight. I'd better rest."

"Tonight, Lord? That's cutting it fine. I'll have to send someone now in order to get a portal placed in time."

"Right. Be careful. Don't alert it. And wake me if it does get excited."

"As you command, Lord."

Shih-ka'i retired to quarters hastily prepared for him. Pan ku and Lord Kuo accompanied him.

Lord Kuo took a chair. "This monster... It's what I sensed back when?" Shih-ka'i nodded. "What're you going to do with it once you've taken it out of the stone thing?"

"I'll consider my options when the time comes."

"Did they notice me? I was too nervous to tell."

"No. Let's get some sleep. I've been too long without."

Hsu Shen himself wakened Shih-ka'i. "Sunset, Lord. I've moved a team to within a mile. Hard on the men. The heat was insufferable."

So are you sometimes, Shih-ka'i thought. "Let's have supper before we go."

"It's ready. I'll have the stewards set it out."

"Give us time for our rituals."

"Of course, Lord." Hsu Shen seemed surprised.

"Yes. I still perform mine. We don't outgrow the need, Hsu Shen."

Pan ku came striding into the apartment as Shih-ka'i

completed his rituals. "Where have you been?"

"Prowling, Lord. To see if there was any talk about our friend."

"And?"

"Nothing. And they'd come to me if they had questions about my master."

"Good. Satisfied, Lord Kuo?"

"Eminently."

"Pan ku, we may have to leave in a hurry if this raid sours. Be ready. In any case, you'll be the last man off the island."

"It's a good hiding place," Wen-chin observed.

"One thing, Lord. I'm not a political man. Don't involve me."

"You've done more than I deserved already. I won't put you at risk."

"Thank you. Pan ku, suppertime."

Shih-ka'i went through the transfer first. One by one, Hsu Shen's men followed him into the cooling desert. This promised to become a chilly night's work.

Shih-ka'i prepared protective spells, then seated himself on the crest of a dune. The stone monster loomed before him. The thing within was sleeping. The transfer had not alerted it.

Hsu Shen settled beside him. "We go in between the forepaws. There's a stairway to its back. Up near the shoulder there's a plug that lifts out. I'm not sure what we'll find inside. I couldn't probe that closely."

Shih-ka'i nodded. "I want complete silence when we go in. I don't expect it sees or hears in mortal fashion, but why take risks?" He stared at the dark bulk. "I wish we knew more about it."

The last men arrived. Hsu Shen spread them in a skirmish line. Shih-ka'i wondered why he wanted so much help. Numbers meant nothing tonight.

"Let's go." Butterflies mated in Shih-ka'i's gut as he stalked forward. What am I doing here? I'm an army commander. I'm supposed to have people do these things for me.

Lord Kuo remained close, spells of his own prepared. Pan ku carried his longsword at the ready.

Shih-ka'i laughed at himself. Arrogant, puny mortal, attacking what might be a god. Such gall!

There was no moon yet. The desert was illuminated only by stars. They seemed more numerous here than in the skies of Shinsan. The darkness seemed more intense.

Shih-ka'i moved into the deeper darkness between the thing's forelegs, carefully picking his way through the rubble. He paused, knelt. Water. Here and there, plants clung desperately to life. Curious.

He had trouble finding the stair. Its base was masked by rubble. Seconds fled. His heart hammered faster and faster. The thing had to know he was here. It must be waiting to trap him… Still, he sensed nothing but sleeping anger.

He began the climb. Pan ku and Lord Kuo were right behind him. From behind them, Hsu Shen whispered, "Lord, must these men—"

"Silence!" Shih-ka'i hissed. He listened. The thing had not stirred. "They go." He resumed climbing.

From the beast's back he could just make out the men below. Again he wondered what point there was to their presence. To comfort their commander?

Hsu Shen eased past him, felt the stone of the thing's battered shoulder. He lifted the plug out. Shih-ka'i felt the godling grow restless. He shook an admonitory finger at his companions.

Pan ku and Wen-chin bore lanterns. These they now lighted. Shih-ka'i took one and started down into the stone thing's heart. It stirred again, but did not waken.

There was one chamber down deep inside, perhaps fifteen feet by ten. At one end stood a stone altar. Upon it rested a small black box.

Once that chamber had been richly appointed. All that remained was dust and scraps, a few ceremonial weapons, and the altar itself. Shih-ka'i advanced carefully, stood over the altar, stared at the box. He returned the lantern to Pan ku.

Still no more than a restlessness in the box. Shih-ka'i reached for it. His hands quivered.

Hsu Shen sneezed. And sneezed again.

The thing in the box stirred.

Shih-ka'i lifted gently and turned, glided toward the stair.

Pan ku sneezed, cursed softly. Shih-ka'i grimaced behind his mask. Carefully, carefully, he climbed the steps.

Now Kuo was sneezing. It was catching. Shih-ka'i felt the dust in his own nose. He fought the sneeze... There was nothing he could do. He hurried to the top, spun, shoved his burden into Pan ku's arms. Pan ku had gotten his own nose under control by grinding at it with his free hand. Shih-ka'i doffed his mask till the sneezing passed.

The god in the box seemed to have settled back into sleep. "That was close," Shih-ka'i muttered.

"What now, Lord?" Hsu Shen asked.

"Back to the island. We'll put weights on the box, spells on one of the boats, and sail it out to sea. It'll run into a storm and go down."

Hsu Shen nodded. He took Lord Kuo's lantern, signaled his soldiers. They began withdrawing. Most of them had departed by the time Shih-ka'i reached the transfer point.

"I'll go last," he said. "Just in case." The godlet still had not wakened. "Be ready when I arrive. Hsu Shen, you go now. Prepare the boat, and begin sending your men on to Lioantung."

"As you command, Lord."

The minutes rolled away. At last there was no one left but Lord Kuo and Pan ku. "Lord," Shih-ka'i said, "I'll give you a few minutes before I come through. Have a good ambush ready. The transfer may waken it."

Wen-chin nodded and departed.

"Go, Pan ku."

"Lord..."

"I'll be there in a few minutes."

"As you will, Lord." Pan ku disappeared.

Shih-ka'i stared down at the box. What would the godlet do? Surely transfer would waken it. Could they control it long enough to put it into a boat? How powerful was it?

He waited five minutes. Before transferring he set the portal to collapse behind him. No one would return the box to the desert should it grab a man as it did the dead. He took a deep breath, stepped into the portal.

The thing wakened as Shih-ka'i reached the island. A finger of power stabbed his brain. He staggered. "You!" the thing in there bellowed. He moaned. Its rage was stronger than he had expected. Its angry, greedy tentacles drove into him, taking control....

Ssu-ma Shih-ka'i was stubborn. He turned, threw the box. It bounced across the floor.

Lord Kuo smacked it with a bolt of power that did no harm at all. Shih-ka'i dove after the box, smacked a fist against its side. It tumbled onward, into the pulsing black maw of the portal.

A dwindling scream faded from Shih-ka'i's mind.

Pan ku reached his side. "Are you hurt, Lord?"

Shih-ka'i allowed himself to be lifted to his feet. "I think I'll live, Pan ku. Damn my bones, I'm afraid I'm going to." He leaned on his batman. "It almost caught my soul."

Hsu Shen came roaring in. "What happened?"

"It woke up," Lord Kuo explained. "My Lord threw it back through the transfer."

"Oh, no! It's back in the desert? What'll we do?"

Shih-ka'i caught his breath. "No. Not the desert. No. Caught in the transfer stream. Done with this world. Forget the boat, Hsu Shen. Let me rest before I return to Lioantung.

We're done here."

Pan ku was helping him leave when the air crackled behind them. A man stepped from a portal. "Lord?" he inquired.

Shih-ka'i turned. "Lord Lun-yu?"

"The Princess Mist is in Lioantung, Lord. Thought you'd want to know." Tasi-feng surveyed his surroundings. He seemed puzzled. Lord Kuo tried to make himself invisible.

Shih-ka'i sighed. "All right. I'll be there directly. Pan ku, let's collect our gear. Hsu Shen, send the rest of your men out."

Lord Kuo remained apart from Shih-ka'i till Tasi-feng departed.

"Pan ku," Shih-ka'i said as they approached their quarters, "I think I've aged a hundred years."

A deputation of nervous Tervola waited in the transfer chamber. Tasi-feng said, "Lord Shih-mihn is entertaining the Princess, Lord."

"What's that racket?"

"Harassment from outside, Lord."

"Tell the lady I'll be with her as soon as I've studied the situation."

"Lord?"

"You heard me. Lord Lun-yu, come with me. Tell me everything she's said." He led the way to a high gallery in the old fortress at Lioantung's heart. From it he could see most of the city and much of the countryside beyond. Pan ku dogged their steps.

"This was a monastery in the old days," Tasi-feng said.

"Really? Interesting. But I'm more interested in current events. What's the Matayangan situation?"

"She gives the impression it's under control. Lord Kuo struck a particularly savage blow before... before..."

"I see. What did she say she wants?"

"She's investigating our position. The army is stretched thin. If either front sours we might have to abandon the western provinces."

Shih-ka'i leaned out a window, watched dragons circle. "The worst is over here. We've eliminated their godling. There'll be no more debacles like the Tusghus. What have they been doing?"

"Getting ready to storm."

"Storm? That's crazy. They don't have the manpower."

"They didn't have it at the Tusghus, Lord."

"So true. But they haven't the weapon they had then, either." Shih-ka'i scanned the darkness. "When will they start?"

Tasi-feng shrugged. "If he follows precedent, not for a few days."

"Don't count on it. He's learning." Shih-ka'i glared at the night. "Damn. I'd like to get my hands on him."

Something skittered behind them. Shih-ka'i whirled. "A mouse, Lord," Pan ku said. "Strangest thing. Sat there just staring at you."

"Let's see what's on the woman's mind," Shih-ka'i said.

"Lord…"

"Not to worry. I'll comport myself properly. I'm as fond of my position as you are of yours."

Shih-ka'i had encountered Mist twice before, during her first reign, and each time his first glimpse had hit him like a blow between the eyes. Though he steeled himself, the result was no different this time. Hard to believe that anything that beautiful was human. Hard to believe that she was the child of that ugly old madman, the Demon Prince.

She rose when he entered the small chamber where she was holding court. As his legion commanders bowed to him, she extended her hand. Never having been formally presented to any of Shinsan's masters, Shih-ka'i was not sure how to respond. He made the slight bow due an army superior. The woman seemed satisfied. "Lord Ssu-ma."

"A pleasure, my Princess."

"The pleasure is mine." She seated herself. Lord Shih-mihn remained at her right hand, a man smitten. "I've been reviewing your campaign."

Shih-ka'i bowed again. "Mercy, Mistress," he said. "I've done my best, but I'm only a pig farmer's son." His tone did not match his words. They were mere formality.

"Mercy isn't necessary, Lord Ssu-ma. Not even the great Lords Chin or Wu could have done more."

Shih-ka'i surveyed his brethren, surprised. They stood tall and silent, unreadable behind their masks. What was this? They had spoken for a pig farmer's son?

The woman continued, "I have complete confidence in you. I'm not here to interfere, only to familiarize myself with your situation. These are trying times for the empire."

Shih-ka'i did not respond immediately. Tasi-feng stepped into the breach. "Lord Lun-yu, Mistress. Commander, Seventeenth."

"A legion I remember well, from times when Lord Wu commanded."

"Those days are gone, Mistress. As is Lord Wu."

"Gone, forgiven, and forgotten."

"Thank you, Mistress. There's a way you could help. The Deliverer has a companion of great power. We're unable to defeat her. To make the point directly, you might match yourself against her."

Shih-ka'i regained his composure. "My commanders tell me she's almost as strong as yourself, Mistress."

"This woman is the Deliverer's source of power?"

"One source. He had another, a godling of ancient times, that resided in the desert to the east. Tonight a Tervola named Hsu Shen and I destroyed it. Now the Deliverer and his woman are on their own."

"They're outside now?"

"Yes, Mistress."

"Let's have a look." Shih-ka'i bowed. His entire staff

started to follow. Mist said, "You gentlemen return to work. Wait. Lord Shih-mihn. Your granaries are full?"

"Yes, Mistress." Puzzled.

"This place is filthy with mice. You might do something if you anticipate a long siege."

"Yes, Mistress."

Softly, Shih-ka'i said, "It won't be long. They're down to the lees of their strength. He's planning another surprise."

Mist glanced over her shoulder, gave Pan ku a look filled with meaning. The decurion was not intimidated. Shih-ka'i said, "Pan ku is my shadow."

"As you will."

Ten minutes later, as they approached the city's northern wall, Shih-ka'i heard a scrabbling sound behind him, then a meaty thump as one body hit another. He spun, saw Pan ku push a large dog away from himself. The hilt of the decurion's shortsword protruded from the beast's chest. The dog twitched, whimpered, lay still. Pan ku retrieved his weapon, separated the beast's head and limbs.

"Pan ku?"

"I'm all right, Lord. Didn't bite through my armor."

"What happened?"

"Came out of the dark straight at you, Lord."

Mist squealed, "Down!" A flash blinded Shih-ka'i for an instant. His vision cleared. Another dog lay at his feet. Its left shoulder had been burned to the bone.

"Maybe we should've let the others come," Mist said.

"I think I see the direction of his next attack."

He was right. Similar attacks were occurring throughout the city.

"Your commanders say he has a huge hatred for the empire. Any idea why?"

"Not the least, Mistress. We don't know who they are, or where they came from." Shih-ka'i resumed walking, "Keep a good watch, Pan ku. He might try again."

From the city wall he could see the woman in white standing atop a knoll a third of a mile away. She glowed in the darkness. "That's her," he told Mist.

She did not respond for half a minute. Then, "Curious. She's not alive. Not in the usual sense. She doesn't have a physical body. Yet there she is."

"There!" said Shih-ka'i, suddenly feeling the presence of the Deliverer. "To the left of her."

Mist shifted her attention, gasped. "It can't be!"

"Mistress?"

She was walking away already. Shih-ka'i and Pan ku trotted to catch up. She said, "Stay stubborn. Give me at least three more days. I think I know the cure for your Deliverer."

Shih-ka'i heard the soft pad of animal feet, but nothing charged out of the darkness. "I hope so, Mistress. I hope so."

14

YEAR 1016 AFE

THE SEED OF DOOM

DAYS HAD PASSED. Varthlokkur was at Mist's home, making certain neither she nor her new subjects had left Kavelin any unwanted gifts. The King walked in. The wizard was surprised.

"Found anything?" Bragi asked.

"Couple of inactive portals. Nothing else."

"Have to leave one working so she can drop in on her kids. Can you fix it so a gang of Tervola don't come tumbling through?"

"I've been considering using a demon guard."

The King made a face.

"I have a particular one in mind. A bureaucratic type. He'll throw anyone but Mist into stasis and defer to higher authority."

The King chuckled. "Come on. Be serious."

"I am. The creature exists."

"What about the others?"

"I shut them down. Radeachar is out looking for any that

might be hidden away from the house."

"What about Maisak?"

"It's clean. We went through it last night. Found four."

"Think she was planning something?"

Varthlokkur shrugged. "My guess is, she used them for communication while she was getting her plot together. Not that she wouldn't take advantage of them later if we overlooked them."

"How's the baby?"

"Perfect. And Nepanthe is up walking around. We decided to call her Smyrena."

"That's an odd name."

"Not so much so in the old days. It was my mother's name. Nepanthe's idea."

"What about Ethrian? Caught anything new?"

Varthlokkur felt the unreasoning anger beginning to rise within him. He clamped down on it, growled, "No. I told you I don't want to talk about it. Let sleeping dogs lie. I think I've finally gotten Nepanthe off the damned subject."

"I got a problem you can maybe help with. Mist's kids."

"Nepanthe was talking about them this morning. They're her brother's kids. We'll take them off your hands as soon as she can cope with them." He had no enthusiasm for the task. He suspected he was too old and set in his ways to father Smyrena properly, let alone to foster a band of stepnephews.

"What are your plans? I'm pretty well through this crisis."

"But this wasn't the crisis you summoned me for. My friend, you played a little game with your eastern obsession and won. That's over. Now you have to come back and face your real problems. And you've got big ones. You've been using Mist's coup to distract yourself."

"Michael and I can handle Kavelin. My big worry is still Shinsan."

Then you're a fool, Varthlokkur thought, but didn't say it. "I doubt it. Well, I'm done here. I'll get back to Nepanthe.

Seeing as you don't need me anymore, she'll want to get ready to travel. She'll want to make long lists of things we just have to drag along with us." He got out before the King irritated him more than he had already.

He thought he'd better stall Nepanthe for a week or two. It shouldn't take Michael that long to show the King how much trouble he really had.

"He's having dinner with the Queen," Dahl Haas said. "I can't disturb him. I thought you went back to Shinsan last week."

"I did. And now I'm back here. And if you don't take that message to the King right now I'm going to bless you with a spell that'll leave you sterile and impotent. Do I make myself clear?" Mist was tired and frightened and angry.

"All right. On your head be his wrath."

"You let me worry about the wrath. Just drag that note upstairs."

Haas returned in five minutes. "All right. He says come on up."

Mist turned away from the mirror where she had been considering herself. She looked older by a decade. She'd had very little sleep for a week. As she followed the King's adjutant through the halls, her legs felt twice their normal weight.

Haas showed her into the Queen's sitting room. The King met her there. "Through here. Been rough?" he asked, leading her through the apartment to a dining room. "It may not be polite for me to say so, but you look awful."

"Hello, Inger."

"Hello, Mist."

There seemed to be a mild frost. Mist shrugged, told Bragi, "I feel awful. Could you spare a meal for a tired old woman? I've been eating on the run since I left. Haven't had anything since yesterday."

Inger said, "Of course." Though she'd never gotten along with Mist, suddenly she was all solicitude. She gestured. One of her women departed.

Mist sagged into a chair. She noted the quick change but was too wrapped up in her misery to care. "I'm exhausted."

The King frowned. "Trouble? What the hell are you doing back? They didn't throw you out already, did they?"

"No. Not yet. No. I came to beg for help. Again."

"What for? You got what you wanted."

"This is something a little different. I got all the troubles, too. I can't handle this on my own."

The King settled himself opposite her. His face became more empathetic. "Go on."

"It's our problem in the east. I got a close-up look. It was worse than I expected. Lord Ssu-ma thought he was on top of things, but... Bragi, he's got his back against the wall. He's been driven back hundreds of miles to an old fortress town called Lioantung. He can't go any farther. He's going to make a stand with what's left of Northern and Eastern Armies."

Bragi looked puzzled. "So? What does that mean to me?"

"He won't just lose a battle if he loses Lioantung. He won't just lose Shinsan. The man is fighting for the world. It lives or dies with him."

"Oh, really!" Inger said. "Mist, that's just too much to swallow."

Mist ignored her. She did not like the woman. She spoke directly to the King, though she answered the Queen's predictable objection. "Bragi, Lioantung is the last obstacle between the Deliverer and the heart of the empire. The last defense of regions where people are packed together several thousand to the square mile. If Lioantung goes, there's nothing to stop the Deliverer from devouring the populations of whole provinces."

"All right. You've got me curious. Start from the beginning. I really don't know what you're talking about."

She went back and began with Lord Kuo's intuition about the eastern desert and his having sent Lord Ssu-ma Shih-ka'i to take command. She meant to edit, but found everything gushing out, without any control. She told every detail she knew, up through her recent visit to Lioantung.

"Armies of dead men?" Bragi murmured. "Really?" He seemed unable to choose between horror and amusement. "And he can take over anyone they kill, too?"

"Exactly. He can even control the living if they're not protected, though it's harder. Animals, too."

"The dead rising against the living. It's a Trolledyngjan draug tale come true... Up where I was raised the old folks liked to scare us kids with tales about the dead coming down from the mountains or out of the sea to carry us off. Draugs, we called them. The walking dead. But those were just wintertime stories." He closed his eyes and looked thoughtful for half a minute. "Mist?"

"Yes?"

"You haven't said why you came to me. You've got the toughest army in the world."

"It's all tied up. And because the Deliverer is going to come after you when he's finished with Shinsan."

"Me? Me personally, or just the west in general?"

"You. Very personally."

"Why? I've put a lot of people in the ground, but none that would want to get even so bad they'd get back up again."

"A grudge, Bragi. Definitely a grudge. This dark Deliverer, this warlord of the dead, is driven by hatred. Something twisted and molded and reshaped him till all he cares about is revenge. On Shinsan. On you. Because, Bragi, the Deliverer is Ethrian. My nephew. Your godson. Nepanthe and Mocker's boy."

She expected the news to smack him like a blow from a club, and she was not disappointed. He gulped air like a fish out of water. "But... but..." He stared, unable to accept. The

Queen stared at him, her face pallid, one shaky hand held at her lips. Bragi tried to say something, apparently could not.

"It's true, Bragi. I'll swear any oath you want. Something in the east saved him from the Pracchia. He's been out there all this time. That something saved him, made him an instrument of destruction and vessel of hatred, gave him immense power, then lost control. I saw him at Lioantung, Bragi. Physically he looks like you'd expect after all this time. But inside he's not Ethrian anymore. He's more like the embodiment of a natural force gone mad."

Inger croaked something. Bragi groaned. "I believe her. Look at her. She's scared silly. Now we know why Varthlokkur was so damned cranky whenever Ethrian's name came up. He knew."

Mist admitted her fear. "You're right. I'm so frightened I can't think. I just want to run... I keep wishing I'd left it in Lord Kuo's lap. I didn't bargain for this. You know what history will do to me if I can't stop Ethrian? If there *is* any history?"

Bragi mused, "I really do understand Varthlokkur now."

"What?"

"He knew. He's known for a long time. He's mentioned Ethrian several times since he's been here. Hinting that he might still be alive. Acting like a man wrestling his conscience. Now I know what he meant when he said he couldn't tell Nepanthe because it would destroy her." He levered himself out of his chair. "He even threatened me when I suggested she ought to know there was a chance Ethrian was alive."

Mist looked up at him. He was pale as death. As frightened as she. He believed. Somehow, that took a huge load off her shoulders. Shared fear is softened fear, she thought, recalling one of the lessons taught young soldiers.

"Let's go talk to him," Bragi suggested.

"I will need his help too," she admitted. "And almost certainly Nepanthe's."

The King winced. "Don't expect him to cooperate. He's determined to keep it from her."

"I'll sell him. I have to."

"Be careful what you say. I've never seen him so touchy. He said he'd pull out on me if I even dropped a hint to Nepanthe."

Inger glanced up sharply, startled. A strange look entered her eyes. What the devil? Mist wondered. "Uhm," she grunted. At another time she would have incorporated that bit of intelligence into her plans. Not now, though. All she wanted now was a way out of her dilemma.

The Queen's servant brought the meal Mist had requested. She snatched the main platter and ate with her fingers as the King led her out into the castle's drafty halls. A few queries about Varthlokkur led them to the small castle library.

The wizard glanced up as they entered. He half stood, dismayed, when he saw her face. He made a sign against the evil eye.

She launched into her tale before he could speak. His dismay became despair. She could imagine the emotional storm inside him. Usually he was a man of stone.

His face hardened. "Enough, woman. The answer is no. I won't touch it. Find another way."

"But..."

"I'm not going to let Nepanthe see what he's become. She's too delicately balanced. She thinks he's dead. Leave him in his grave."

"What are you going to tell her when his dead men get to these parts?" the King demanded.

"Mist is exaggerating. His armies will fall apart."

"*You* are sticking your head in the sand," Mist snapped. "They've held up against the finest we could put in their way. He made mistakes in the early going. He's still a child. But he's learned. He's bottomed out. From now on he'll only get stronger. Unless the three or four people who mean most to him emotionally shatter the chains of hatred binding him."

Anger reddened the wizard's cheeks. "You speak with conviction and passion, but you don't know what you're asking. The answer has to be no."

Bragi suggested, "Then don't go yourself. Send the Unborn. Make the lie truth."

"Lie? Truth?"

"Have Radeachar kill him."

"No. Listen. You don't understand. I can't help. It's your problem, Mist. You deal with it. Bragi, I told you before, if you tell Nepanthe about this...."

"Yeah. Yeah. I know. I won't. Even though I think you're wrong. Totally, insanely wrong. I won't."

"You're behaving irrationally, Varthlokkur," Mist said.

"Try to understand. I want to protect my wife."

"You don't give her enough credit," Mist said. "She looks neurotic, but she's a lot tougher than she pretends. She's had to be."

And the King: "I don't think you're protecting her at all. I think you're protecting yourself. From your own insecurities. You're just scared of change. Change might alter your relationship..."

"Be still!" the wizard snapped. And, "Just remember what the Thing did to you the other day, with the succession. Recall how the vote went? You understand what it means?" He smiled evilly. "You can't afford to lose me now."

"Wizard, I get nasty when people try to twist my arm."

"Better get used to it."

"We've been on opposite sides before. I can live without you."

"You've been warned. Stay away from my wife." Varthlokkur shifted his gaze to Mist. She rocked under the impact of his glare. "The Deliverer is your problem, woman. Ethrian is dead."

She sagged, defeated. The King took her arm. "We're

wasting our time here. He's gone goofy. Maybe the Brotherhood will help. You have friends there."

"It's not sorcery I need," Mist replied. "We have that aplenty in Shinsan. I need people who can reach Ethrian emotionally."

"We'll think of something." Over his shoulder, Bragi said, "I'll remember this, wizard."

Varthlokkur was startled by the man's intensity, but only for an instant. He slammed a book to the floor. Mist jumped. Her nerves were raw. Outside, she asked, "What now?"

She didn't like this feeling of helplessness, this having to come west to petition aid. It made her feel impotent and incompetent....

"You and me, I guess. Maybe an aunt and a godfather can do the job. Come on. I have to tell Gjerdrum and Derel where I'm going. Old Crankwort back there was right about one thing. I've got trouble, judging by the tricks the Thing pulled while we were setting you up. I have to make sure my ass is covered while I'm gone. Otherwise I'm liable to come home and find myself out of a job."

"There's not much point to just you and me going. We represent everything Ethrian hates. I don't think anyone but his mother could reach him now."

"We'll have to try, won't we? If he's as dangerous as you say?"

"I suppose."

"How long can you wait? Maybe Varthlokkur will come around."

"Not long. Lord Ssu-ma is a stubborn man, but he can't hold out forever."

"If you have a favorite god, send up a prayer. Maybe if Varthlokkur calms down, he'll take a closer look. If things are as bad as you say. He's basically a decent sort. He has a conscience."

"Maybe. And maybe he's just a blind old fool."

Varthlokkur eased into his apartment an hour after his confrontation with Mist and the King. His hands still shook. He was scared. It had been centuries since he had flown into so towering a rage. He'd had to use old fear-fighting tricks from apprenticeship days to calm himself this much.

There was something wrong with him. Some madness smoked through his mind, twisting and knotting. It wasn't like him to lose control. Was Bragi right? Was his real problem a childish insecurity?

Could Nepanthe handle this? Was she more resilient than he believed?

Had he sold himself a false hope when he'd decided Ethrian would be defeated by sheer entropy?

He lighted a candle, sat, tried to read an old, handprinted text which claimed to be a true history of the origins of Man upon his world. The calligraphy kept sliding out of focus.

Damn! His world was falling apart. It had taken him ages to put a decent life together, and now, suddenly, the whole thing hung by a thread. Hell yes, he was insecure. And when you had fought as long as he had, you damned well deserved something good out of the rest of your life....

A shadow fell across his lap. He jumped, startled. "Nepanthe! What're you doing out of bed? You had your exercise. You should be resting...." His heart sank as he saw the look on her face. Fear hit like a hammer's blow.

She was dressed for heavy weather. She had the baby bundled and wrapped. "I need my son, Varth."

"Oh, no," he said softly. "Oh, no. Why?"

"Ethrian is alive, isn't he? You've known it all along. You've been lying to me."

"No, dear. I told you..."

"You told me lies. Lies and lies and lies. He's at a place in Shinsan called Lioantung. And you didn't want me to know."

The rage welled up again. "I told him..."

Nepanthe herself was powered by a cold anger. She

weathered his outburst without flinching. "You warned who? What are you doing to me? Varth, I want to see my son. Do you hear me? Mist is here somewhere. She came to see you. I'm going back with her."

Varthlokkur ignored her. He ambled into their bedroom, stared down into Smyrena's empty cradle. After a time he went to the window. "Come, Radeachar. Come, my only friend."

"Why did you lie to me?" Nepanthe demanded. "Damnit, Varth, I'm talking to you. Answer me!"

He whirled. "Did they tell you what your son is?"

"What *they?* Who are you talking about? Tell me."

"Ragnarson and that Shinsaner bitch."

"I haven't seen either of them. What have they got to do with it? Never mind. Tell me about Ethrian. Then find Mist and tell her I'm going with her."

Anger fed upon anger. Their shouting increased in pitch and intensity. The Unborn arrived at the window and hovered there, unremarked.

"All right, damnit!" Varthlokkur suddenly shrieked. "We're going. Be it on your head, woman." He whirled, stamped out of the room muttering, "Bragi, you'll pay. You cut your own throat this time. The wolves are circling you right now. I'm just going to sit back and laugh while they pull you down."

Nepanthe watched her husband go, baffled behind her anger. What was that all about? she wondered. All that noise about Bragi and Mist. And she hadn't seen either in ages... They must have known too. They must have been keeping it from her. She never would have known had not the Queen come to see Smyrena and mentioned it in passing.

Poor Inger. Now she would get yelled at too.

The hell with them. All of them. She was going to see her son. What they liked didn't matter.

15

E THRIAN'S DEAD WARRIORS brought a chair plundered from a manor near Lioantung. He settled into it. Sahmanan seated herself on the earth beside him, leaning against the chair. "Can you tell me your idea now?"

"I suppose." The fun had gone out of teasing her. "I'll use their animals against them. And the bodies of those the animals kill."

"Won't they destroy them?"

"Probably. The dogs, cats, horses, and such, that they can catch. But how do you guard against rats that attack you when you're sleeping?"

"It might work. You're planning a siege?"

"We can afford it. They don't expect help. This's the battle that'll make or break us."

"What about the army?" She nodded toward the nearest dead warriors. "They're only good for a few days."

"They won't go to waste. Let's get started. Guard me." He

dropped the ties to his body, drifted into the city. Lioantung was a maze of twisty streets and alien architecture. Whole quarters were empty. He would recruit among abandoned animals....

The enemy were busily preparing for his assault. They seemed unconcerned. The battle in the forest had restored their confidence. Only the Tervola themselves were uncertain.

They were debating what to do about the animals....

He flung himself into the darkness-haunted streets, found a stable. He seized a horse's dim mind. It reared, broke down its stall, hammered a stableboy to the earth.

Ethrian seized the body, found a hayhook, slipped into the night. He stole up behind a legionnaire....

So it went, hour after hour. The enemy responded. By dawn no soldier went anywhere alone. Next day Lord Ssu-ma ordered all animals destroyed. Ethrian returned to his body.

"You look exhausted," Sahmanan told him.

"A little. Did they try very hard?"

She gestured at their surroundings. The earth was scorched. His chair had been reduced to toothpicks. "I thought they had us once. I barely hung on."

"They're going to kill the animals. It's time to send in the dead."

"Don't you want to rest?"

"I don't have time."

"Ethrian..."

"Be still." He reached out, gathered the threads. Corpses shambled toward the city. Dragons took the air. Some carried multiple riders, some supported the storming of the walls. The legions left off slaughtering livestock and rushed to the battlements.

Ethrian continued the attack till almost nothing remained of his army. He and Sahmanan were the only survivors outside the city. Inside, in the abandoned quarters, he squirreled away a thousand bodies.

He roamed the city in his out-of-body state, occasionally slipping into an animal to listen. His enemies were as tired as he.

Wearily, they resumed the slaughter. Some commenced a house-to-house search for the dead.

Ethrian returned to Sahmanan. "Rest, Ethrian," she insisted. "You're killing yourself."

"One more thing, just to keep them busy. Then I will."

He went back into Lioantung, seeking rats. And rats he found, of course, for Lioantung was an old city, well stocked with vermin.

He began in Lord Ssu-ma's citadel headquarters. In a hundred places rats suddenly streaked across rooms, overturning lamps. Most of the fires were extinguished immediately, yet a few started where there were no witnesses.

Ethrian returned to his body. "That should keep them occupied. Wake me if anything important happens."

He slept fourteen hours and wakened still only partially refreshed. "What's happened?" he demanded.

"Nothing. They've been too busy fighting fires."

He went into the city again. The last conflagrations were under control. Weary legionnaires were staggering to their barracks, cursing him, praying for rest. He gave them no respite.

Here, there, he sent rats to the jugulars of the sleeping. The dead he raised against the living. He shuttled from barracks to barracks. The Tervola mounted sleepwatches. He shifted his attention to the headquarters itself, then to the wall, hurling animal after animal at the sentries. He used dead men to open a gate, brought in beasts of the field and forest. Confuse and frighten, confuse and frighten, he chanted to himself.

When doing nothing else, he moved his hidden soldiers inward from the empty quarters. Slowly, slowly, they closed on Lord Ssu-ma's headquarters....

There were no more large city animals. He had no time to recruit in the forest. The Tervola turned their art to the destruction of mice, rats, and squirrels. "It's a race now," he told Sahmanan. "I have them diverted, though. With luck, my next attack will kill so many Tervola you can overpower the rest."

His attack lasted three hours. Afterward, he returned to Sahmanan. "That should do it. We'll finish after I've rested."

"Ethrian, something's happened to the Great One."

"What?"

"I don't know. I don't feel him there anymore. It worries me."

"Does it matter?"

"Maybe. We might need him again."

"Is he up to something?"

"I don't know."

"We'll go see when this is done."

"We can't. The flyers are gone."

Ethrian gave her a sharp look. He did not like her tone. "You trying to say something?"

"No... Yes. Ethrian, you're Nahaman all over again. Just as filled with bitterness and hate and unreason."

"Be quiet. I have to sleep. We finish them when I wake up."

A morning sun hung low and red when Ethrian sloughed his haunted dreams. Sahmanan was shaking him. "What?" he grumbled.

"Wake up. They're up to something. Look." She pointed toward the city. Soldiers had come forth. A squat, chunky Tervola bore a white flag. His bodyguard spread out near the gate. Strangers moved up on the Tervola's sides. Next to him, on either hand, a woman walked. A man walked outside each woman.

"Oh, Lord," Ethrian said, stricken. "Oh, Lord, no."

"What is it? What is it, Ethrian?"

His breathing became ragged. Deep inside him, something stirred. A shadow uncoiled. He shrieked. The darkness welled up. The world disappeared.

"Ethrian!" Sahmanan chafed his wrists, slapped his cheeks. "Wake up! Please?" She glanced toward the city. "They're almost here. I need somebody to tell me what to do."

Shih-ka'i stood at a stiff parade rest, ignoring the pain of his wounds. The Princess and her party entered the command center. He snapped to attention. His surviving commanders saluted. Mist eyed them, appalled. "What happened, Lord Ssu-ma?"

"We held, Mistress." Shih-ka'i studied her companions. Two men and a woman, of western stamp. The woman carried an infant. The younger man had the warrior look. His gaze did not rest. His lips were taut and pale. The older, thinner man looked angry. Shih-ka'i faced his Princess, his question implied.

"The wizard Varthlokkur," she said, indicating the older man. A chill scrambled down Shih-ka'i's spine. "His wife, Nepanthe, and their daughter."

Shih-ka'i bowed to the woman. "My Lady."

Mist said, "I'll have to translate."

Shih-ka'i nodded, considered the third man. The wizard's bodyguard?

"King Bragi of Kavelin," Mist said.

Shih-ka'i went rigid. His commanders stirred angrily. He admonished them with a gesture. "The Ragnarson of Baxendala and Palmisano?"

"The same."

One of the Tervola stepped forward...

"Meng Chiao! Comport yourself. Mistress, because of this man he lost three brothers, four sons, and his legion." Shih-ka'i planted himself before Ragnarson. The westerner towered over him. He removed his mask, stared into the man's eyes. He saw no fear in those pools of blue. The man said something.

Mist translated. "He says you look like an honest soldier. The first he's seen among Tervola."

Shih-ka'i smiled, replied, "You'd find me more stubborn than Lord Ko." He awaited Mist's translation, asked, "Mistress, what is this?"

"These people were close to the Deliverer once. His grandfather. His mother. His godfather."

The commanders stirred again.

"Mistress?"

"And he's my nephew by marriage. Lord Chin kidnapped him during the Pracchia thing. We thought he'd died. Somehow, he survived, made an alliance with your godling, and came after us, assuming we were behind his misfortunes."

Shih-ka'i paced. Finally, "What do you propose, Mistress?"

"That we go talk to him. That we shatter his illusions. That we steal away his cause for destroying the empire."

Shih-ka'i surveyed the visitors. "These people have no reason to help."

"They will. For their own reasons."

"Then let's try it. Pan ku. Bodyguards."

"Lord!" Pan ku saluted snappily, departed. He returned in minutes. "Ready, Lord."

Shih-ka'i explained, "The Deliverer has made it impossible to walk the streets unguarded."

The city was a ruin gutted by fire, shattered by blows from the skull-faced things. Every street boasted its heap of charred bones.

Mist said something. Ragnarson grunted, conceding awe at the devastation. The wizard betrayed no reaction at all. He had a big anger on. His wife seemed included in the flame of his ire. Shih-ka'i dropped back, doffed his mask, examined the baby. He expressed his approval with a smile. The woman responded in kind.

"Why is it so quiet?" Mist asked.

"The calm before the storm. He's resting."

"Could you have stopped him again?"

"I doubt it. This's our last cast of the dice."

They reached the gate. Soldiers swung it wide. Pan ku handed his master a stick with a white cloth attached. Shih-ka'i stepped out of the city. "Hold the guards here, Pan ku."

"Lord?"

"If the Princess, the wizard Varthlokkur, and I can't hold our own out there, there's no hope anyway."

"As you command, Lord." Pan ku wheeled, rushed inside, hurried to the ramparts, found a light ballista. He laid it with all the care his master gave preparation of a spell. The Deliverer would hear from Pan ku if he attempted any treachery.

Shih-ka'i walked toward the hummock where the woman was waking the Deliverer. He kept his stride purposeful. He would not betray his fear to these westerners.

The Deliverer rose, brushed his hair back, stared, went down. The woman knelt over him. He rose again, exuding arrogance. He gestured. A panther came round the hummock and curled at his feet. A bear appeared, seated itself at his right hand. A huge forest buffalo, its eyes wild, stationed itself to the woman's left.

Shih-ka'i told Mist, "Keep your eye on the woman." Then, "What's wrong with him?"

"He knows these people. He's imagining what they think of him."

"I see." He halted five steps from the Deliverer. A short leap for the panther, he reflected. He glared. This whining child had destroyed two armies?

Mist stopped when he did. Ragnarson and Varthlokkur followed suit. The woman with the infant did not. "Ethrian?" she said in her own tongue. "Ethrian? Look. This's your sister. Her name is Smyrena."

Torment filled the boy's eyes. He started blubbering. "Mama. I thought they killed you. I thought they killed you. They told me...."

Nepanthe shifted Smyrena to her left arm. Her right she slipped round the boy, pulling him against her shoulder. "It's all right. It's all right, Ethrian. It's over now. It's all right."

The air was still. The world was silent but for the boy's weeping. And yet, the hair and clothing of the woman in white stirred as if blown by a rising wind. Shih-ka'i glanced at Mist. "Mistress?"

"Not to worry. She's happy for him." Silent communication passed between the women. Mist nodded.

Something drifted down from the sky. It hovered behind the hummock. Shih-ka'i looked only once. "The Unborn," he murmured. He had heard of the thing. Its presence was more offensive than he had believed possible.

The woods buffalo snorted, loped away. The bear followed, breaking into a wild shamble. The panther rose elegantly, licked a paw, strolled toward the wilds. Nepanthe started walking her son toward the city.

Shih-ka'i glanced at Mist again. "It's over, Lord Ssu-ma. It's really over. Go ahead."

Mother and son passed him. He turned. The wizard and King kept pace as he followed. He glanced back, saw Mist and the woman trailing. The woman floated more than walked.

His tension drained away. He felt limp. Almost disappointed. He hadn't realized how tense he was....

It began suddenly. He did not know anything was wrong till his mother was hurled away, and he went rigid. A dark nimbus surrounded him.

The air crackled. Shih-ka'i had felt the same thing just before the disaster on the Tusghus. "Mistress! Princess!"

Varthlokkur flung himself forward, caught his woman before she fell. Ragnarson had sword in hand with almost magical quickness. He crouched, growling in his harsh western tongue.

Mist shrieked, "Ethrian! Stop!" Shih-ka'i heard echoes of the other woman in her voice.

He tackled the youth. The boy remained rigid. Shih-ka'i clamped his fingers round a stiff throat.

Something moved on Lioantung's wall. Bodyguards scrambled. The western King bellowed. His sword hammered the air above Shih-ka'i's head.

The youth bucked violently. Shih-ka'i bounced to his feet as the King plucked a broken spear from the earth, a ballista shaft diverted from its deadly arc. "I owe you, westerner." He faced the Deliverer.

Madness filled the boy's eyes. His mother wept against the wizard's chest. The boy's mouth slowly opened.

The woman in white stepped past Shih-ka'i. A faraway voice said, "Ethrian?... Oh, no! It's *Him*. The stone god has taken him."

"Impossible," Shih-ka'i snapped. "We destroyed him." He and Hsu Shen, Pan ku and Lord Kuo... Hadn't they?

Gently, Varthlokkur passed his wife to Ragnarson. There was some trust left there. He made a small gesture. The Unborn drifted closer.

"No. Don't," said the woman in white. "I summoned him. It's only just that I banish him."

The fury of an immense inner struggle distorted the boy's face. His mouth opened wide. He began filling his lungs. He tried forcing his hands to his lips. They hovered, palsied, a few inches away.

The air crackled as it had before the disaster on the Tusghus. Shih-ka'i snatched up a handful of earth, flung himself forward, forced the soil into the Deliverer's mouth. His off hand he drove viciously into the boy's chest. He felt bone crack under his fingers.

Sahmanan's voice seemed to come from everywhere and nowhere, like the wailing of the mothers of the thousands when they learned what had become of their sons in Lord Kuo's ill-fated western campaign. The youth faced her, pale, clutching his chest. He croaked, "Sahmanan! No! I beg you... I'll give you anything. All the power I gave him. I'll give you the Word. You could be queen of the world."

The keening grew louder. Shih-ka'i ground his palms against the earholes of his mask, could not shut it out.

The Deliverer's mouth opened wide. Vomit gouted. Again he drew breath for a shout.

Sahmanan's voice cracked. The youth went rigid. He seemed to flicker, to fade, to spin, to become two distinct Ethrians, one of which was a shadow of the other so bleak and dark light shied away. A scintillant mist gathered, spiraling inward. Then only the black Ethrian could be seen, rocking slowly, trying to widen its mouth.

Cracks of fire ran over the boy of darkness. Smouldering flakes fell away. Smoke drifted on a rising breeze. Suddenly— whoosh!—the rest of him flung skyward in one roaring, expanding black cloud.

Shih-ka'i felt that same despairing cry he had sensed after hurling the box into the portal on Hsu Shen's island. The earth trembled and glowed where the boy had stood. A dome of air shimmered overhead.

"He's gone," said the woman in white. "And when he goes, I must follow. We'll trouble you no more." Though the breeze persisted, her clothing no longer stirred. She faced the woman weeping against Ragnarson's chest. "I'm sorry. Tell her I'm sorry. I didn't want to hurt anyone. I just never found the will to...."

Shih-ka'i could no longer hear her. Light passed through her now. He shouted, "You're forgiven." He turned to Mist. "Princess, are you all right?"

"Yes. Just a little shaken. I thought you'd disposed of it."

"I thought I had. We dumped the thing into a transfer with no exit side. How could it have escaped?"

The wizard Varthlokkur spoke for the first time. He sounded contemptuous. "Use your reason, Lord Ssu-ma. Time doesn't obtain in the transfer stream. Neither does death. Now, finally, we know the nature of the horror that's lurked there since Tuan Hua opened the first pair of portals. It was that thing.

"He found himself alive after you thought you were rid of him. He cruised back and forth across the centuries preying on unlucky travelers. He searched out the one time Ethrian made a transfer, penetrated him, and hibernated till his own absence from the present wakened him. Why do you think the boy assumed the thing's madness so willingly? He wasn't that sort of child. Had he not had his father's strength and stubbornness he would have succumbed far more swiftly and completely."

Varthlokkur turned away, took his wife from Ragnarson. "I'm sorry, dear. I tried to protect you from this."

"You were wrong, Varth. You shouldn't have shielded me. I'm not a child. We might have saved him if we'd come earlier."

Pain filled the wizard's eyes.

Shih-ka'i considered the dark pillar of cloud, the coruscation doming the fallen Deliverer. He searched himself for some sign of elation. There was nothing there. His war was over and won, and he felt like a loser. He started trudging toward the city. The others followed, except the foreign woman. She remained near her fallen son.

Tasi-feng hurried to meet Shih-ka'i. "Lord... It's your man Pan ku."

"What?" Shih-ka'i ran, his stubby legs wobbly.

Pan ku lay across the engine that had discharged the shaft that Ragnarson had turned. His throat had been cut. At his feet lay the remains of another man, a man almost wholly putrefied. Tasi-feng said, "He died trying to protect you, Lord."

Moisture stained the inner faces of the jewels in Shih-ka'i's mask. He did not correct Tasi-feng. The stone thing had had its revenge. It had slain his man and used him to launch a missile against his master. "He was like a son to me, Lord Lun-yu. Like a son and a brother. We'll see him off with a hero's honors."

Shoulders slumped, Shih-ka'i faced the rising sun. Lord Ssu-ma Shih-ka'i, pig farmer's son, Commander of Armies and Victor Over the East. He snorted derisively.

Nepanthe approached the darkness and scintillation as nearly as she dared. She looked within herself for some deep feeling about what the morning meant. She could locate nothing but a hollowness. She couldn't feel more than mildly bitter about Varthlokkur having kept the truth from her. Her knowing or not knowing had been irrelevant. Ethrian had been lost the moment those devils of the Pracchia had forced him through a transfer.

Could she blame anyone but herself? She had gotten them into that situation....

The sun pushed through the pillar of darkness. She glanced up. It was beginning to dissipate. The woman in white was now no more than a twitch in the air, like heat rising off bare stone. The coruscation where Ethrian had fallen was losing its color, turning milky, threatening to go watery.

She glanced toward the city. The chunky little Tervola had outdistanced everyone. He was at the gate already. Bragi and Mist were ambling along, apparently talking. Bragi's gestures looked dispirited.

Varthlokkur had stopped. He faced her from two hundred yards, waiting. The Unborn floated above his head. She stared back at him. There lay the new life. The last vestige of an old life lay dead at her feet. The end of an era was written....

The coruscation died. And there lay the body of her son. "But..." she murmured. "I saw him explode. I did." Frantically, she beckoned Varthlokkur.

The wizard approached reluctantly. Too many sharp words had been exchanged. Their relationship was severely wounded.

Ethrian groaned.

"Oh! Damnit, hurry up!" Nepanthe shrieked. "Varth, please!"

The wizard sensed the quickening in the boy. He ran.

Ethrian's eyes opened a crack. "Momma?" he croaked.

Nepanthe flung herself on him and wept.

The orders from the Princess were terse but explicit. Shih-ka'i reported as directed. Like his brethren, he had remained in quarters while Ragnarson and Varthlokkur remained in Lioantung. The two meant less to him than they did to most Tervola, but he had gone along in the interest of morale and solidarity. He had a good team here. He had to stand with them as they had stood with him against the Deliverer.

"Mistress?" he inquired, standing at attention in the wreckage of what had been his headquarters.

"They've departed. Cancel the games."

"As you command, Mistress."

"I wanted to commend you, Lord Ssu-ma. And reward you. I have a new task for you, if you're willing to undertake it."

"I'm a soldier, Mistress. I am the empire's to command." What new task? The Matayangan front? He wouldn't relish being tossed into that bloody cauldron.

Mist smiled. "No. Not Southern Army. The command every Tervola wants: Western Army."

Shih-ka'i's eyes narrowed behind his mask. Western Army? A plum, certainly. The glamor command. He was blunt. "Why? What of Lord Hsung?"

"I want a western commander who'll keep his mind on business. Not one who'll be plotting against me or taking off on his own. Someone who isn't foaming at the mouth for revenge." Softly, with humor, she added, "Besides, I can't stand Lord Hsung."

Shih-ka'i had only a passing acquaintance with the man. Nevertheless, he nodded. The one favorable thing he knew of Lord Hsung was that he could be a very good commander— when forced to concentrate on his calling.

He asked, "When would you want me?"

"Moving him out will be ticklish. But before the end of the year. Take the intervening time off. My friend Lord Ch'ien will take over here."

"I'll use the time to familiarize myself with the western situation." And, he thought, begin the fruitless search for someone able to replace Pan ku.

"Very well. I can't force you to take a vacation, though I wish you would."

"I've been in harness too long, Mistress. One more question. Did Ragnarson and the wizard patch it up? That will be important."

Mist smiled, rose, stepped down, embraced him momentarily. "Thank you, Lord Ssu-ma. For everything you've done." And, as she started away, "No. They didn't. The woman tried to make peace. Varthlokkur has much too stiff a neck."

And inside his beastmask Lord Ssu-ma Shih-ka'i smiled himself.

After the challenge in the east anything else looked easy.

✝

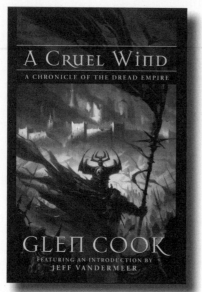

ISBN: 978-1-59780-188-1 ❦ Paperback $14.95

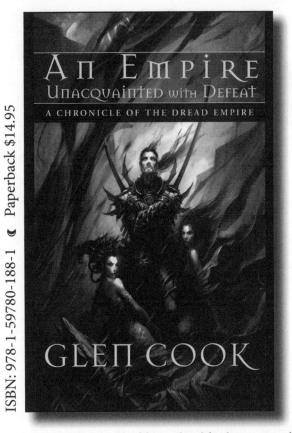

The Dread Empire, a gritty world of larger-than-life plots, nation-shattering conflict, maddening magic, strange creatures, and raw, flawed heroes, all shown through the filter of Cook's inimitable war-correspondent prose. The Dread Empire, spanning from the highest peaks of the Dragon's Teeth to the endless desert lands of Hammad al Nakir, from besieged Kavelin to mighty Shinshan, the Empire Unacquainted with Defeat, with its fearless, masked soldiers, known as the Demon Guard...

An Empire Unacquainted with Defeat collects all of Glen Cook's short fiction set in the vast world of the Dread Empire, from "The Nights of Dreadful Silence", featuring the first appearance of Bragi Ragnarson, Mocker, and Haroun bin Yousif, to the culture-clashing novella "Soldier of an Empire Unacquainted with Defeat"; from "Silverheels", Cook's first published work of fiction, to "Hell's Forge", a haunting tale of cursed pirates and strange lands, appearing here for the first time.

Also including a detailed introduction and extensive story notes by Glen Cook, *An Empire Unacquainted with Defeat* charts the development of this influential American author and the massive, multifaceted world that he created.

NIGHT SHADE BOOKS IS AN INDEPENDENT PUBLISHER
OF QUALITY SCIENCE-FICTION, FANTASY AND HORROR

ISBN: 978-1-59780-321-2 ℂ Paperback $14.99

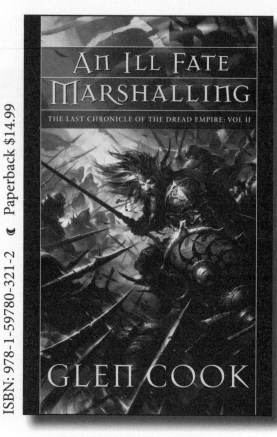

COMING DECEMBER 2011

King Bragi Ragnorson decides to join Chatelain Mist's coup against the Dread Empire. Varthlokkur—the King's wizard—tries to dissuade Ragnarson from this chosen path, but only the drum-beat of war is heard. The King's Spymaster Michael Trebilcock joins with the wizard to stave off The Ill Fate Marshaling, to no effect.

Many of the characters from past volumes take center stage, and the climatic events of this book shake the world of the Dread Empire to its very core, creating *A Path to Coldness of Heart*.

ISBN: 9781597803298 ❧ Hardcover $25.99

A PATH TO
COLDNESS OF HEART

THE LAST CHRONICLE OF THE DREAD EMPIRE: VOL III

GLEN COOK

COMING JANUARY 2012

At long last, the conclusion to Glen Cook's Dread Empire saga has arrived…

King Bragi Ragnarson is a prisoner, shamed, nameless, and held captive by Lord Shih-ka'i and the Empress Mist at the heart of the Dread Empire.

Far away in Kavelin, Bragi's queen and what remains of his army seek to find and free their king, hampered by the loss… or desertion… of their best and brightest warriors. Kavelin's spymaster, Michael Trebilcock, is missing in action, as is loyal soldier Aral Dantice.

Meanwhile, Dane, Duke of Greyfells, seeks to seize the rule of Kavelin and place the kingdom in his pocket, beginning a new line of succession through Bragi's queen, Dane's cousin Inger.

And in the highest peaks of the Dragon's Teeth, in the ancient castle Fangdred, the sorcerer called Varthlokkur uses his arts to spy on the world at large, observing the puppet strings that control kings and empires alike, waiting.

For the time of the wrath of kings is almost at hand, and vengeance lies along a path to coldness of heart….

Glen Cook is the author of dozens of novels of fantasy and science fiction, including *The Black Company*, *The Garret Files*, Instrumentalities of the Night, and the Dread Empire series. Cook was born in 1944 in New York City. He attended the Clarion Writers' Workshop in 1970, where he met his wife, Carol. "Unlike most writers, I have not had strange jobs like chicken plucking and swamping out health bars. Only full-time employer I've ever had is General Motors." He currently makes his home in St. Louis, Missouri.